CONTEMPORARY NORWEGIAN WOM

Some other books from Norvik Press

Sigbjørn Obstfelder: *A Priest's Diary* (translated by James McFarlane)
Hjalmar Söderberg: *Short stories* (translated by Carl Lofmark)
Annegret Heitmann (ed.): *No Man's Land. An Anthology of Modern Danish Women's Literature*
P C Jersild: *A Living Soul* (translated by Rika Lesser)
Sara Lidman: *Naboth's Stone* (translated by Joan Tate)
Selma Lagerlöf: *The Löwensköld Ring* (translated by Linda Schenck)
Villy Sørensen: *Harmless Tales* (translated by Paula Hostrup-Jessen)
Camilla Collett: *The District Governor's Daughters* (translated by Kirsten Seaver)
Jens Bjørneboe: *The Sharks* (translated by Esther Greenleaf Mürer)
Jørgen-Frantz Jacobsen: *Barbara* (translated by George Johnston)
Janet Garton & Henning Sehmsdorf (eds. and trans.): *New Norwegian Plays* (by Peder W.Cappelen, Edvard Hoem, Cecilie Løveid and Bjørg Vik)
Gunilla Anderman (ed.): *New Swedish Plays* (by Ingmar Bergman, Stig Larsson, Lars Norén and Agneta Pleijel)
Kjell Askildsen: *A Sudden Liberating Thought* (translated by Sverre Lyngstad)
Svend Åge Madsen: *Days with Diam* (translated by W. Glyn Jones)
Christopher Moseley (ed.) *From Baltic Shores*
Agnar Thordarson: *Called Home* (translated by Robert Kellogg)

The logo of Norvik Press is based on a drawing by Egil Bakka (University of Bergen) of a Viking ornament in gold, paper thin, with impressed figures (size 16x21mm). It was found in 1897 at Hauge, Klepp, Rogaland, and is now in the collection of the Historisk museum, University of Bergen (inv.no. 5392). It depicts a love scene, possibly (according to Magnus Olsen) between the fertility god Freyr and the maiden Gerðr; the large penannular brooch of the man's cloak dates the work as being most likely 10th century.

Cover illustration: Fam Ekman: from 'Little Red Hat and the Wolf', 1985.

CONTEMPORARY NORWEGIAN WOMEN'S WRITING

AN ANTHOLOGY

Edited by Janet Garton

Norvik Press
Norwich
1995

British Library Cataloguing in Publication Data

Garton, Janet
Contemporary Norwegian Women's Writing — (Norvik Press Series B)
   I. Title II. Garton, Janet
   839.82099287

ISBN 1-870041-29-1

First published in 1995 by Norvik Press, University of East Anglia,
Norwich, NR4 7TJ, England.
Managing Editors: James McFarlane and Janet Garton.

Norvik Press has been established with financial support from the University
of East Anglia, the Danish Ministry for Cultural Affairs, The Norwegian
Cultural Department, and the Swedish Institute. Publication of this volume has
been aided by a grant from Norwegian Literature Abroad (NORLA).

Printed in Great Britain by Page Bros (Norwich) Ltd., Norwich, UK.

Contents

Acknowledgements

Norvik Press is grateful for permission to print the extracts in this anthology from the following authors and publishers:

Bjørg Vik and Cappelen forlag: 'Er det sant at kvinner er undertrykte?', from *Sirene* Nr.1, 1973, pp.7-10; *To akter for fem kvinner*, 1974, pp.16-36.

Liv Køltzow and Aschehoug: *Hvem bestemmer over Bjørg og Unni?*, 1972, pp.69-100.

Eldrid Lunden and Det norske samlaget: *hard, mjuk*, 1976, pp.39-49.

Bergljot Hobæk Haff and Gyldendal: *Gudsmoren*, 1977, pp.157-72.

Marie Takvam and Gyldendal: poems from *Falle og reise seg att*, 1980; *Brevet frå Alexandra*, 1981, pp.22-25.

Karin Moe and Aschehoug: texts from *Kjønnskrift*, 1980.

Mari Osmundsen and Oktober: 'Sju minutter på seks', from *Wow*, 1982.

Gerd Brantenberg and Aschehoug: *Favntak*, 1983, pp.257-79.

Lisbet Hiide and Gyldendal: 'Adam drømmen om løvinnen S', from *Alices særegne opplevelse av natt*, 1985.

Sissel Lie and Gyldendal: 'Min skog brenner aldri forgjeves', from *Tigersmil*, 1986.

Herbjørg Wassmo and Gyldendal: *Dinas bok*, 1989, pp.9-29.

Cecilie Løveid and Gyldendal: *Dobbel nytelse*, 1988, pp.9-34.

The excerpt from *Dina's Book* is reprinted with the permission of Arcade publishing, New York. Translation copyright © 1994 by Nadia Christensen.

The editor would like to thank all of the above for their assistance and enthusiasm, and also to record her thanks to the University of East Anglia for granting research leave in order to work on the project.

Foreword

1973 was the sixtieth anniversary of the year in which the women of Norway, among the first in the world, won the vote. It was also the year in which a new journal began to appear, celebrating the jubilee in its first issue: *Sirene* (Siren), with the subtitle 'A signal of the times for women and men'. 'Siren' has a double meaning in Norwegian as in English, as the first editorial points out; it refers both to the seductive mythical temptresses who lured men to their deaths and to a signal warning of danger. The aim of the journal is firstly to make women (and men) aware of the reality behind illusion and pretence, and secondly to warn of the danger of explosion caused by the constant pressure of repression.

The journal was launched at a time of intense activity in feminist circles in Norway. The end of the 1960s had seen a politicization of culture, which had led several writers from the so-called 'Profil' group to join the Marxist-Leninist branch of the Communist party in Norway, and had made women writers more conscious of their social and political status. Although in one way the sixtieth anniversary of suffrage was a cause for celebration, in another it was an occasion for sober reflection on how little advance had been made since then. Women's standing in public life, as political representatives, senior managers, academics and the like had, with few exceptions, hardly improved over sixty years, and changes in the law had had little practical effect on the way they lived their private lives.

The early 1970s saw the formation of women's groups such as *Nyfeministene* (The New Feminists, 1970) and *Kvinnefronten* (The Women's Front, 1972), which set about raising awareness of inequality and making women more visible. Much effort went into improving the ratio of women in political bodies, both at local and at national level, which bore fruit over the next two decades, as the proportion of women in local councils increased from 9.5% (1967) to 31.1% (1987) and in the national Storting from 9% (1969) to 35.7% (1989); by 1990, the Prime Minister and half of her cabinet were women. Legal advances included a much-delayed law making abortion finally freely available to all (1978) and an Equal Status Act (1979) which went further than most European ones in allowing for positive discrimination, acknowledging that the removal of formal barriers was not in itself enough to achieve real equality.

In literature too, there was a shift in sensibility; echoes of increased political awareness can be traced in the work of several women writers. *Sirene* was one of the focal points for the activity of those who wanted to effect change in laws and attitudes. Its first issue, as well as the article by Bjørg Vik quoted here, also contained an article by Berit Ås, an academic who set up a women's university, about women and the law; a short story about women's work and men's work by Margaret Johansen, whose novel *Du kan da ikke bare gå ...* (You Can't Just Walk Out ..., 1981) caused a stir with its disturbing depiction of a battered wife; and a slightly edgy interview with Liv Ullmann about the problems of being a single mother. Some previously established writers, like Bjørg Vik and Liv Køltzow, became more politically radical in their works from this period; and writers who were beginning their literary careers, like Gerd Brantenberg and Mari Osmundsen, debated the dilemmas of women in the sexual and the social sphere.

The didactic nature of these books gave them a popular appeal at the time, but one which the authors themselves now feel is somewhat dated. It is interesting in this connection that the authors who raised objections when I contacted them about the excerpts I had selected for inclusion in this anthology were Bjørg Vik and Liv Køltzow, who both felt that they had moved on from the way they wrote in the early 1970s, and that the excerpts did not really represent their achievement. Bjørg Vik wondered whether such an old article as the one from *Sirene* was of any interest any longer, and Liv Køltzow was more emphatic: 'I regard this book as anything but representative of what I want to do — *precisely* as a *woman* writer. This exaggerated problematization of femininity and women's lives is a phase which I passed through as an author for a short period only.'

Looked at from a vantage point of twenty years later, this directly committed writing was a phase in the careers of most of the authors concerned, but an important one nevertheless, from which many went on to develop in many different ways. Women writers in Norway during the last twenty years have been so prolific and so various that sketching in any general trends is a risky business, and bound to be hedged around with reservations. But if one can see any dominant tendency, I believe that it is in the direction away from politics and towards fantasy, towards a less realistic, more imaginative fictional form.

Women writers have become less apologetic, more confident in their creativity; they have moved from middle-class Oslo flats to the wilder shores of invention and experiment. Fictional characters who were career girls or working mothers have become authors who write with their vaginal muscles, lionesses who tear their prey, artists who create mind images through controlled orgasms. Women's sexuality too has become freer and more freely expressed, as female desire and pleasure become central, not secondary, and actively demanding, not passively receptive.

This anthology represents an attempt to convey an impression of the great variety of contemporary women's writing in Norway. The excerpts are arranged more or less chronologically in order to give some sense of the development outlined above, from the factual and analytical *Sirene* article to the sensuality of Herbjørg Wassmo's sexual meeting and Cecilie Løveid's playful interchanges. In terms of genre, they include excerpts from novels (Køltzow, Haff, Brantenberg, Wassmo); short stories (Osmundsen, Hiide, Lie), excerpts from plays (Vik, Løveid); poems (Lunden, Takvam, Moe) and letters (Takvam). They are contemporary and realistic (Køltzow, Vik, Osmundsen, Brantenberg), historical (Wassmo), historical-fantastical (Haff, Løveid), futuristic or science fiction (Hiide, Lie). They deal with women's attitudes to their own sexuality, from the shock of a child's sudden awareness of danger (Osmundsen) to an older woman's love for a younger man (Takvam). They include explorations of lesbianism (Brantenberg), the Madonna/whore syndrome (Haff), incest and mother/daughter relationships (Løveid). Some are humorous (Moe, Haff), some use religious themes (Wassmo, Haff). Language is important; several texts are innovative or outspoken in their use of language, and some are about language, its appropriation as a weapon of power and the need for women to find their own language (Køltzow, Moe).

Notes on the Authors

GERD BRANTENBERG (b.1941) began her career as an author somewhat late; she published her first book, *Opp alle jordens homofile* (What Comes Naturally) in 1973, when she was 32. Part of the reason for this was that the sexual liberation of the 1960s did not extend to lesbianism, which was what she needed to write about; once these inhibitions were conquered, she produced a humorous account of the adventures of a lesbian in modern-day Oslo, followed by a novel which was a major international success, *Egalias døtre* (The Daughters of Egalia, 1977). The latter is a parody of patriarchal society, which imagines what life would be like in a modern matriarchy; women not only wear the trousers, but rule social and religious ritual through their mysterious link with nature via birth and menstruation, whilst men must curl their beards, shave their chest hair and constrict themselves with penis holders to make themselves attractive. Even language is affected, since the male is derived from the female and not vice versa; thus man/woman and male/female becomes manwom/wom and mafele/fele — a distortion which remarkably quickly comes to seem entirely natural.

Lesbianism is a consistent theme of Gerd Brantenberg's writing; she rapidly became a figurehead for alternative sexuality in Norway, and an outspoken participant in cultural debate. Her major project in the 1980s was a semi-autobiographical trilogy about a girl growing up in Fredrikstad in the 1960s, watching helplessly as her tyrannical father exhausts her once confident and exuberant mother, and coming to terms with her own difference from the social norm, for which she has no name because it cannot be named.

Favntak (Embrace, 1983), from which this excerpt is taken, is a novel about a love triangle with a difference; into the marriage of Torgeir and Irene comes the other woman, Aud, who falls in love with Irene and makes her realise that she is bisexual. Torgeir reacts with predictable fury and disgust, and refuses even to try to understand; although he has had a mistress for several years, he regards that as a different matter altogether, and it is his implacable opposition as much as anything which drives Irene towards Aud. For Irene, Aud brings the realisation not just that her marriage is repressive but that she has lacked the space in which to think her own thoughts, develop her own projects; the room which Torgeir burns is more than just a study: 'the letters he had burnt, the room he had destroyed, they were her slow journey towards understanding herself.' (p.288)

BERGLJOT HOBÆK HAFF (b.1925) has a long career as a novelist behind her, having begun publishing in the 1950s; but it is not until fairly recently that her work has received the critical attention it deserves. Her works were not considered topical in the 1960s and 70s, as they never followed any school or political direction. She has always gone her own way as a novelist, and from the start has written novels with an allegorical, quasi-mythical flavour, such as *Bålet* (The Fire, 1962), in which the battle between good and evil is fought out between two mystical male figures, the gentle, humble cobbler and the sardonic rabble-rouser, fighting for the love of a woman; or *Skjøgens bok* (The Prostitute's Book, 1965) where the central figure is a kind of eternal feminine, a woman who can become whatever men need her to be, as well as helping them into life and out of it.

The mixture of fantasy and workaday realism which characterizes her stories has found a more appreciative audience recently, as literary fashion has caught up with her. *Den guddommelige tragedie* (The Divine Tragedy, 1989) transposes the story of Christ to South Africa under apartheid; God is a rather incompetent divinity, who fails to make Mary pregnant (her husband has done it already) and eventually tumbles from the sky, only to be taken prisoner, classified as coloured (being neither black nor white) and sent to work in the mines. *Renhetens pris* (The Price of Purity, 1992) is set in Spain during the inquisition and narrated by a self-righteous priest who refuses to recognise his burning desires until they drive him to rape.

Acknowledgement of the close links between the sacred and the corporeal, the fantastic and the realistic, is also at the centre of *Gudsmoren* (The Mother of God, 1977), from which this excerpt is taken. The central character is a little prostitute, the meekest and most exploited of all, who is made pregnant by a fine but brutal gentleman; she carries her unborn child through all the degradation of the streets, and finally gives birth in a freezing room with the assistance of three tramps called Caspar, Melchior and Balthazar. The child is a girl, which is rather unexpected, and the little mother is left completely bereft (her comrades have been arrested) until the trial with which the novel finishes, where those who have betrayed her are called to account, and she then slips out through a gap in the narrative into a most prosaic urban scene.

LISBET HIIDE (b.1956) is the youngest of the authors in this anthology, and has not written so much as most of the others. She published two volumes of short stories in the 1980s, *Alices særegne opplevelse av natt* (Alice's Peculiar Experience of Night, 1985) and *Dame med nebb* (Lady with Beak, 1988). Many of her stories depart altogether from reality into a surreal world where people can take on the properties of animals or machines and the boundaries between one person and another can become unclear. Some of the stories can be read as a comment on female neurosis, like the title story of the first volume, in which the story of Alice growing bigger and bigger suggests a bulimia-like obsession with eating enormous quantities of food. Some deal with male fantasies exaggerated to the point of grotesqueness, like 'Playmate of the Year' in which a man's fantasies of making love to a pin-up girl are rudely shattered by the arrival of the girl herself as a castrating monster; or the story included in this anthology, in which the incarnation of feline sexuality fulfils a man's wildest dreams and leaves him bleeding on the pavement.

LIV KØLTZOW (b.1944) was a member of the 'Profil' group of writers in the 1960s, and derived important impulses from them; she points out herself that she has always felt closer to some of her male literary colleagues than to other women writers in terms of the way she writes. Her first book, a collection of short stories called *Øyet i treet* (The Eye in the Tree) was published in 1970; the subject matter of the title story is a game of hide and seek, but the whole course of events is described by a girl hiding up a tree, observing intently both the minutely-detailed patterns of leaf and trunk and the larger patterns of the children's game through sunlight and shade. The seeing eye is a motif of much of her writing.

After a more 'political' period at the beginning of the 1970s, Liv Køltzow returned to writing in a less didactic way, registering rather than inviting judgement, about people and the patterns of their relationships. Novels such as *Løp, mann* (Run, Man, 1980) and *Hvem har ditt ansikt?* (Who Has Your Face?, 1988) are studies of contemporary life and comments on verbal and sensual communication, or the lack of it. The latter novel purports to be based on the 'wild notes' of Helen, an artist who falls in love and finds her life disrupted in a chaotic manner;

her attempts to make sense of it are equally chaotic, and the novel poses questions about the whole idea of a story, and whether it is possible to tell one.

The excerpt from *Who Decides About Bjørg and Unni?* has been chosen as a document of the early 1970s. The novel is set on a modern housing estate, with two young women as its central characters: Bjørg who is married and resentful of her role as a housewife with children, and Unni who is an unmarried mother, juggling the demands of her job with the problems of childcare. Like the other women of the estate, they regard politics as a distant male domain; but faced with the local threat of a new trunk road through the estate, bringing pollution and danger to the children, they slowly realise that politics does concern them and that it is possible for the little people to stop the bulldozers.

SISSEL LIE (b. 1942) is both an academic (Professor of French Studies at Trondheim University) and an author, although creative writing is her second career; her first book, a collection of short stories called *Tigersmil* (Tiger Smile) was not published until 1986. The lure and the danger of sexuality is very much in evidence in these stories, sometimes as erotic fantasy (in 'The Chauffeur'), sometimes as exhibitionism ('Naked under a black plastic mac'), sometimes as violence, as in 'Tiger', a multilayered story within a story where an author is writing about a rape, only to become the victim of rape in a similar fashion herself.

Since 1986 Sissel Lie has written several novels. *Løvens hjerte* (Lion's Heart, 1988) is a story of two women; one, a modern girl who has been betrayed by her lover, travels backwards in time to the sixteenth century to meet the French poet Louise Labé, whose poems have meant much to her and who demonstrates an enviable independence in her life and in her writings. The novel includes translations of her poems and paints a vivid picture of medieval French society. *Granateple* (Pomegranate, 1990) develops from a prosaic beginning — a conversation between three women in a cafe — into a fantastic fable where the characters take on a mystical dimension.

The short story 'Strange things happen when my forest burns' is taken from the author's first book. Like most of the other stories, it is also about a sexual meeting, but in this case set in a futuristic dimension with science fiction overtones, in a thought-policed society where sexual excitement is regulated to produce images for hygienic purposes, rather than being a private affair. The central character rebels and seeks her own pleasure, but her resistance is doomed in a collective dystopia where intimacy is public property.

CECILIE LØVEID (b.1951) has written in many different genres, and often in a mixture of genres which is difficult to categorize, on the borderlines of prose and poetry, of epic and drama. Her earlier works were mainly poems or prose poems, which announce themes which recur throughout her work: that of abandonment by father/husband/lover, and that of the sea. The subject of her works is nearly always women, both in the literal sense and in the sense that they are written around women's bodies and women's desire. Language is a central preoccupation, as in *Sug* (Sea Swell, 1979), a cycle of texts tracing Kjersti's involvement with her own creativity and with her lover who leaves her; it ends with the wish for a new language in which to express a new meeting: 'a language without words...without colour...one with a fine "touch me" structure...one with warm "come into me" calls'.

Her more recent works have been mainly dramatic texts, and have been staged with varying success; although most critics agree that she is an exciting and innovative dramatist, productions are not always popular. Her dramas are unconventional and unrealistic, often containing references to other texts and moving between ballet, pantomime and musical, with elements of the lyrical and the grotesque. Her radio play *Måkespisere* (Seagull Eaters, 1983), which won the Prix Italia, is about a poor Bergen girl during the second World War with aspirations to be an actress; the text is intercut with quotations from the housekeeping manual of Henriette Schønberg Erken, which provides an ironic commentary on the failure of her dreams.

The excerpt from *Dobbel nytelse* (Double Delight, 1988) is taken from the beginning of the play, where Siri's daughter Cat, who is both a feline temptress and a modern version of the medieval St Katarina, has come to disrupt the archeological investigations and the marriage of Siri and her husband Guy. The dancers Tutti and Frutti and the androgynous guitar-playing pig, whose bizarre appearance contrasts with his singing of plaintive medieval troubadour songs, observe and comment on the jealous triangle which develops. In this play, however, it is not the man who abandons the women but the women who dispose of him; as the play ends, Siri sets sail into the past in a medieval boat, and Cat is left alone on stage holding her baby sister 'like a Madonna'.

ELDRID LUNDEN (b.1940), like Liv Køltzow, drew some of her creative stimulus from her association with the 'Profil' group of authors. She is both a poet and an essayist; she teaches creative writing, and has written critical analyses of other writers' work alongside her own poetry. There have been seven volumes of poetry so far, from 1968 to 1990; she became well known in the 1970s with volumes like *hard, mjuk* (hard, soft, 1976) and *Mammy, blue* (1977). Both in her poems and in her essays she is preoccupied with problems of language and its cultural connotations; she writes in Norway's second official language, New Norwegian, and has written about the different culture of the two languages and particularly about their availability to women writers. She explores the links between language and gender, though in a non-separatist way; she defines her writing as 'an attempt to speak a language which I believe can convey feminine values. And this language is one which does not belong to women alone.'

Her poems in *hard, mjuk* are compact and intense, often employing unexpected combinations of words to suggest new perspectives. The poems explore the idea that love perhaps is possible; 'hard' and 'soft' are not simply male and female poles, but are shared between the sexes. The poems included here make up the third section of the four in the volume, which ends inconclusively; many of the poems in the last section are formed as questions, uncertain as to the outcome, tender and vulnerable and aware of the impossibility of ever fully knowing.

KARIN MOE (b.1945) has from the first appeared as an experimental author, not afraid of taking risks in her writing and with a lively sense of humour. She too combines writing as a critic with her creative activity; the book *Sjanger* (Genre, 1986) contains essays, interviews, poems, lists, pictures on a whole range of subjects from Irigaray and Baudelaire to strawberries and coke. French literature and criticism are a source of delight and inspiration.

Kjønnskrift (Sextext, 1980), her first book, was also her most straightforwardly feminist statement, and one from which she now feels somewhat detached. It was followed by *39 Fyk* (1983) and *KYKA/1984* (1984), books with titles impossible to translate — she has invented the words — and difficult to summarize, as are her most recent books, *BLOVE 1.bok* (1990) and *BLOVE 2.bok* (1993) — again an invented title. All her texts are elements of a cultural critique, combining deep seriousness with a zany humour, which has been called 'an attempt to portray the patriarchal structure in us... or the layers in us which give free rein to unrestrained 'freedom' in such a way that greed and crazy excess gain a power over people's thoughts which leads to destruction... which leads not only to a breakdown of the immune system or the destruction of the rain forests, but also to a human type which exceeds the fantasies of Dr Mabuse in its evil.'

The texts which have been selected here from *Kjønnskrift*, in a mixture of poetry and prose, amount to comments on and criticism of the male domination of culture and opportunity. Some of them are comic, explaining the problems faced by a female author writing about the male organ when she has seen so few of them, or the dilemma of a female author wanting to write a body-centred text: if the pen is a metaphorical penis, how can a woman convey her sexuality on paper? Some express frustration with all the men who stand between a woman's work and its publication, solidarity with other women menstruating, or a horrified recognition of the way in which a rejected single mother can turn on her own baby.

MARI OSMUNDSEN (b.1951) is unusual amongst modern authors in that she writes under a pseudonym. Her early novels were typical examples of the left-wing writing of the 1970s, such as *Vi klarer det!* (We'll Make It!, 1978), describing working-class life in a modern factory environment, and the necessity of political organization. The central characters are women, doubly discriminated in an environment where their work is undervalued; the central character is a young girl who becomes pregnant, and realises that abortion is as much a political issue as poverty.

In the 1980s Mari Osmundsen's writing has been quite different, as if freed from a straitjacket of political correctness into a more personal and idiosyncratic form. *Gode gjerninger* (Good Deeds, 1984) is about two modern Oslo girls who both have contacts in another dimension; Karianne has a pact with her own personal demon who grants her wishes but exacts a toll in the form of her soul after death, and Rut is thrown suddenly into another world which has no contacts with the universe she knows, and for which she is never given any explanation. *Familien* (The Family, 1985) is also about two worlds, the everyday one of work, relationships and childcare problems, and a separate female 'wild zone' which is a refuge for witches, pin-up girls and runaway single mothers. Beneath the fantasy there is always a political element in Mari Osmundsen's works, which becomes more overt again in a recent novel *Gutten som slo tida ihjel* (The Boy Who Killed Time, 1990) about the problems of refugees from the Third World in modern Norway.

The short story 'Seven Minutes to Six' is taken from the collection *Wow*, from 1982. Most of the stories in this collection are realistic, often concerned with situations which demonstrate the resourcefulness of women in a tight corner: the woman attacked by a rapist who knifes him, the battered wife who gets her husband arrested, the woman determined to cope with a 'man's job'. 'Seven Minutes to Six' contrasts the lives of two young girls, both meeting a pervert who cannot see any difference between them: Kajsa is an innocent child who receives a shock she will never forget, whereas Anne, only a little older, is an experienced prostitute who agrees to his suggestions to earn money to buy drugs.

MARIE TAKVAM (b.1926) is a poet who, like Eldrid Lunden, writes in New Norwegian; it is a language which lends itself particularly well to poetic expression. Since her debut in 1952, she has produced a volume of poetry every five years or so. As well as writing frankly about sexuality and physical pleasure, and attacking the traditional 'woman's role' with gusto, she has also become increasingly environmentally conscious, protesting about the wasting of scarce resources and more especially about the unequal distribution of wealth and opportunity between the Third World and the affluent West.

Marie Takvam's concern with Western indifference and a way of life which takes exploitation for granted is in evidence in several of the poems selected here, which contrast the narrator's trivial concerns with a world of suffering she does not see. She drinks a cup of coffee in comfort whilst a naked woman staggers under the weight of the coffee beans; she thinks about her nail varnish whilst millions are starving; she tries to tie her shoelaces whilst being bombarded with more information than she can absorb. The matter-of-fact tone of the poems underlines the contrasts starkly. Other poems, like 'Please don't bar my path', have a more erotic theme, which is also present in *Brevet frå Alexandra* (The Letter from Alexandra, 1981). The latter is a novel composed of letters from an older women, Alexandra, to a younger lover who has now left her; the letters express a defiant assertion that love transcends age and the convention that says that it is all right for older men to take younger women but not vice versa, but at the same time admit to a niggling worry that by transgressing the code she has nevertheless exposed herself to ridicule.

BJØRG VIK (b.1935) became an influential figure during the late 1960s with her collections of short stories (she began publishing in 1963) and her participation in public debate; both in her fiction and in her polemics she was a pioneer of the new feminist movement in Norway. She was on the editorial board of the magazine *Sirene* at its inception, and her stories of contemporary life highlight the dilemmas of modern women. Some of her early stories had a certain *succès de scandale* because of their frank acknowledgement of female lust; others told of the quiet desperation of the lives of many. The collection *Kvinneakvariet* (An Aquarium of Women, 1972) is a cycle of stories which traces the way women are trained to conformity, from young schoolgirls dreaming of filmstars and white weddings to middle-aged married women struggling to cope with the burden of double work in factory or office and in the home; some of the stories explore alternative lifestyles, and the problems of those who try to defy the rules.

Bjørg Vik has had considerable success as a playwright, writing for radio and television as well as stage plays. Her plays, in total contrast to Cecilie Løveid's experimental pieces, are naturalistic studies of middle-class life, which yet expose the tensions beneath the well-ordered surface. She has continued to write short stories, a genre which many critics think suits her style best; more recent collections have been less sensational, with melancholy titles like *Snart er det høst* (Soon It Will Be Autumn, 1982) and *En gjenglemt petunia* (A Forgotten Petunia, 1985). Recently she has produced a series of autobiographical novels about growing up in Oslo after the war.

To akter for fem kvinner (Two Acts for Five Women, 1974) is a committed play about women's lives. The only characters are the five women, a group of former schoolfriends in their thirties having a reunion and comparing notes on their experiences; during the course of the evening they face up to the fact that their lives are not all they would have them be. Hanna is the most aware, a single parent who has left her son with his father and has to cope with the disapproval of other women and her own grief. Lilleba is an 'earth mother' who has diverted her feelings of inadequacy into a cosy world of child-rearing and domesticity, whilst Gry is a bachelor girl who is secretly terrified of sex. Anne Sofie is exulting in a new lover, and does not want to admit that she is cheating her husband, and Ellinor has a perfect marriage and a perfect career — until she finds out during the evening that her husband has a mistress. The discovery of the pain behind the facade is not entirely negative, however, as at least some of the girls leave prepared to confront their situation with a new honesty.

HERBJØRG WASSMO (b.1942) is a writer from the north of Norway, whose works nearly always have a flavour of her own home region. She trained as a teacher, and made her debut as a writer rather late, in 1976, with two volumes of poetry, but soon turned to writing prose, and has had her main success as a novelist. Her major achievement has been with two series of novels about two very different women from different times, Tora and Dina. The 'Tora' series is a trilogy, published 1981-86, whose central character is a young girl growing up in the north of Norway after the second World War, carrying the double burden of being the bastard child of a German soldier of the occupying forces and being the victim of sexual abuse at the hands of her stepfather. The abuse is her secret shame, for which she has no words even to herself; despite the support of loving friends, she never manages to free herself from the guilt and the fear. The trilogy was a bestseller, and seen as an important contribution to a topical debate.

The two novels about Dina are *Dinas bok* (Dina's Book, 1989) and *Lykkens sønn* (The Son of Fortune, 1992) — the latter purports to be about Dina's son, but his fate is always overshadowed by hers. The novels have a historical setting, in a northern Norwegian fishing and farming community in the mid-nineteenth century. Dina is a woman who appears, in this excerpt from the very beginning of the novel, to be as strong as Tora is weak; she acts decisively and takes what she wants, getting rid of a husband who has become a burden and taking a young lover on the day of his funeral. Yet despite her independence and ruthlessness, she too is a betrayed child; she caused the death of her mother in an accident as a child and was rejected by her father, and has grown up to expect betrayal every time she trusts anyone. The novel is also about language; Dina loses her powers of speech twice, after her mother's and her husband's deaths, and the novel is interspersed with quotations from the Old Testament, with its patriarchal language which is a constant reminder of the law she has transgressed.

For more information on these authors, see Janet Garton: *Norwegian Women's Writing 1850-1990*, Athlone Press, London 1993.

Janet Garton
Norwich, April 1995

BJØRG VIK

Is it true that women are oppressed?

Patriarchal society
Manipulation
Indoctrination
Role models
Sex Discrimination
Oppression of women

The words resemble smooth balls in the air. Clean kicks,
long balls crossing the sideline, angry headers at the crossbar.
Goal?

The defence bunches together, determined and scared: The
Status Quo must be protected.

The words remain mere words, until we are able to unveil
their contents. Since for a number of us the oppression confus-
ingly resembles privileges, it is difficult to recognise it, and
even more difficult to get within range of it.

Haven't we achieved what men have *not*? That is, we are
spared working full-time, we are spared having responsibility
for society or we are able to take it on if we really want to?

Aren't 'all roads open to us'? Don't men work themselves to death for our sakes? Aren't we the ones who with simple, tried and tested tricks are manipulating men and bringing up the children, and thus also forming the people of tomorrow?

On the surface we can answer, 'Yes'. It is this surface which is deceiving us. It is a viscous dough of old thoughts, habitual attitudes and handed down opinions.

One day you start scratching at the old scabs, and yes, it hurts. Under the scabs you will find yourself raw and vulnerable. Suddenly it stings a lot. You experience a jerky, painful awakening from a dream you thought was good. And the new skin grows thin and sensitive. It provides precious little armour. However, the fact that you know that there are more of us, that we are many, is the best fact to sustain you.

You think back. You try to tack experiences and half-clear memories together to form a pattern. Was I (or will I be) really discriminated against? Was I (or will I be) influenced to do this and this? Was I – or will I always be – trained to have typical women's attitudes.

You can't avoid seeing it: you have grown up in the shade, in the shade of those who were going to develop themselves, who had to get used to having responsibility, who had the right of the firstborn to decisiveness, self-confidence, opportunity for development and the drive to get things done. You are a distorted shadow plant. What self-confidence and initiative you have rescued, is diseased. It has been nourished on defiance and bitterness, on the silent or open condemnation of those around you, on guilt and shame.

You look around. You start to gather proof. You must be specific. The slogans rumble like empty barrels if you don't give them content. From when you open the morning papers to when you see the last picture on the late night news on the TV, you are continuously confronted by the fact that it is *men* who matter in society. It is men who express themselves, who exercise administrative control and debate, who have opinions about something, who do something, who are something. And who have developed a terrifying power ideology and cult of leadership, so as to keep each other in check – and not least: to keep us in check.

Now you can see it everywhere. You see it in the supermarket where men are shop managers and we sit at the till or serve at the vegetable counter. You see it in the corner shops which are practically all owned by men and where we are poorly paid shop assistants. You go to some kind of office, the social services, the tax office, the bank, the post office, the school office. In all these places you see us in subordinate positions. Exceptions do exist, and some people try to make them the rule. But the rule is: men are at the top, men are in all significant leadership positions, in all institutions, from the government to the church, the legal apparatus, education and industry. All are dominated and led by men.

You are still living in the shade.

A male culture? Of course.

Now you start reading statistics. You didn't realise that figures made such exciting reading matter. Black on white, you see what you experienced in the bakery, in the bank and at the factory. A tiny percentage of us reach management positions. An unreasonable difference of salary between men and women in many professions. Some professions become typical female professions, which is tantamount to typical low wage professions. Some jobs are put in the lowest wage groups. They are always women's jobs.

Are we predestined to pack sweets, wash floors, write out invoices and hand out testers in supermarkets? How many intelligent people are earning a living by sewing lamp shades, selling make-up or writing address cards? The statistics do not exist. Maybe we should be grateful for that?

But why?

Why do we give up our education? What happens to our ambitions, our responsibility, our ability to make decisions with people and about ourselves?

There is something or someone who takes it from us, and we let them take it – in order to be accepted by the system, to continue to be allowed to belong to the group (read: the established society). And it is easy to give up a responsibility which no-one has taught us to take, either for our own life or for that of others. The fact that we have learnt to sacrifice ourselves for other people, does not mean the same as responsibility. Those who sacrifice themselves the most, become the most dependent, the most helpless. The fact that we have learnt to serve others (family, employers, lovers, husbands, children) has little to do with self-determination and social responsibility. It is an irresponsible (or calculating?) system which creates so many dependent women. But as long as we fool ourselves that we 'choose' for ourselves and continually mistake dependency for 'privileges', – we will remain in the vicious circle: Parasitic people (women and men) breed parasitic children, who in turn will find a parasite to live their parasitic life with. If the middle-class woman or the working-class woman sponges off her man and his effort at work, then *he* also sponges off her dependency on him and her housework. If the children sponge off the continual care of the women who work at home, then to an equal extent they sponge off the exhausted working women's feelings of guilt. And as long as we are played off *against each other*, the bitterness can be directed against other women, instead of against society and the hard-boiled role patterns which form us all, which lead us astray and abuse us, both in working life and at home. And the ingrained thoughts and attitudes which govern us in all our interactions with people.

Manipulation? Of course.

One day you start flicking through your 10-year-old's

school books. 'Father is reading and mother is sewing' must now be a thing of the past? Not at all, only now it occurs in a more crafty, thinly veiled way. For example, if you flick through an 11-year old's maths book, you will see that all the professions are defined by men. Men drive cars in several problems, are electricians, tailors, ditch diggers, salesmen in 11 problems, earn money, *are* something. Women, for their part, are represented by a continually baking and meal-making mother. She is baking in 4 problems, sewing in 8, buying food and making meals in 15. Whilst girls buy food in 14 problems and sew and knit, preferably in whole classes of 20-30 knitting girls at a time, the boys sometimes buy oranges, otherwise they stick to buying skates, footballs and tools.

The other school books tell indefatigably about men and men's achievements in the long and disputed history of the human race. There are pictures of men and stories about men, from the Viking Age to NATO, from Our Lord to Wergeland and Lenin.

You start to wonder. Haven't we women ever done anything? And why haven't we done anything? Why aren't these books interested in why some 50% of the world's population was sentenced to passivity? And why then don't they draw attention to those women who *despite everything* managed to create something? What happens inside half of the class reading these books, what happens inside the girls? What kind of picture do they create of their own sex and of themselves? What happens to their *self-image*?

You flick through story books, through children's books. You listen to children's stories on the radio and watch television. It is there all the time. The exceptions are few and far between, like drops in the sea. A flood-tide washes over us every day, in nearly every connection: Boys (men) have a monopoly on initiative and drive, on being focused on as the real midpoint, as the *main person*, whilst girls fall into line as secondary figures and get first priority on feelings, care and passivity.

Indoctrination? Of course.

Is it because we are mothers that our lives should be so different from those who become fathers? But what about those who never become mothers? Or who have to be mother, house-worker and working woman? Or all of those who want to be both a mother and a professional person, like most men who want to be both fathers and professionals.

Should the whole of society be arranged around those of us who become mothers and wish to work at home and have the opportunity to do so?

When will we understand that there are actually many, there are a lot who are in different situations – and that it actually is a matter of *solidarity*? In a revolutionary way, it is a matter of solidarity amongst women. We, who are used to measuring our own well-being against our co-sister's despair. And who on the whole have only shown solidarity with our closest supports (husband, family), because we did not dare to do anything else? Because who dares to take on their protector and the society that protects them – when we have never learnt to live unprotected?

What we need is the will to destroy a pattern which is destroying us all, both women and men. A pattern which continues to press itself around our personalities, which im-pedes and deforms us, which is continually pressing the chil-dren into new straitjackets of 'masculine' aggression and self-assertion and 'feminine' relinquishing of self and subordina-tion, which splits people into neurotic opposing relationships, a division of sexes which is as hysterical as it is straining to seem 'natural'.

Role models? Of course.

You watch films, read books, magazines, newspapers.

You see women's bodies abused in advertising, entertainment, pornography and art. You are pumped full of fashion articles about how you should dress, mask your natural woman's face and falsify the true shapes of your body.

You walk on the street, to the cinema, to a restaurant.

You are a woman and are primarily viewed as a woman, that is, as a *sex*. Some look at your body, your legs, your hips, your backside. Women also look at you, just as you have looked at women. We are *so* instilled in looking at ourselves and each other as sexual objects, and normally as competing objects, that it is more important than what we might think, feel, believe, be, work for or with.

You read the job advertisements. Dividing the jobs into two sections: 'women' and 'men', is still actually allowed. People are employed not according to their qualifications, but according to their sex. You also know that women are continually passed over in important appointments, in both public administration and private industry alike.

You read books. They are often about women. A great deal of 'women's literature' is pure sex role propaganda. Unfortunately, the lower levels of literary quality do not correspond to lower circulation. The damage caused can only be surmised. In serious literature women are also to be found. Sometimes we are dumb geese, hysterical creatures, mystical creations, randy unaccountable bitches or glorified saintly figures. Most often, we are only trivial, boring and frustrated, but nice to look at, acceptable for a screw and the production of children. The descriptions of our bodies, thoughts, attitudes and behaviour reflect a truly vivid contempt for women, sometimes in the form of fear, sometimes in the form of perverse idolatry.

The most favoured tool for down-rating women is probably ridicule. There is hardly a newspaper, show, film, theatre production which does not ridicule women in some context or other.

Our bodies are a territory subordinate to men. Over large

parts of the world men have colonized us, made us into a sexual caste with low status, socially and psychologically.

Men try to control our bodies financially, aesthetically, morally and sexually. They decide what we should use our bodies for, what kind of employment, at the workplace or at home. They decide how our bodies should look, uncomfortable fashions (largely created by men or male indoctrinated women), falsifying our natural shapes. They also tell us who we should love, how many and in what way. Preferably in life-long monogamous marriages – here the self-sacrificial ethos comes in handy – and we must not destroy our own market value by 'using ourselves up' on too many men. Here the feelings of shame for her own body and sexual urges instilled in women are used as an important method of control. Furthermore, we hear how so-called normal women experience an orgasm. It is often men who tell us that too.

Sexual discrimination? Of course.

A man is virile. A woman is a nymphomaniac. A man has had many women. He has a certain aura around him. A woman has had many men. She has a certain aura too ...

Madonna or whore. A brilliant either-or, they can whore with the harlots and marry the Madonnas. The triple standard is flourishing: Level 1: what the man can allow himself to do; Level 2: what the man's wife can(not) allow herself; Level 3: what 'other' women can allow themselves to do (mistresses, prostitutes).

Society knows how to distinguish clearly between married and unmarried women. It is part of the means of persuasion. In contrast to men, we change both our surname and 'title' from *Miss* to *Mrs* when we get married. A man is surprisingly content with being *Mr* throughout his life. We are to be considered as incomplete creatures, without a husband, in the eyes of society. Of course the inflated self-image of many men will burst at that moment when they can no longer create it at the expense of the suppressed woman's dependence.

Many of us can measure our independence and our own intrinsic value in what (or how little) we are without a husband. We borrow the status of the man and let ourselves be used as a platform for his professional effort. We give birth to children and bring them up for a society which does not consider this work to be of a professional nature – in spite of this being the actual *basic production* of society. It is society (state and industry) which will make use of the children's ability to work when they grow up, and not us, who have used ten or twenty years of our lives to make them grow up.

Washing floors and giving birth to children gives no rights to be involved in decisions within society, and it also gives us a minimal right to making decisions about ourselves. Looking after a three room flat gives no status. And we can shout as loudly as we like that we are doing a worthwhile job! 'Of course,' they answer, 'an invaluable job.' *It is so invaluable that it cannot be evaluated as work!* And then we are so privileged. We do not have to clock in at the factory. We do not have to be stressed to death at our writing desks and at conference tables. If *that* is true, then we should *share* these privileges.

'No, it is anatomized,' we hear. It is the order of nature. It is 'a woman's vocation'. We must be financially dependent, or be grateful for poorly paid jobs, or exhaust ourselves in double work. We must live isolated with children in a society where the opportunity of self-realization and freedom of choice is restricted to men, as far as it is possible to talk about freedom of choice in a capitalist society.

No, this is not biology. It is politics, male politics.

Female subordination? Of course.

We can say it as simply and as straight as this: All our thoughts and attitudes are subordinate to men, because we are all influenced by a three-thousand-year-old male culture.

But the myths are coming undone.

It is painful to wake up. It is painful to see so many scared and distorted shadow plants. You feel empty and confused and scared when you must throw overboard most of what you have learnt and believed.

As time goes by, the feeling of new opportunity will come. Then you will be able to try to think differently, think in a new way, live differently.

It feels good to stretch towards the light.

Translated by Angela Shury-Smith

LIV KØLTZOW

Who decides about Bjørg and Unni?

CHAPTER 6

Bjørg walks up towards Grefsenkollen. On the way, she drops Marit off at the park gate, passing her rucksack over the fence to the playground supervisor, and carries on between the blocks of flats. She takes the paved path along the side of the grassy hiking path, up to the residential road. The gardens are laid out with green lawns, but are withered except for a few small red-brown roses against the walls. A woman in skirt and anorak is slowly raking up the leaves under the apple trees and burning them in a heap beside the fence.

Bjørg has to take a detour to get Jon and the pushchair along the path through the woods. Between the trees, she catches glimpses of the town, Fornebu airport, church spires, Bøler, Tveita.

It is the morning after she went to the Triangle with Bjørn. Through her sleepy dullness, she feels her whole body and mind looking back and trying to sort out the mess she has landed in. She wonders how much Arnfinn noticed this morning, and is not convinced she'll be able to keep her thoughts to herself.

Eventually she reaches the sledge run. Jon's head bounces up and down as the pushchair bumps on the gravel. The crushed stones poke up like eyes everywhere, watching.

Frosty bilberries. Still quite a lot of colour around. Red-brown patches of bilberry bushes, brown-gold bracken and straw, but only a few leaves left, fewer than yesterday. The woods seem naked. There is a breeze and it is clouding over. The air is milder than it has been and grey mother-of-pearl clouds move over the sky from the west.

After a while, Jon tires of being bounced about. She takes him out of the pushchair and lets him toddle around the cones and pebbles along the edge of the path. She sits on a piece of rock beside the hiking path to Trollvann, with the cushion from the pushchair underneath her. Shivers a little and wraps her arms round her legs, resting her chin on her knees. She doesn't know if she will say anything to Arnfinn. Wonders if it's possible to tell him. Thinks again about how it happened.

When she went in, she panicked for a moment. A red light shone over the emergency exit beside her. She hesitated, not knowing what to do. Once she had stopped, she found she was unable to make herself go either down the steps or along the gallery. She didn't know where to find Bjørn. The place had been refurbished since she was last there. A continuous crowd of people swarmed past her, talking, shouting. A cloud of smoke and the beat of the music from a room below. A faint sweet smell beside her — could be hash or incense or after-shave, she didn't know which. She stared at the other girls' permed hair, long spotted skirts, flowered blouses, indian shawls, corduroy coats and shiny patent boots, looked down at herself and then around for a mirror.

The memory of being eighteen, sixteen, seventeen hit her

like an icy cold blast: watch other people, use your eyes, hang on, find someone, survive, don't get lost, watch your clothes, laugh, smile, dance, don't faint. And she longed to be home with Arnfinn, their adult life, the flat, the children.

Then she felt two large hands come over her eyes. Dark. The panic changed to expectation. Bjørn? When she turned round, it was Kjell. She was pleased to see him again, and to find Bjørn straight away with Kari Andresen when they went down.

She gave Bjørn a hug, ordered a beer and leaned back in the chair, warmed by the sense of freedom, by the music and the familiar voices of her old friends, by Bjørn's arm which she felt round her back.

During a break in the music she asked the others about their work. Kari worked in a bank and added that she hadn't been to the Triangle for ages. She had bumped into Kjell that afternoon and come with him. Kari asked Bjørg if she was still a physiotherapist. Kjell had studied technology and was working for some company. Then there was Bjørn. It went quiet. She got the feeling he had messed around more than he had let her know. Different music jobs, tried being a playleader in a music creche but didn't have the necessary training, maintained he was studying for his university entrance exams in the spring. She thought he seemed thinner and more uptight than in the morning, his sarcasm not so funny any more. It made her feel unsure of herself.

When the disco started, Bjørn wanted her to dance. The music washed away everything except dancing. She was breathless, lost in the rhythm, body like a brass instrument, shining, full of different tunes trying to get out, her fingers itched, her feet, her shoulders moved around. Bjørn laughed towards her in the red halflight as she kept the rhythm with her feet and felt how good things were between them now. The same old feeling of being with Bjørn, taking a break from everything, having a bit of peace, nobody interfering.

Hot from the dancing, she drank two more beers, getting a little drunk. The ashtray overflowed with white cigarette ends, wet beer stains, empty cigarette packets. Kari and Bjørn talked about travelling, hotels and music jobs. Kjell wanted to talk to her about being a technician. It was just working with technical things, more and more technical things, whereas Bjørg, she was a physiotherapist and Mensendick teacher. She just mended and repaired — people. It began to feel like every other Saturday night out drinking she had ever had. People came to their table, sat down then disappeared again, or hung around Bjørn mumbling incomprehensibly about music. God knows, how much everyone seemed to need to chatter on a bit to someone, dance a bit, have a beer or two, escape for a while. She felt strangely sleepy thinking about it, wanted to go. Suddenly there were too many drunken people around her with too many of the same problems.

She picked her bag up from the floor, put down her cigarette and said she had to get the bus. She took Kari's telephone number and gave her own. They hadn't had much chance to chat now but they could ring each other couldn't they. She gave Kjell a hug. Bjørn stood up and they went out together.

Outside it was a clear, starry autumn night. They walked slowly down some street or other. Bjørn had his arm round her. She looked up at the facades of the buildings and the rows of high narrow windows with heavy curtains inside. And outside the plaster decorations, rows of broad cornices, and black shiny sloping roofs with windows. She had a strange feeling of being back in a time that was really past. The dry sound of their shoes on the pavement, the piles of leaves flying up whenever a taxi rushed past, the chestnuts with waxy yellow leaves under the streetlamps, a woman clattering along in high heels turned into a side street.

Bjørn stopped to roll a cigarette.

'Will you make it to the bus?' he asked. He was quieter again, like he had been in the morning. She had plenty of time, she said. He rested his hand on the back of her neck as they walked on, and after a few paces turned and bent to kiss her. Deep inside, beyond the warmth of his arms around her, she thought about the bus home and Arnfinn, but pushed it to one side until they started walking again, side by side. She realised she would have to go now if she wanted to catch the bus. And she would have to hurry if she wanted to avoid this turning into a major complication.

She couldn't decide and waited until the bus had gone, decided to wait for the next one at quarter past twelve and went with Bjørn up to his room in an old house in one of the streets nearby.

In a shop window just before they got there, she saw them reflected. Bjørg and Bjørn. Tall and slim. Dark clothes. A couple. Bjørn's worn old jacket, his hip-hugging jeans, her hair hanging fair down her back, her coat, her womanliness — it was all there. It was perfect. As perfect as it never had been when they were teenagers. Only now that it was really over, had it become perfect. Bonny and Clyde, she thought, her white teeth smiling at Bjørn, at the adverts, at everything that had fascinated her for so long. Bjørg and Bjørn. Bjørn and Bjørg. It wasn't quite real. And behind the lovely picture of them in the window glass, towers of coffee jars, labels on tins, disposable nappies, bars of soap, oranges, price tags, special offers. Expensive, a bit cheaper and then expensive again. The other life she lived during the day. Reality forcing its way back in.

The thought of it cooled her down a good deal and, when they went up, she sat in the corner of the sofa rubbing her hands warm while Bjørn boiled water for tea, put some records on and filled her once more with a feeling of refuge and rest. At the same time she knew she was on a dangerous slope, but that she had started it and couldn't talk her way out now. She thought about the clothes shop that morning. The jumper she had bought, yellow and fashionable with her round breasts in it. Was it just that marriage put a lid on all these things and when she lifted the lid they were still there? Everything was just as before, the icy blast from her teenage years when she went into the Triangle, the feeling of being no-one but trying to be someone by the clothes you wore, by holding on to a man's arm, and when it didn't work out, doing the same thing all over again? This could be just the same old trap she had fallen into again.

Bjørn came over, poured the tea into the cups and sat beside her on the sofa. She looked at him. He was thin, his neck gaunt, his hair black. It was no trap, just a short moment of honesty between them, a moment of trust. They couldn't help touching each other, feeling each other.

When they had taken off their clothes, she looked at him and felt he was a stranger. His chest was narrower than Arnfinn's, his penis smaller, the hair on his body thicker, his knees bony. The whole time they made love, she felt the strangeness of him, like an unfamiliar smell, despite the familiarity and intimacy of the whole experience. She missed the feeling of belonging she had with Arnfinn's body. At the same time, she felt on the point of a white-hot, thrilling ecstasy linked to Bjørn, Bjørn from this morning, Bjørn's hands, his black hair, and she swayed around in the feeling, giddy from it, but came no further. It seemed to her almost before they began that intercourse was different from just being together normally. It was like an eye, honest and sharp, following her to make sure she was really involved in what she was doing. For a while she was sure they wouldn't be able to finish and thought helplessly, this mustn't be something that only Bjørn felt pleasure in. Then she remembered that she had started it. It was she who decided. She was in control. She could stop whenever she wanted, go whenever she wanted, carry on if she wanted. She felt a glow of fondness for that and looked at Bjørn's face.

She slept for five minutes afterwards, woke as if it were morning but saw the white streetlight outside the window and a glimpse of something that could be the moon beyond the rows of roofs on the other side of the street. She sat on the edge of the sofa and put her clothes on while she drank the cold tea in large gulps. Thought about all the shortlived moments of peace there were. Now this one was disappearing already.

She hadn't had time to talk to him but didn't want to leave without doing it. Thought about who he was and what sort of life he led, and wanted to ask him about it, but felt how clumsy it would be and how impossible to do it properly. Instead she chattered about what a good night out it had been, talked about Kjell, about how Kari was, whether she and Bjørn would see each other again. She wrote down his address and said she might drop into the shop some time.

Bjørn put on his jumper and trousers, went out with her, gave her a hug. The same feeling of taking a break from herself and her whole life stayed with her in the taxi home, the city full of light behind her as she got out and her heels clacked along the quiet paths towards the flats.

In the hall she put the light on. Outdoor clothes, rubber boots, carrier bags, umbrellas, a crust on the floor, a fire engine, a cloth, plastic pants. Suddenly she was back again. It was hard to return to her unresolved family life. She came home, found everyone asleep, everyone who expected something of her, depended on her, always took it for granted that she would serve them with her work, her presence, her body, her mind.

She crept around in her stockinged feet, brushed her hair, knowing it had meant a lot to feel the old freedom again and her old independent life. She wondered how she would manage to hold on to it, keep it now she was back here.

In the morning she woke with a fit of black conscience. At the breakfast table, Arnfinn asked if the film had been good.

'Not particularly,' she answered, 'but I met Eva. We went for a beer afterwards.'

'So, you were women's-libbing?'

He looked relieved. She twisted her large features into an exaggerated ironic grimace.

'We had so much to talk about.'

'Yes, I can imagine.'

He picked up his packed lunch and the newspaper, put on his jacket, kissed her and left. She sat at the table unsure of herself again. She hadn't reckoned on it being so awful to talk about something that hadn't happened. She felt at once that her whole marriage stood in the balance. This was how trust between people was undermined. She saw before her how everything broke up into small incomprehensible pieces and became meaningless the moment you no longer stuck to what, after all, had happened.

Marit came pattering out to her, just awake and still sleepy in her pyjamas, with bare feet. She stuttered a little, rubbing her eyes.

'Mummy, I had a horrible dream. There was, there was a great big bear.'

Bjørg started. A bear — Bjørn. She took Marit onto her lap, with the child's arms round her neck, her cheek next to her own, chatted to her about the bear without being able to rid herself of the growing feeling that the ground was disappearing from under her feet.

Bjørg watches the smoke rise from the factory chimneys at Økern and Alnabru, sees the spire of Tonsen church, the cranes way down in the harbour. She hears the drone of the traffic and the sound of work right up here on the moss where she and Jon are sitting sticking twigs into cones, making barns, cows, sheep. She thinks about Arnfinn who will be in the printing room now, the noise, the mess of the ink. He would no doubt swap with her if he could see her. And why couldn't he? Why couldn't they swap? She would give a hundred thousand kroner to be standing there in dirty overalls doing a proper day's work, talking to grown ups during the morning break, not always living in a child's world, not always having to mess about with cows and fir-cone pigs, and play her way back into a childhood she has long since squeezed dry and got sick of.

She thinks about Arnfinn. Arnfinn this morning. What he is like and why she married him. She feels the vitality has gone out of their relationship. Just an unsteady piece of ground left beneath her. What happens if he finds out?

Arnfinn is tall, heavily built with broad shoulders. He is practical, clever with his hands, can always mend cars, fridges, motorbikes, radios, put windows in, lay floors. He is active, reads technical journals, newspapers, talks about things that interest him, the news, films, what politicians have said, Arctic expeditions, technical innovations, ideas about the future. He dominates their home completely in all these areas. In between times he can be absent-minded, distant or just tired. He is maybe not particularly bright. She has often thought his domination is caused by his need for action rather than a desire for power.

Now she thinks about him in relation to Bjørn, she feels Arnfinn is like a machine. He never really sees her, is not really interested in her world, is completely swallowed up by his own men's world, his mates' world. There is nothing wrong with him really, she thinks, except that he is used to his mother waiting on him, takes it for granted. Otherwise he is a decent person. She likes the way he wants to take a stand in politics, likes his desire to get things done. She likes it better than Bjørn's leanings towards hash and dropping out, towards a closed-in environment where nothing can be achieved.

When she met Arnfinn, she liked his adult ways, his manly body, his earthiness, his strength. Now it has changed. She is sick of struggling in the shadow of his self development. She enjoyed herself with Bjørn yesterday and for a moment she allows herself to succumb to the hopelessness of working her way back to where she was with Arnfinn.

Jon begins to sulk. He is fed up with the woods and all the things he keeps falling over. He wants to put the cones in his mouth. He needs his nap. She has to go home and tidy up.

She picks up the cushion and anoraks and struggles with Jon who decides he doesn't want to get in the pushchair after all. He twists himself around and cries, his body stiff. She gets angry and a bit heavy handed. While he sits sniffling on the way down, the sun comes out through a couple of pale blue gaps left between the clouds. It shines burning hot on her and Jon and on the aspens, thin and golden along the edge of the path, with their last leaves. Colour bursts out for a moment over the whole city and on the hill above her, then disappears again immediately. Before she gets home, it begins to spit with rain. She manages to put the hood of the buggy over Jon but gets wet herself. As they get home it starts to pour, and she has to lift him out sleeping and go, wet and warm, up to the flat which is in a complete mess after two days of letting it go.

She feels a rush of energy and decides to get all the cleaning done in an hour, starts wading through it a room at a time. The bedroom, lounge, children's room, bathroom, kitchen. Dirty socks, sweaty shirts, nappies, socks with holes in, buttons that have come off, split trousers, stiff ironing in a pile waiting to be done, trousers with dark stains, dirty bed linen. Handfuls of paper tissues, disposable nappies which smell, apple cores, ash trays, toilet rolls on the window ledge, milk cups, withered autumn leaves in vases, hundreds of soggy lumps of bread under Jon's chair. Toys everywhere, in the double bed, the bath, on the bookcase, on the veranda.

She fetches a bucket and cloth and runs while she dusts. She thinks about slavery and peasant revolts and about Arnfinn who just drops his dirty socks on the floor while he broods about the latest wage settlement or how they should deal with the local union leader's latest initiative.

She sorts the clothes, putting them in drawers, to soak, into the washing machine, into the sewing basket — everything back in its place. She thinks about all the men in the world. Tall or strong, powerful or weak, they can't clean their own mess up. They couldn't keep the dirt away for a week. They don't know how to keep themselves clean, how to get food or clothes. She imagines a world-wide washing strike and enjoys the thought of the worlds of work and world politics drowning in dirt, the smell of sweat, dust, sick, washing up, smelly socks.

She finishes and sits in a chair. The sparkling flat shines icily at her. She will get angry when the children and Arnfinn start messing it up again later today.

She feels that one way or another she has to start fighting against Arnfinn. There is no point in running off with a new man every time they disagree. She sees that clearly. She could exchange Arnfinn for Bjørn, could imagine being married to Bjørn — Bjørn at work all day, her at home. Nothing would have changed.

Arnfinn. Arnfinn and her. For the last few months she has felt with her whole being that it was Arnfinn who stood in her way. Like having his hand clasped round her neck all the time. Her game, being housewife, mother, began to fall apart just as Unni's interest in politics began to grow. It was then she suddenly realised that nothing the others talked about had anything to do with her. She felt betrayed. She had one thought in her head: they belonged and she didn't. They met adults every day while she was dependent on Arnfinn, and him alone, whenever she needed openness, trust, new ideas. She had the feeling she just emptied her meagre ideas over into Arnfinn's head and he immediately put them into practice. She felt stillborn, useless. No rings radiated out from her. She took no part in anything. Except the humiliating consolation of making bread, recipes with cheese, overalls, bookcases, lamps, shopping, flowers in the window boxes, painting the walls a different colour each year, a new sofa, kitchen curtains in a different colour. She experienced things with her children, but couldn't share them with Arnfinn because he wasn't with them and didn't notice the same things as her. She made it plain to him that the children were her sphere and only she had any real grasp of them. At the same time she was angry with him because it was like that. She never finished reading a newspaper, never knew what the others were talking about. She lived in her own era. Not the eighteenth century, not the Stone Age, but her own twentieth century with sun and wind, weather, frost, clothes and the smell of washing, blue hills and dusky evenings, good wide yawns at bedtime and newly washed sheets. She had no part in the others' century, didn't know what happened in their time. She hasn't been living in time.

She thinks about politics — and the growing feeling that she must either begin to take an interest or stay out of it for good. It is hard to imagine she could spend her whole life indifferent to what is happening in her own country, indifferent to who has the power. Wouldn't she, at some time or other, sit there and feel like one of the many millions of oppressed and apolitical women that pro-EEC campaigners say don't exist in the EEC countries? She knows a bit about politics. Inside herself. But she'll never get any further than now if she carries on clearing up after Arnfinn.

She goes over to the window. The rain pours down the

panes. In the distance there is a light outline of clouds over the hills. She remembers last night and can't help rejoicing that such things happen. At the same time she imagines it happening again with someone else in six months, a year. Afterwards, each time, back here to wash the window sills, tidy up underwear, overcome her bitterness towards Arnfinn, take nourishment from her secret life when she is alone. Should she carry on being unfaithful to Arnfinn just because she daren't ask him to wash his own socks?

And yet, as she stands there tapping her nails on the smooth window sill, watching the rain getting heavier, all the time feeling uneasy about Jon whom she can't be bothered to get up yet, still with the same old sense of imprisonment lying in wait inside her body, standing in her cage in the flat, she refuses to reject her experience with Bjørn. Never in her life, she thinks, will she feel any guilt for that evening.

She turns away from the window thinking obstinately about Bjørn, and her eye catches the pile of newspapers overflowing out of the bookcase. She forgot to tie them up and get rid of them. She fetches string and scissors. There are a week's papers at least, perhaps two — except for today's which Arnfinn takes every morning. She gets angry. It is just not on that he assumes the paper is his and that it is more important for him to read it than for her.

She starts to leaf through the pile. Folds out the pages, rustles the paper, forgets to tie them up and reads them instead. Politics, sports pages, car pages. Car pages, sports pages, politics. Sports pages, car pages, politics. Hats, ties, muscles, briefcases, wrestlers' vests, politicians' smiles, politicians' suits, guerilla uniforms. Weapons, racing cars, briefcases, football boots. No wonder the paper is more important for Arnfinn than for her. Men's smiles and pompous statements, an ocean of trickery and corruption, disguised and open power battles, intrigues. She rips up the paper in her hand in anger.

One thing is certain, the capitalist system Arnfinn talks about is inseparable from the sick worshipping of power-hungry men every day in stupid, obsequious newspapers. Inseparable. A soap advert she came across when she was little suddenly comes to her. 'A soap without parallel'. Parallel? Did that mean the edges of the soap? You couldn't have soap without edges. Otherwise it would be flat. It isn't possible. Without edges it doesn't exist. In just the same way, she thinks, the world, politics and the newspapers would not exist without this cockfighting between the boys.

What was the soap called? 'Goma', 'Greve'? Heavens, how tired she is. Jon wakes, mutters, starts to fret. He is always bad tempered after his nap, hungry. She thumps her fist on the table. She won't tell Arnfinn what happened yesterday until ten years from now. She'll go straight out and get a job. There can be no talk of sharing the housework with Arnfinn until they are equal. As long as she stays at home, she stays at home. As long as she has time to do all that is needed in the house for four people, it is ridiculous to put pressure on Arnfinn to share it with her. What would she do instead? She knows Arnfinn does a hard day's work with a full-time job and his union activity as well. If she wants to change anything at all, she will have to start working herself. The children will just have to suffer at first. They will probably end up better off than before.

Bjørg ties string round the papers and tries to imagine how it would be, if she could manage it. To get a job sorted out seems easier to her than getting Arnfinn to change his habits. She has no intention of getting into a situation where she has a job and all the housework. She'll have to make a plan of action. She feels it will be best to keep quiet about Bjørn, best to keep quiet about a lot of things.

She throws the pile of papers under the hall table and tiptoes over to put on the record she bought yesterday before

Jon wakes properly. She remembers how easy it was to talk to Bjørn, and suddenly realises, blushing at her own naivety, that it would be far too brutal a revenge on Arnfinn to tell him anything at all. It isn't his fault after all, even if it feels like it all the time. She dances by herself to the Stones music and smiles at the thought of all the women's lib comments she will hear and put up with hearing. When it comes down to it, it is her own fault she has been at home so long, messing about and allowing herself to get bitter. In fact, it is she who has been brutal. She who has betrayed Arnfinn. In a way, she is quits with him now. So it is easier to start again.

Jon whimpers. She picks him up and takes him into the living room with her, holds him in her arms and carries on dancing. He wrinkles his forehead crossly, whilst he looks around for the music. Doesn't he like Mick Jagger's sly voice? She thinks about Mick Jagger and why girls still fall for those who treat them roughest, hardest, most aggressively, abuse them and deceive them. It is Arnfinn she is thinking of — all that she found so irresistible in him at the beginning. Maybe it is because of some wish to be taken seriously, to be treated as an equal, as someone who can live through trials, someone who is given a fair chance to develop herself without being protected. Maybe. On the other hand, it could just as easily be the remains of an old masochism, helplessly falling into old patterns of womanhood — I cannot be anyone's equal, I must be helpless, I must be wretched and spineless. This is the one thing I have learnt. I know all there is to know about guilt, reckoning, washing up and how to avoid anything other than the guilt disappearing until the next load of washing-up. I don't know anything else.

And why do people believe that as soon as an opening is visible in someone's face, as in Bjørn's face yesterday morning, they have to creep into it straightaway? Instead of using the opening for something else. As a chance to make friends

49

for example, to find more people to trust. It is a way of dragging the idea of marriage with you everywhere. 'It is only possible to trust one person at a time.' Trusting several people is polygamy, and trusting many, even most, people only something that exists in a fantasy world. For most people, when someone shows them friendliness, openness, the first time they experience it, it is so exceptional that they throw themselves at it, swallow the whole of it, decide to suck on it for the rest of their lives, get married.

She goes over to the record player. Jon looks at the knobs and tries to reach them. Bjørg takes the record off, listens to the silence after the music and puts the record in the sleeve. For a moment she longs for Arnfinn to come home, for the disturbance and noise of people back in the flat, lots of people — for there to be lots of them there all the time.

CHAPTER 7

Bjørg does her coat up and looks for the umbrella in the cupboard. They are in the hall of her and Arnfinn's flat. Unni says, 'It will be fine, Arnfinn. If she wakes up you can give her an apple.'

'Yes, go on you two. The longer you stand here fussing the worse it will be.'

He comes in from the living room with the coffee pot in one hand and a cigarette in the other. The television flickers. In the kitchen, the washing machine is rinsing clothes.

Bjørg and Unni go downstairs and smile at each other.

'Damn, I forgot to tell him where I put the apples.'

'It doesn't matter. He'll cope for two hours without apples. Even if they make a pact and all three of them scream the whole time.'

It is raining. The water streams down the road, splashing

out of the gutters.

Unni stops outside the door to put up the umbrella and turns to Bjørg. 'I hope it's OK to do this, Bjørg. It was a bit of a struggle with Kristin being so tired when she came back from Merete. I think Arnfinn was a bit annoyed with me. But still, I think he can manage to babysit for once.'

They walk up the road which shines wet in the lights. The rain slants down in the wind. She is getting cold and wet on her legs above her short rubber boots. That wasn't really what she meant to say but she is tired and just started chattering. At least it was about what she wanted to say.

'Oh yes', says Bjørg. 'Yes, it was a good idea. I just wish you'd found a better excuse for him to babysit than going to a meeting. In this weather too.'

Unni starts to feel angry. For heaven's sake, she thinks, are you completely stupid? No-one moans more than you about how awful it is living next to the Trondheim road with kids. It's you who will suffer most if we get yet another road. She feels like giving up and is on the verge of regretting it all. Could go home instead to a warm flat and have a cup of tea.

'Anyway, Arnfinn babysat last night too,' says Bjørg.

Oh, thinks Unni. Where were you yesterday then? What's happened? In the halflight under the umbrella, she looks at Bjørg's profile, her nose, mouth, chin and the little smile which is suddenly somewhere in her face. So, finally something has happened. Bjørg's stupid secrecy under the umbrella. Doesn't she understand how things are, doesn't she understand anything. It's like seeing a horse in flight. Couldn't you have thought of something better, Bjørg. Couldn't you have thought of something else. No, you couldn't. She recognises Bjørg's prison, under the umbrella, in the rain, between the flats, rain water trickling around their boots and down the windows at home. Yes, she knows it inside out. Does she really believe anything has changed?

Unni doesn't want to talk to her about it, doesn't want to see inside her head. She is dreading the meeting, knows hardly anyone who is going, wishes she wasn't and says, 'Heavens, two days in a row. Not bad. Did you go to the pictures?' She turns to Bjørg. Her face is not like she expected after all, not secretive. No, Bjørg laughs aloud and at once Unni feels stupid. It is Bjørg's old rebellious laugh. It is good. Unni feels her sense of responsibility catch in her throat. She has to smile at Bjørg's laughter. Now she is really dreading going to the meeting and talking to people she doesn't know. 'No, let's go home to my flat, Bjørg,' she says nervously and jumps when two more umbrellas suddenly appear behind Bjørg. Two other women going to the meeting. They nod and ask if Unni and Bjørg are going. Two women in their forties. Unni has seen one of them before, lots of times, but not the other.

They go into the hall, down a flight of steps. The warmth, rainwater in the corridor outside, steel chairs and small tables and right at the top, the dais. Metal ashtrays, worried faces, friendliness, smiles. Mineral water from somewhere. There are a lot of people here. Curiosity. Unfamiliar faces. Who is it who lives around here? Not alone in their living rooms with short-lived entertainment in front of the television, but in a hall in a cellar, meeting together to see if they can get anything done.

They find their way to an empty table together with the two women who came in with them. They all look round, hesitate, smooth folds out of skirts, sit down.

'Well, what awful weather. Coffee would have been nicer,' says the eldest of the two women and smiles at Unni, as she plays with the straw in her mineral bottle and thinks about how meetings used to be. 'But everything had to be organised so quickly. I think this meeting should have been held yesterday, anyway. The diggers are already out. They start properly tomorrow. I can't see there is anything we can do.' She looks at Unni and wants to know what she thinks about the proposal to be discussed, stopping the digging and demanding that the issue is taken up by the authorities again.

'Yes, aren't we just going to stop the digging, then?' says Unni, who doesn't really have much of an opinion just at that moment. 'Isn't that all we are discussing?'

Perhaps the woman beside her is against the proposal? She feels nervous and starts to read the circular again to make sure she has understood everything. With half an ear, she listens to what Bjørg and the other woman are talking about. Bjørg looks animated. Unni hears her strong, slightly husky voice and then the milder, thinner voice of the woman who is called Mrs Martinsen. 'It's ridiculous how we've let it get so difficult with children here along the Trondheim road. It's something I've only really realised now, unfortunately, with my children almost grown-up. But it is the hill that has saved us so far. Without the hill it would be hopeless. Now we have to fight for it.'

She smiles and adds, 'Remember this, you young people. If there is something you want, get together and fight for it. We were so cautious when we were twenty. Now people are beginning to understand that they have less and less to lose by taking things into their own hands. I think it's marvellous. The less cautious I become myself, the better I feel it is to be alive.'

Cautious? Is that what they are? Bjørg and Unni sit and feel cautious. Old maids. Young girls from the 1850s disguised as elegant women in trousers. Unni puts her bag down and looks at Bjørg. Bjørg is sitting in her chair and talking pleasantly with the woman next to her. Glad to have found someone she likes at last. This is not Arnfinn or Unni forcing on her something they don't believe themselves. A forty year old woman with so much life left in her. This is something Bjørg has to believe in. Bjørg carries on the conversation, talks about herself too, but not as she usually does. More easily, more open. Is she making fun? Is she being smooth and sarcastic? Does she mean to sit through the whole meeting like this? 'Yes, that's right.' 'Yes, absolutely. That's just what I think.' And then come out afterwards and say, 'What a load of shit!' But she seems honest. Her voice sounds serious, her face is normal. No sideways glance at Unni. Bjørg at a meeting, thinks Unni, dust on her brain, a general meeting of the residents' association. Everything Norwegian films have always made fun of. It isn't true that people are like that. Behind her someone laughs. She thinks, it looks as if people are enjoying themselves, without their televisions, with each other. She feels a small, no, a major sense of achievement that she has managed to get Bjørg to come and organised Arnfinn as babysitter.

It is not long before she sees politics raise its head again. It is after a dry, cautious man has assumed the task of explaining the situation. 'Yes, you know most of it, but can we just look at the main issues again.' After he has 'reported', 'referred to', 'discussed', 'authorities', 'the Head of Planning', 'the letter of such and such a date to such an office' and a 'new letter of such a date to another office', 'where it was pointed out', 'rejected', 'opposed' and 'Housing Officer', 'City Planning Office', 'Expropriation Office', 'City Councillors', 'Sports and Leisure Office', 'Parks and Gardens', 'Traffic Chief', 'Building Commissioner', 'Executive Committee', 'Highways Commissioner'. After Bjørg has sunk into her body and sat thinking of Bjørn's face, the metal bracelet round Bjørn's wrist. After Unni has felt annoyance fight with boredom for supremacy inside her, God, this is impossible. It's hopeless. After a few other men have taken the stand and carried on about Highways Commissioner, Heads of Office, authorities, Traffic Chief, statues, busts, plinths and endless lists of filed letters. After a woman has stood up and said 'straight out' that 'this meeting is pointless. It has all been discussed before and we know very well there is nothing else to be done. I don't want to be part of any demonstration' and, now she has sat down again, added, 'I don't believe in such things. It only causes trouble.'

The sudden unpleasant wakefulness in her body. Everyone is all too aware of their body at the meeting. Biting their lips, pressing their fingers together, blushing, sitting with their hands half raised, looking round the tables, reassuring themselves that at least one person near them agrees with them, holding the edge of the table or taking a cigarette out of a packet, asking for a light and turning round when they hear a new speaker. A young man has stood up. They listen politely.

'I don't think it's so terrible to cause a little trouble to those who have had something to do with this. It would trouble me if we became the victims of some bureaucratic tactic to wear us out when the issue is so important to us. Some of us have tried to think how we could do it. It is quite simple really. There's no harm in trying when we have so much to lose. I think we should go down tomorrow and get the workers to stop the digging and at the same time, send a group of people from our housing group down to the office that is dealing with it. I think it's wrong to stand around and let the authorities run completely off the rails. It's important to do something when we actually see that a mistake is being made. Otherwise all this talk about democracy doesn't mean anything at all. They haven't considered those of us who will be affected at all. It doesn't make any difference that the bulldozers are already there. They can even fill in the hole they've dug today. I don't think we should let ourselves be frightened off by the bulldozers or give up yet. I'm sure we can get the authorities to delay the project. It's just a matter of making sure they can see us behind their piles of paperwork.'

Long speech. Unni doesn't like the last sentence. All well and good for well-meaning young men but it is not enough and people wince at the word 'democracy'. When she looks around she meets a sea of worried, averted, closed or insecure faces. Or is it not really like that? Something else can be glimpsed in the face of a middle-aged housewife and ends as a movement of her hand towards the table on the dais. She begins to speak without being sure whether to stand or sit, with her body bending forwards and her arms leaning on the table top.

'All of us who have had children in this area are sick of running round and herding them through the traffic, and now it will be worse than before. No, I want to do something. My children may be nearly grown-up but I think everyone who lives here should stick together over this. We will lose what sleep we have left. I would be ashamed if we didn't do something. Think of our children. We are adults. I support your proposal, you ...'

Someone shouts his name, 'Berg'.

'Yes, Berg, yes.' She nods and sits down looking around for a response. It becomes quiet. Are Berg and the others waiting to see what everyone else thinks? Doesn't everyone agree, thinks Unni, apart from the ones who have already spoken out against doing anything?

Unni frowns and wants to say that she supports the proposal, but daren't. Bjørg sits smoking with a slightly distant look in her eyes.

'If we do something like this,' says a voice a little distance away, 'it will end up with people in other districts doing the same. And in the end no-one will get what they want. How would it be if the authorities listened to every argument and suggestion people flood them with all the time?'

Yes, how would it be then? Unni has to smile, but at the same time thinks, now we have been stupid. We have lost our grip again. Can't we just get on with it? But they can't because there are lots of things that have not even been thought of yet, several people are saying. A man stands up and calls Berg's suggestion unrealistic. The people working the bulldozers cannot just stop. They have to do their jobs. It is making life difficult for them too. And those who make the decision, they cannot possibly take a new decision just like that. Who would keep a watch on the diggers in the meantime? They have already started digging up at Krokveien as well. How can you believe it is possible to stop something like that?

Unni is bored stiff. What is wrong with people who talk like this? What is wrong with what they say? A fairy story she reads Kristin about just what they are doing. 'Cow, cow, give me a bowl of milk. The cat won't kill the rat, the rat won't gnaw the rope, the rope won't hang the butcher, the butcher won't kill the ox, the ox won't drink the water, the water won't quench the fire, the fire won't burn the stick, the stick won't beat the dog, the dog won't bite the pig, the pig won't jump over the fence and I shan't get home tonight.'

The people speaking now are the ones who hang onto this same back-to-front jingle. Those who are hypnotised every time someone raises a new difficulty. Those who are moving further and further back.

However, there are still a lot of people who have not said anything yet. She can't tell by their faces what they think. She thinks, dreamily, just imagine if there is something else behind their silence. Why don't you say something yourself? I suppose you think they can see by your face that you support the proposal?

Why daren't she confront the worried tones, the hostility towards those who want to do something? In the distance she can smell the burning smell of politics. Can a measly demonstration about a piece of road reawaken the old fear of communism? A smell of fear. Unni daren't speak. She feels blocked. Her voice would sound thin and girlish. Who would she look at? Mrs Martinsen, the floor, the ceiling, the back of the woman's head in front of her? She would go bright red as usual, and if she said something stupid, she could ruin it all.

She's only there to follow what the others do. Who has spoken so far? Six men and two older housewives. Is it so difficult to be a young woman and speak up?

In any case it is much more difficult than to overcome the idiotic difficulties the four men and one of the women keep putting forward. All five of them are completely overwhelmed by these fantastic problems that no-one has properly considered before. One mountain after another in the fog, chasms, slippery wooden bridges, high fences, walls and more. No, Unni does not believe in their difficulties. They are just rubbish. Old people's problems. Will there be any problems left as soon as you manage to open your mouth and get people to listen to you? They just act as if there are problems. Or is it a real prison they are stumbling around in?

She wonders if they will manage to get others in behind their grey walls of pessimism with them. If they will get them too to see the talk of protest with grey, rational eyes. So the faces of those who want to do something suddenly appear to shine with white, trusting naivety. So the idea of doing something appears childish to them, naive. Naive, blank faces. Like dumb Indians who believe they will not be shot down as long as they wave their white flag.

She looks around. Are the others bothered about it? Are they having a rest and thinking about something else? The woman at the next table, with the strange look in her eyes, is there something wrong with her left eyelid or is she just staring? Are they thinking about the bathroom floor at home which was wet when they left home, after the shower? Unni guesses. What are they thinking about? a razor, soap in their hands? Being at their holiday cabins? Painted red after the summer, the warm air through the tops of the fir trees, bare feet on the gravel path, ice cream adverts at the campsite? Have they forgotten all that is happening here? Is it autumn in their heads? The rain that began this morning, and a rotten remark at work. The horrible feeling has stayed with them all day, heavy, what did he mean by that? Or are they thinking about being alone? Chopping wood in the shed when no-one else is around. Pieces of bark in the grass, the smell of sawdust. Alone with chocolate on the bedside table, porno magazines with greasy creases and white flesh on all the pages? Fights? Do they wish they could break out of their indecision, with clenched teeth and punches? Are they thinking about how they normally live in their blocks of flats? Attempts to make friends when they are up on the hill in the summer when it is warm? Everything they want to protect?

Unni dreams. The woman beside her nudges her in the back and nods. She forces herself back to reality with a questioning look on her face. Has someone spoken to her? Is she supposed to do something?

But it is not her. It is a young housewife talking. Unni listens to her. The woman supports the protest. It is surprising. It takes a while to comprehend. She doesn't say anything new or special. She is not particularly clever, but she supports the protest and wants it to happen. She manages to save it as it seemed to have died completely. She ignores the man who spoke before her. She begins with a different angle, begins with herself, and Unni feels she recognises herself in her face.

The woman who thought a protest would only cause trouble gets up again. Unni holds her breath. 'Naive', 'senseless', 'uninformed' she says again. The words hang in the air after she has sat down again. Unni thinks angrily, they mustn't be allowed to turn this argument about 'sense' upside down again. They are the ones who don't have any sense. I have got to say it. I have to. It's too important. They are standing everything on its head and no-one has said so. I'm going to say it. Unni raises her hand. Her voice comes back at her from every wall, saying, 'The ones with sense must be those who are trying to keep the traffic away from our children. It must make sense to try to keep the right to decide how our children will grow up, or if they will grow up at all. And what about us? How will it be for us? I support the protest. Can't we take a vote on it now?'

She sits down and feels confused. What did she really say? 'And what about us?', 'Support the protest'. Did anyone understand? Has she said something stupid? All the eyes that turned to look at her and the surprise on Bjørg's face. The woman next to her is friendly and lights a cigarette for her. It has all been said before. Why did she do it?

But afterwards when they start to discuss a vote seriously and to talk about how the protest should be put into action, she thinks it must have been good. She lets the surprise rush round inside her head, lets a warm wave of pleasure at herself wash through her. She feels that the similarity between what they are tackling now and the way she is taking up her own case with Kristin's nursery place shows there is only one way to get things done. This is something she knows about: pen and paper, write down all the difficulties and overcome them, one by one.

'Do we need a vote?', 'Can't those who want to protest just do it?', 'It's important to have the support of the whole community behind us.' 'What about the protest to be delivered to the authorities?', 'Someone has written a draft. Can it be used?' 'The office, the address, which people there are sympathetic, names?' 'What do we do about the loss of work to the building company?' 'Who is responsible for compensation?'

The vote. Slips of paper and silence. The count. A large majority in support of the protest, quiet jubilation, a quiet sense of excitement in most faces, then back down to earth, feet back on the ground because it is on the ground that this is happening. People like to find a use for the practical experience they have. She can see that. What time tomorrow? Who will stay at home in the morning? The count. Should the committee deliver the protest? Protest committee? Who will speak to the workers? Nominations to the committee are made.

At the last moment, a new warning about the problem of the building company, discussion of whether they should talk to the builder, put it aside for later.

Then they are finished. The meeting breaks up.

It is nearly eleven. Unni and Bjørg are tired and talk mechanically to each other on the way home.

When they come up to the flat, Arnfinn asks who was voted on to the committee. He sits while they talk. He asks questions, makes comments, puts forward objections which they have to think about before they can answer. Finally he says that it sounds good and is about to go to bed but Bjørg asks him to carry Kristin home.

They wrap Kristin in a blanket without her waking and Unni thinks how nice it is to walk beside Arnfinn with Kristin asleep in his arms. A sort of peace pipe atmosphere after the peaceful conversation just before, no sarcasm, Bjørg not fighting. At the same time it is strange to talk to him when he doesn't know she is wondering who Bjørg has been with. It isn't important, she thinks. It's nothing to do with me. But she cannot help watching him from the window as he walks home again.

Translated by Julia Norman

BJØRG VIK

Two Acts for Five Women

Ellinor: How we used to sing all night! Are we getting old?

Lilleba: Old?

Gry: Not old –

Anne Sofie: Something is happening to us.

Gry: Happening? Of course something is happening.

Anne Sofie: I mean, it's happening now. I can see it in the mirror, you don't have to tell me. I think turning forty is awful.

Gry: Life begins at forty.

Anne Sofie: It's over, nearly everything is over. Oh God, I wish I was twenty –

Lilleba: And what would you do then?

Gry: You go swimming and to the gym and –

Anne Sofie: And dye my hair and use sweeteners and try to get rid of my wrinkles with make-up and wear long trousers to look young. It's just ridiculous, all of it.

Hanna: (*with a smiling negro mask in front of her face, wiggles around*) Big man like me? Big white man love me? I soft and obedient, like you want me. Give birth, breast feed, wash children. Wash, cook, scrub? Everything you ask for. (*on her knees*) Little woman look up to big man, big protector.

Lilleba: (*naively*) What fun! It's like being at the theatre.

Hanna: You rule over my body, my thoughts, my life. You lock me up safely in your house, you look after money and the big bad world. I look after the little nest –

Anne Sofie: That's enough. I think we understand what you mean.

Ellinor: (*in male role*) No, little woman, you cannot stay here and gather dust. Get out! Go out to work!

Hanna: As my lord and master decrees. I go to factory, I wash big long floors, I serve in shop, I empty potties, I sell clever gadgets at doors, I look after the old, look after the young, look after the sick. I rush home, boil potatoes, bake bread. No-one notice that I work –

Ellinor: You're so tired in the evening. You're no fun any more. I'm going out for a walk.

Hanna: Kind sir, don't go. I'll be a wonderful lover, read all about it in books. I get new nightdress, perfume. I make sure there's no baby. I do everything!

Ellinor: You're too stupid to talk to.

Hanna: Oh, I go on course, learn clever things, become educated person, speak nice words.

Ellinor: Your body is so old, wrinkled, flabby. Your breasts droop.

Hanna: I buy new bra, new super bra, I buy corset, go on diet, go to keep-fit. Dye my hair! Red? Blue? Use spray, floral spray, here – and there. I am a flower, pick me, pick me, big bumblebee!

Anne Sofie: OK, OK, we get the message.

Hanna: (*removes mask*) Do you?

Lilleba: Can you remember when Hanna and Anne Fi —

Hanna: As you can see, woman is mankind's best friend.

Lilleba: Can you remember when Hanna and Anne Fi acted in that play at school, the one about the pilot, both of them were in love with a pilot –

Ellinor: You're going a little over the top, Hanna. But OK.

Hanna: You have to say it with capital letters now and then.

Lilleba: And the handsome pilot was that one in the same year as us. What was he called? The one who squinted so amazingly. It looked as if he was looking at both of you at the same time.

Anne Sofie: And at the first night party we drank home-made wine and beer and the pilot crash-landed in the shower.

Hanna: Without a parachute.

Lilleba: And Anne Fi's petticoat was showing throughout the performance and that was the worst thing that had ever happened to you.

Ellinor: It seems to me that you aren't so uncertain and deprived of freedom, Hanna. Not the slave type if you ask me.

Hanna: I have risen above it all, at last. But it took some time.

Ellinor: I seem to recall quite clearly that you stood on your own two feet before as well.

Hanna: Yes – but, with crutches.

Ellinor: By that, do you mean poor Magnus?

Hanna: I clung to him, yes.

Ellinor: Do you mean that Anker is my crutch? My crutch and support — ?

Hanna: You've got to find that out for yourself, Ellinor.

Ellinor: When people start using that old phrase 'you've got to find that out for yourself', then they've found it out for you, that's for sure.

Lilleba: You haven't taken much with you, Hanna. All those beautiful things, the new dresser, the leather chairs —

Hanna: I had a bad conscience, you see.

Lilleba: (*naively*) Did you?

Hanna: Lilleba – !

Lilleba: Did I say something wrong again? I am sorry, I didn't mean to —

Anne Sofie: Would that be so strange?

Hanna: What?

Anne Sofie: I mean, if you had a bit of a bad conscience.

Hanna: Aha, there we have it. It's really quite strange, but people love to talk about divorces. Especially those who are married.

Ellinor: That was underhand, Hanna. Defensive.

Lilleba: I don't understand what you're talking about.

Anne Sofie: Me neither.

Ellinor: What a shame you don't have the guitar any more.

Hanna: (*gets up*) Yes, what a shame I don't have the guitar any more.

Gry: What, have you still got it, after all?

Hanna: Got what?

Gry: The guitar.

Lilleba: (*suddenly, concentrated*) Hey everyone, women must be allowed to struggle free and liberate themselves and that kind of thing, take the path they want to, I mean where *they* want to, just like Hanna. If it is right, I mean? To realise themselves, all alone, don't you think so? (*The others look at her, astounded.*)

Anne Sofie: My goodness.

Lilleba: Yes, I think it's wonderful. (*eagerly*) Several of Doris' friends aren't married at all, just living with a man —. It's quite wonderful, isn't it? Well, I wouldn't dream of it. Mother would be beside herself and my mother-in-law —

Anne Sofie: You wouldn't have a mother-in-law then.

Lilleba: Oh? Oh no, that's true.

Ellinor: Liberation — . I don't know.

Hanna: I used to go round looking at myself in the mirror all the time, I remember, I put my hair up in different ways, thought about clothes, tried to change myself, 'be a new person' —

Gry: I remember you dying your hair red, I almost died of shock.

Anne Sofie: And blue-black. You looked as if you'd been imported, and those earrings!

Hanna: As if it changed anything. Took pictures of myself with the automatic timer, moody self-portraits. Good God.

Anne Sofie: Was that so crazy?

Hanna: And then I bought all kinds of things. Candlesticks, tooth mugs, flowered toilet rolls, tablecloths, baskets, umbrella stands.

Lilleba: You've always had good taste.

Hanna: Housewife neurosis, a classic case. Washed the floor twice a day. Couldn't manage anything in bed.

Lilleba: But —

Anne Sofie: So we're back to that again.

Gry: What else.

Hanna: When I won the photo competition Magnus pretended he was happy, bought champagne etc. No, he wasn't really jealous, just sad. Yes, that's it, sad. As if he felt how unused I was, got a bit scared. He said, 'There's only room for one climber in a marriage', that's what he said.

Ellinor: Climber. Is that what you are? And me?

Hanna: And then he got drunk.

Lilleba: I don't think climber is a very nice word to use. It's completely wrong, if you ask me.

Hanna: You are wonderful, Lilleba.

Lilleba: Have I made a fool of myself again?

Hanna: Just think girls, just think what we could have done, could have created! If we'd had the same opportunities as men.

Anne Sofie: Why don't we do something then? All the opportunities are there.

Gry: Of course.

Hanna: Are they?

Anne Sofie: In our part of the world women have all the opportunities.

Hanna: In our part of the world women are still women. Don't forget that.

Lilleba: No – ?

Ellinor: Hanna's negro theory.

Hanna: The most important thing isn't whether a school or university is open to you, but whether it is open to you – here. (*taps her forehead and chest*) That you have learnt to trust yourself, your own way of thinking. Self-respect is the key to everything.

Anne Sofie: Do you remember – do you remember Gunhild? (*The others go quiet*) (*Hanna nods slowly*)

Lilleba: She was so pretty. Beautiful.

Gry: She had everything in a way.

Anne Sofie: Musical, beautiful, intelligent. Finished with top grades.

Gry: She started studying, didn't she?

Lilleba: She really had everything.

Anne Sofie: Studied Russian. I meet her mother now and again when I'm at home. She's got really old.

Lilleba: And Gunhild – ?

Anne Sofie: (*shakes her head*) No hope. Completely out of it. Her mother visits her. Apparently Gunhild doesn't recognise her very often.

Lilleba: How awful.

Hanna: Yes.

Lilleba: That long, heavy hair, a fantastic red — .

Gry: The way she played Tchaikovsky gave me goose pimples.

Anne Sofie: Her mother and father didn't want her to go to university. They wanted her to go to business school. She cried till she got her own way. Afterwards she wanted to travel.

Lilleba: (*resigned*) Yes, yes — . (*silence*)

Lilleba: Yes, yes.

Ellinor: Things don't always go the way you think they will.

Anne Sofie: No — .

Lilleba: No, they don't.

Gry: They often go in totally the opposite direction.

Anne Sofie: With all of us — ?

Ellinor: (*breaks the mood, tries to be cheerful*) Do you remember Inger Marie? The little grey mouse in Class B, the one who always had curlers in her hair and a chiffon headscarf, the one who always had a tummy ache when we were taking sports badges?

Lilleba: Inger Marie?

Anne Sofie: The one who lived down by the brewery in the old block by the dairy?

Ellinor: I was at Margaret's exhibition, and this incredible lady sails in wearing a fur coat, larger than life, sports car and bleached hair. 'Very sophisticated', she said, 'The colours are very sophisticated'. 'Good God!' I said, 'Is it or is it not Inger Marie?' Yes, the wife of Managing Director Samuelsen or Gabrielsen or God knows what. That was a lady who'd got somewhere in life. House in Italy and —

Hanna: Her father worked for the tram company.

Ellinor: She bought three pictures. The blue would match the curtains or something like that, at her country residence.

Anne Sofie: She failed German, tried again and failed again. Got a job in the perfume department.

Ellinor: She had it all down to a fine art. The way she talked – 'very talented artist'. I just stared.

Hanna: Girls can go far on curlers.

Lilleba: I wonder what Gunhild looks like now.

Gry: Sports car too-.

Anne Sofie: I visited her a few years ago. Fat, pale. Totally apathetic. It made me so depressed, couldn't face going again. I wrote some cards. Now I don't even do that. (*Sound of ambulance sirens*)

Lilleba: Oh there it goes again. It always makes me think of the children.

Gry: Relax, Lilleba.

Ellinor: It was quite strange with my mother.

Lilleba: (*to* Gry) You can say that, you don't have any. You can't help worrying. This fear —

Ellinor: It was quite strange with my mother. It was like a mental fixation with her. We were to have a proper education, even though we were 'only' girls.

Anne Sofie: It seizes me up. My whole body seizes up - .

Ellinor: It makes me ashamed to think how she wore herself out. She was fantastic. But then she experienced what it was like to be alone with three children – and a sewing machine.

Hanna: She was amazing.

Anne Sofie: When someone comes over to us when we are out, I seize up when we remain seated. I think: I wonder whether it looks strange, if I get up now? It's as if I am caught in a trap, everything gets knotted up inside.

Hanna: Didn't you want to go to university too, Gry? Physics?

Gry: Chemistry. That's a long time ago, I'm happy with my lot.

Hanna: Yes, happy — .

Lilleba: I'm also happy with my lot. (*emphasises*) I'm as snug as —

Ellinor: (*drily*) a bug in a blender.

Lilleba: Funny.

Hanna: I thought there was so much I hadn't experienced, that was the worst. The way things are now, is how it will be for the rest of your life. And then the pot boiled over.

Anne Sofie: Was it worth it?

Ellinor: I don't want to live alone, it's so difficult living alone.

Hanna: I had to work it out. All the fuzzy moralistic laws. Everything they stuff down our throats. Had to puke it out and start all over again. Not use the reproachful faces of others to judge right and wrong, but – but my own personal experience.

Lilleba: Personal experience — ?

Hanna: My body, its energy, the actual joie-de-vivre in a way – like a thermometer for right and wrong.

(Gry *polishes her glasses nervously*)

Anne Sofie: You are such a romantic, Hanna. A moralistic romantic. People who live in a community with other people must naturally fall in line with both written and unwritten laws.

Hanna: Sounds like you're marking a Norwegian essay. A good deal of those unwritten laws of yours aim to destroy us girls. Don't you understand that? We're being castrated in both body and soul. But never, never again will I allow myself to be struck down by guilt!

Anne Sofie: If I'm marking essays, you're giving a lecture.

Lilleba: And what about me? Whispering at the back of class?

Hanna: But Anne Fi, look at the girls in your class, what do you think they're thinking about?

Anne Sofie: Them? Oh yes, they're wondering whether their trousers are tight enough, what kind of hairspray they should use, if anyone can see that they've got their period, if they'll be asked to the cinema, whether —

Hanna: You see!

Ellinor: And some of them are desperately waiting for their periods, or maybe they're already pregnant, I remember that nightmare.

Anne Sofie: That's how they are.

Hanna: No! We *make* them like that, that's the difference. The unwritten laws, amongst other things – .

Ellinor: (*stretches*) Yes it's wonderful, wonderful to be an adult.

Gry: (*carefully*) Yes, in a way —

(Ellinor *gets up, walks around the room a bit*)

Lilleba: (*resigned*) Yes, yes – .

Anne Sofie: (*to* Lilleba) Why do you do that all the time?

Lilleba: What?

Anne Sofie: (*moves her hand to her head, to her hairline, copies a movement characteristic of* Lilleba) It's as if you're checking whether your hair's fallen out.

Lilleba: Oh? Maybe I'm scared that will happen, that it will fall out.

Anne Sofie: Men go bald. (Ellinor *moves on the floor in slow parodic dance steps, humming softly*)

Hanna: You're all hopeless.

Ellinor: (*whilst dancing*) What did you expect?

Hanna: Oh, expect. I never expect anything in particular.

Lilleba: That's clever, because then you won't be disappointed.

Hanna: Precisely. Then I won't be disappointed. (*shuts her eyes*) Good God. (Ellinor *sings louder, dancing.*)

Lilleba: Did I say something wrong again?

(Hanna *drinks*)

Anne Sofie: (*rummaging in her bag*) I thought I had – no —

Ellinor: (*quoting a poem*)

> 'Some words
> Bloom late
> One day when the wind tires
> when hands release each other
> to be alone, to be open
> to the sun
> which also tires
> A thirsty day which leaves the wine undrunk.'

Gry: We should have had the guitar.

Lilleba: How strange, that it only happens to men. That only men go bald?

(Ellinor *goes to the window*)

Anne Sofie: You can never find anything in this kind of bag. (*puts it away*)

Lilleba: It must have something to do with hormones. Don't

you think so?

Ellinor: (*looks out of the window*) Fish & Game. Petrol station. Cemetery. Traffic lights.

Lilleba: I started on a course. Maybe I told you about it?

Ellinor: How nice that you can see the trees in the cemetery.

Hanna: And all the funerals.

Lilleba: It was an English course.

Ellinor: Are they elm trees? They look like elm.

Lilleba: Not that there's anything to tell. But he was quite good-looking, the teacher. Mister Lofthus.

Gry: How did it go?

Lilleba: I stopped, I couldn't manage to concentrate. A button was missing off his jacket, so I didn't listen to what he was saying. He had such strange ears, like that. (*puts her hands up to her ears*) Sad, doggy ears. Felt like scratching him behind the ears.

Hanna: And sewing on his buttons for him.

Lilleba: He reminded me of the man who used to be after you ages ago, Anne Fi, the one who stood whining at the gate when you came home at night, the one with the big shoes, the one who never dared kiss you.

Anne Sofie: Gunder, poor thing. Actually, he's a gynaecologist.

Lilleba: Really? So you could have been a doctor's wife.

Anne Sofie: Indeed.

Lilleba: That used to be my dream, a doctor or a captain.

Gry: Hans is a shop manager.

Lilleba: But there's only him and the sales manager. And the secretary.

Hanna: (*to* Ellinor) Why aren't you saying anything?

Gry: He's listed in the telephone directory as a manager, and he's just as good as any other manager listed there.

Ellinor: No.

Lilleba: (*happily*) Do you mean that?

Hanna: (*smoothly*) The perfect hostess ensures that all uncomfortable topics of conversation are avoided, that the food is
easily digested, the lights are low —

Ellinor: And that the hangover isn't fatal.

Hanna: You sobered up quickly enough.

Ellinor: Yes.

Hanna: Is something wrong? (Ellinor *shakes her head, sits
down*)

Lilleba: He never had a packed lunch.

Gry: Packed lunch?

Lilleba: The teacher. Mister Lofthus. I think he kind of looked
forward to every Tuesday —

Anne Sofie: How strange that I started thinking about Gunhild.

Gry: (*touches* Lilleba) Lovely soft material in this dress.

Lilleba: Do you like it? Doris was with me. 'You have to wear
soft clothes,' Doris says, 'You must – '

Anne Sofie: Who is Doris?

Lilleba: Doris? Lives in the house next to us, she's married to
the brother of one of the top bosses at Esso. 'You must wear
soft clothes,' Doris says, 'You are a duck.' she says, 'A duck
with a flock around you. You must be soft.'

Anne Sofie: Anne hasn't worn a skirt for years, apart from on
Christmas Eve for her grandmother's sake.

Lilleba: Very sweet people. You should see the conservatory
they've built on the veranda. Flowers and creepers, fountain
with built-in light. Magnificent! And a fish with luminous eyes.
Magnificent! Electric you see, the eyes —

Anne Sofie: I drove past Kitty —

Hanna: What do they use that for?

Lilleba: The fish? Decoration of course. It's completely ...
completely oriental.

Anne Sofie: I drove past Kitty in town today. How's life
treating her?

Hanna: Quite hard. Where are the matches? Klaus has the

children and she's going to take her exam.

Anne Sofie: And that half-starved sculptor she ran around with, didn't it work out?

Hanna: No, it didn't work out.

Lilleba: Hans says she'll look like a wreck within five years. Klaus is quite an alcoholic and the children are seeing the school psychologist.

Anne Sofie: And that's what's called liberation. – Poor girl, they had such a good relationship, Kitty and Klaus. And then to run off and fall in love with a pasty-faced artist, leaving her husband and children and starting all over again with bedsit life and canteen stew. She's welcome to it.

Lilleba: There was something about Kitty —

Hanna: Klaus sat on her, owned every hair on her head. Kitty did the only right thing. That she had to fall in love to get out of it, is the same old story. Women often liberate themselves in that way, liberate themselves from one man so as to bind themselves to another. Cheers!

Gry: Nicely put. It's as if we can't breathe without a man to cling to.

Lilleba: There was something about Kitty, something or other, the way she walked, the way —

Anne Sofie: I think Kitty is having a really hard time. Such a miserable bedsit in such a godforsaken area and then meeting her children once a week. Oh yes, it's great that she's taking her exams and all that, but she must be pretty miserable.

Hanna: At least she's her own boss.

Anne Sofie: Do you really believe that?

Hanna: There isn't a man telling her what to do any more.

Anne Sofie: No, not one. Several.

Lilleba: (*wide-eyed*) Is she living it up so much?

Hanna: Maybe you're a bit envious of her?

Anne Sofie: Me? Envious of Kitty? Jesus, why should I be envious of her? I've seen her face, all worn out and dreadful,

74

with those bags under her eyes. And I've seen her medicine cabinet. You can't make me believe that she's moved into the Garden of Eden.

Ellinor: Nor do I believe that the garden of Eden lies in Grünerløkka, the heart of the East End.

Hanna: Maybe she's discovered that the safe harbour of marriage was not the best place for a woman to realise herself, to develop —

Anne Sofie: I don't see the point. And those poor children, doesn't anyone think about them?

Lilleba: Yes, the school psychologist.

Ellinor: Klaus sat like a horrible owl in a corner watching over Kitty. Practically strangled her with all that jealousy.

Lilleba: But there was something about Kitty. Her eyes. Was it her eyes?

Ellinor: Do you think Klaus would have coped with her staying on at school, paddling in a sea of men all day? He would've had a breakdown.

Gry: That's why it's important to lock us up.

Anne Sofie: What do you know about it? You've never been married or locked up, as you call it.

Gry: I have eyes in my head, is there anything wrong with that?

Anne Sofie: Eyes in your head! And knees which are shouting out, my girl. And so has Kitty.

Gry: (*polishes her glasses*) Do you think it's so very difficult to get hold of - a little sex.

Anne Sofie: I don't think that's so difficult, no, but I think there can be some problems in getting hold of a friend who will stay, who will come back the next day and the day after that, who in short sees it through and is worth keeping hold of. At our age, dear friends, this is a bit of a problem.

Lilleba: What a horrible conversation.

Anne Sofie: I'll tell you why. The best men are sitting in their cages with wives and children and dogs and canaries and mortgaged up to the hilt. If I leave out those who are gay or impotent, there's a little group left who are scared stiff, who've had so much or so little to do with girls that they neither dare nor can. And if they dare and can, it's only to use us as door-mats and mattresses.

Hanna: Sounds as if you've thought it out carefully.

Anne Sofie: Thought what out?

Hanna: What opportunities you have – without Dagfinn.

Anne Sofie: Yes, I have. (*surprised, with bravado*) And I don't want to risk it. I've got a damned good life, very good, to-gether with Dagfinn and the children. I'm happy at school and earn a good wage. We work well together at home. Dagfinn makes better food than me. I love the children. I think it's nice raking up the leaves and mowing the lawn and –

Ellinor: But then there isn't any problem.

Anne Sofie: Precisely. You're the ones who're making prob-lems – by talking about cages and freedom and all that rubbish. You should try growing up soon.

Hanna: You were the one who said it. 'The best men are sitting in cages', you said.

Lilleba: Shh! (*The others are silent for a moment*)

Lilleba: Someone's crying.

Anne Sofie: It's not a cage for me. I've chosen it for myself. I didn't 'have to' get married. I chose Dagfinn and he chose me and we've stuck together and we aim to —

Hanna: One moment, do you really imagine that you 'chose' for yourself, as you say? Of course you didn't. None of us did.

Lilleba: So I should be unhappy, because I 'had to'?

Gry: Let Hanna finish.

Anne Sofie: Good God, you're all giving me a headache.

Hanna: You were just as chock-a-block full of implanted opinions as the rest of us. You read just as many magazines, short romances and teenage books and watched soppy films.

You loved wedding pictures and reports of weddings just like the rest of us. Don't imagine that you chose for yourself. We walked right into the trap, that's what we did.

Lilleba: Do you mean that I should be unhappy because I 'had to'? Or you, Hanna?

Hanna: Magnus was so happy. I've never seen a man so happy as when I told him that I was pregnant. He had me where he wanted me then. He realised that. Men understand that – intuitively.

Anne Sofie: I don't understand this hatred of yours.

Hanna: Hatred?

Ellinor: Of course, he's a little happy. Without him she becomes someone to be pitied, in the eyes of society, and is treated in that way.

Lilleba: To be pitied — ?

Hanna: Good God, if I'd known then what I know today. We all got married, Kitty, Anne Fi, Lilleba and I, it was so infectious. It was only Ellinor who didn't dive in straight away. And Gry of course.

Ellinor: I felt as if I kind of belonged to another race because I wasn't part of the great rush. There had to be something wrong with me in a way.

Lilleba: It had something to do with feeling safe, don't you think?

Hanna: Without the ring and the conjugal bed, we felt kind of shabby – and scared. It's quite ingenious, you see.

Anne Sofie: You can talk, Ellinor. You don't have children. What do you know about being together, about —

Hanna: (*quickly*) No, Anne Fi, you've gone too far now. You're hitting below the belt now.

Anne Sofie: Am I? And that's what *you* say — ?

Hanna: Yes, that's what I say. And I've got children too.

Anne Sofie: Precisely. You've also got children, Hanna.

Hanna: What do you mean?

Anne Sofie: You shouldn't forget it. (Hanna *drinks quickly*)

Ellinor: Maybe it would be a good idea to find another subject? Besides I think my lack of children bothers you more than it bothers me. (Anne Sofie *takes her bag, looking for something again.*)

Lilleba: I never played with dolls. It's quite strange, but I never played with dolls. Mother thought there was something wrong with me. 'It'll come,' my grandmother said. 'Just you wait.'

Hanna: (*with forced enthusiasm*) Cheers! Cheers girls!

Lilleba: Pictures were what interested me. They tried to teach me to knit. I couldn't manage that either. I was only bothered about pictures, completely crazy about pictures. Strange, I had nearly forgotten it — . (*resigned*) Yes, yes — .

Hanna: (*gets up*) Cheers, I said. A toast to sisterhood and solidarity! A toast because we support each other and respect each other!

Ellinor: (*drily*) Yes, let's drink to that. (*The others nod, toasting hesitantly.*)

Hanna: (*rhetorically*) At last! At last we women have raised our consciousness! At last we have opened our eyes to the three thousand years of suppression at the hands of the patriarchy! Now we are no longer on our knees, but bravely, with straight backs and heads held high, we reach out our hands to each other, we take our future in our hands —

Anne Sofie: Heil Hitler!

Hanna: If we take our lives into our own hands, we let our lives unfold like large, beautiful flowers, spread waves of warmth and happiness, the power of life! Gone are the all old battles for power, we shall love and work as equals, together we will find the forgotten sources, our wonderful sunken Atlantis...

Ellinor: Wonderful, Hanna. More.

Gry: Frightful rubbish. The world doesn't need any more

visions.

Ellinor: Of course we need visions, the world has always needed them.

Gry: The world needs action, justice. All you lot are doing is gossiping.

Anne Sofie: When I hear Hanna giving those feminist speeches of hers, I'm not sure that the ability to speak is a gift to the human race.

Lilleba: Shh — . There *is* someone crying. I said there was. (*The others are silent, distant crying*)

Ellinor: Who is it?

Hanna: It's next door.

Gry: We're talking too much.

Hanna: It's one of the children.

Ellinor: Are we being noisy?

Hanna: You should have heard her, her in there, when Henrik was here. 'Oh darling, have you got a son as well?' 'Yes,' I said, 'I have.' And then I gave her a really horrible look.

Anne Sofie: You're scared too, Hanna. You're scared too.

Hanna: (*sits down*) What I wanted to say was, how nice it is that we're not working against each other any more, not talking behind each other's backs and distrusting each other, like we've always done, in order to survive — .

Ellinor: Not so bitter, Hanna. Sodom wasn't built in a day either.

Lilleba: I'd like a brown carpet in the loft extension, mocha brown, maybe the kind that won't last so long?

Anne Sofie: Now you're doing it again. With your hair.

Lilleba: Doris has mocha brown in her bedroom and Brazilian rosewood beds. It's so elegant. I can paint the door green, moss green, maybe? But what about the curtains, what shall I do about it?

Anne Sofie: (*automatically*) Them.

Lilleba: Do you think yellow would be all right? Of course, it depends on the covers on the divan –

Anne Sofie: Good God! I'm getting one of my migraines again.

Gry: To survive — . What did you mean by that?

Hanna: Is it so difficult to understand? I mean quite simply that we've always kept on stepping on one another. We've never seen where the true enemy is, we had to just cling to – the system. So as not to be frozen out!

Anne Sofie: Frozen out — ?

Ellinor: (*recites a poem, slowly, defiantly*)

> 'Your new lethargy
> tastes of wild honey
> our hands intertwine.
> The time is here for – '

Anne Sofie: (*cuts in, angrily*) What do you mean by frozen out?

Ellinor:

> 'The time is here for a song
> about the rain meeting with grass
> don't wait
> the seconds have gathered
> on the outermost branch, fall'

Hanna: Look around, open your eyes! Divorced women, unmarried women, women without children, single women with children. We are all frozen out, more or less!

Anne Sofie: Widows and orphans.

Ellinor: (*faster, rhythmic*)

> 'the seconds have gathered
> on the outermost branch, fall
> one by one
> light up as they fall, extinguished
> against hands and eyes
> against tears and sleep
> against everything,

fall
one by one
how long — '

Hanna: And then we use any means to keep hold of the man we've got, if we've got one. And we accept everything. But you're all deaf and blind and don't want to see or hear! Sitting here so smugly, so happy-on-the-outside that it makes you sick —

Gry: But —

Hanna: But Gry, you should at —

Gry: (*quickly*) I'm trying to understand what you're saying, but you're so aggressive.

Anne Sofie: Very aggressive.

Hanna: Do you all think it was easy for me to leave Henrik, to leave him behind with Magnus? What do you know about what's inside me? Magnus needed the boy, he'd have gone to pieces without him, I know he would. Shouldn't a father have rights and duties? Isn't that what we're talking about? Is it all just talk?

Ellinor: We don't blame you, Hanna. You're the one blaming yourself. Can't we talk about something else?

Hanna: You're trying to make me feel frozen out, because I did it!

Anne Sofie: Are we?

Hanna: Just like you talk about Kitty. Just like you talk about everyone who breaks out.

Anne Sofie: Kitty's different.

Hanna: But don't you understand, that what you are saying, what you believe, is only contributing to keeping everything the way it is! We must submit to the woman's role, be like this and that, that is, how it suits men, even if we're not like that! (*Walks back and forth whilst talking. Stops, leans her head against the doorpost.*) It makes me so desperate. You don't want to understand, don't want to open your eyes, are just scared – (*The others sit silently, thoughtful.*)

Ellinor: (*low*) I'm scared. It's true. I'm scared of living alone, that's just how it is. I admit it. Maybe I'm clinging to Anker. Maybe I would've worked with greater strength, in a better way, if I was alone. I don't know —

Anne Sofie: You who live alone with your dogs in that godforsaken fisherman's shack half the summer.

Lilleba: Why do you do it? (Ellinor *doesn't answer*) When I think that Hans could have a heart attack and die, it scares me to death.

Gry: Oh, Lilleba.

Lilleba: Maybe I'll be a widow? Nearly all of us will be. What will I do? Me?

Ellinor: Not everyone's like you, Hanna.

Anne Sofie: I'm sorry for what I said – about the children. It's my head. But not everyone's like you, you're so strong.

Hanna: That's not what you mean. You don't mean that I'm strong. You mean that I'm different. You want to make me an exception. It's easier to explain away in that way.

Ellinor: You're strong, Hanna.

Hanna: I'm not stronger than any of you. I've just started fighting. That's the difference.

Translated by Angela Shury-Smith

ELDRID LUNDEN

hard, soft

Does she live in a man's world? Yes, indeed, and the man
in her was once
a caring person, the woman
at times quite sensible; has this all
vanished?

The upbeat
dreams, the young girls
huddled close with clear boundaries
of vibrant skin between them.

Young girls in a room, emitting
their gestures, narrow
messages in their fingers
or chubby ones
way down to their heels.

The graceful contours
of that other
woman softly forcing her way
inside her. Is she in
there yet?

Night in the forest
and someone gently
engulfing her in a warmth
of his own,

waiting until morning
for the night sky to darken
inside her and go to bed.

Mornings
with a new balance point in her body,
the earth spinning softly and the trees
surprisingly tall above
them. She moves across
the earth with soundless strength
in her steps.

The gentle light
inside him, pale along his lower arms,
faintly pulsing at his throat, and
her hands so suddenly scared
of the lifeforce beneath his skin.

Voices and words that
cause her to turn around
and scan the horizon for meaning,
sun-starved throughout.

The back that starts
to straighten up, trembles
briefly halfway, then it
shoves the chair into place and leaves.

He, a large dark pulse
with many shadows
beating lightly
on his lips.

He who plunges deep
inside her with a smile and
finds her
filled to the mind with
tears.

Translated by Frankie Shackelford

BERGLJOT HOBÆK HAFF

The Mother of God

A HARDENED SOUL IS CALLED HOME

In the last hour, before time and eternity merged together, she was sitting on a bench in the inner city when something strange befell her.

The cold loosened its grip on her body ever so slowly, the child she held in her arms stopped its whimpering, and the never-ending stream of pedestrians who hurried by gradually abated.

All at once it seemed as if the street were closed off on all four sides, and she was sitting in an enormous, illuminated hall where a multitude of people had gathered waiting for someone or other to appear. From their growing unrest she understood they'd been waiting for a long time and had reached a degree of impatience that signalled that something had to happen soon. Not far from the bench where she was sitting, the room was partitioned by a bar, and right behind it, in a sphere of over-powering light, was a table with a record book and some writing implements.

Suddenly she felt a strong draught moving through the room, and turning her head, she saw a door that was open exceedingly far away, and a female figure approaching with quick steps. Her appearance intensified the murmuring unrest in the hall, and as she made her way through the crowd it was easy to see that many only grudgingly made room for her.

When she reached the table, she stood looking out over the assembled for a few minutes, as if lost in deep thought and with a look that seemed both distant and penetrating.

'Why, it's the face,' thought the little one, wide-eyed in speechless wonder. 'Then she hasn't forgotten me after all. Then she has finally come to plead my case on the last day.'

After the woman had taken her place at the table, she sat absolutely still for a moment, resting her head in her hands, as if she were preparing herself for an assignment that demanded complete presence of mind. Then she began to leaf back and forth in the record book, and the expression on her face was continually shifting, from fairly mild to nearly awe-inspiring. A breathless silence descended over the hall, and the only sound that could be heard was the beating of the little one's heart and the faint rustling of paper when one of the pages was turned in the big book. Occasionally the woman lifted her face, sending deep, rather searching looks around the hall, then she finally raised her voice and named a name with unexpected force and authority.

No sooner was it pronounced, than a person broke away from the throng and walked stiffly towards the bar with laborious steps. At first it appeared to be a very old woman, bearing the affliction of the whole world on her back. But as she moved into the sphere of light around the bar, her age became more indeterminate and the entire figure seemed ravaged by an incurable sorrow. As she dragged herself across the floor, she sighed constantly, and putting one hand on the bar, she lifted a corner of her dress with the other and dried her nose and eyes.

'But that's ...' shot through the little one with painful and powerful force. But before she could think the thought to its conclusion, she felt an invisible hand touch her shoulder directing her to be silent.

After the old woman had dried her eyes and sniffled for a long time, she looked curiously around the hall, and her sunken face took on an almost indignant expression.

'What's the meaning of bringing me here from such a long way away?' she whined. 'I thought I'd said once and for all that I don't participate in out-of-town meetings.'

'Don't you see who's sitting over there on the bench?' the woman asked gravely. 'Her newborn child, wrapped in a bunting, is in her arms and she doesn't know where she's going to spend the night.'

'I've said I don't participate in out-of-town meetings,' the old woman repeated with a grumble. 'What an ungodly draught there is here. There ought to be a law against summoning people to outdoor meetings in the winter.'

'Go over and reconcile yourself with your daughter,' the other woman said in a commanding, yet mild voice. 'It's still not too late, and if you hurry, you might both be able to catch the evening train.'

The woman she was speaking to cast her eyes quickly to the side, barely glancing at the two on the bench. Folding her arthritic hands on her chest, she said in a self-righteous tone:

'My daughter died several years ago, and thank the Lord for that. Once I had the Salvation Army conduct a missing person search, but I never should have done that.'

'Did you perhaps learn something about her you weren't able to bear?'

'Able to bear,' cried the old woman with a contemptuous snort. 'It was nothing but a pack of lies from beginning to end. It only taught me one single thing: That you should beware of having dealings with people from other religious denominations.'

'And that is your last word,' asked the other. 'Even though the two of them over there are in dire straits and on the verge of perishing.'

The old woman pressed her lips together and looked obstinately down at her hands, then, after a long while, reached out and ran a critical finger along the woodwork on the bar.

'Just as I thought,' she squeaked, bringing her hand right up to her eyes. 'Dust and filth as far as the eye can see. Dear me, may the Lord look in mercy upon all who are distressed and troubled. But I think my time would be put to better use giving this railing a once over.'

She lifted the same corner of her dress with which she had dried her eyes earlier and started rubbing the handrail with quick, almost angry movements. She was soon so absorbed in her task that she didn't see or hear a thing, and as she continued wiping the bar high and low, her face, taut with determination, gradually relaxed and took on an expression of deep satisfaction.

'Thank you, that will be all,' the other woman said with a nearly inaudible voice and reached for an eraser that was lying on the table. As she shook her head and moved her hand across the paper, the busy shape shrivelled up, becoming more and more pitiful to behold. And even as its arms toiled and kept at it until the very end, it disappeared from its place of refuge in time and took flight into eternity.

THE ELEGANT GENTLEMAN IS BACK IN TOWN

Some time after the old woman's passing, an unknown gentleman came into the hall, as if from a long way away and clearly in a hurry.

'What's going on here,' he called out in a loud voice. 'How often do I have to repeat that judgement is mine alone.'

At this late point in time the woman was already turning the last pages of the book, and a large portion of the crowd had by now left the place. As the trial proceeded and a long list of people had tried their cases, a kind of regularity descended over everything that happened. The few eyewitnesses remaining no longer looked so thunderstruck, and more and more often the horrified exclamation: 'look, he's disappearing' was replaced by the more prescient: 'pretty soon he'll disappear' or: 'he'd better watch out, or he'll be gone.'

When the woman showed no sign of relinquishing her place at the table, the newcomer took his place a little ways from her and, hands on his back, observed her activity with an air of condescension.

'Well, what do I see,' he began, raising himself onto the tips of his toes and gently rocking back on his heels. 'I surely haven't acquired a competitor since my last visit to these parts? Well, I'll be damned, a female omnipotence, with eyes like two big question marks and disfiguring dashes across her forehead. Gracious me, how she sharpens her pencils and keeps a cool head in order to give everyone their due. Just a pity she approaches her task in such an unorthodox manner.'

'What are your objections to my procedure,' the woman asked, lifting her eyes from the book with interest.

The stranger furrowed his brow and refrained from answering right away, but took his time lighting a cigar which little by little enveloped him in a thick cloud of smoke. 'Oh, these disappearing acts,' he sighed and made a rueful gesture with his arms. 'I must confess that I have a little difficulty interpreting them as entirely realistic.'

'I understand,' replied the woman, who couldn't quite manage to conceal the little smile on her lips. 'No more apocalypses and burning bushes! Realism has made its entry at the very highest level, and woe to him who is disobedient and knoweth not the time of his visitation.'

'I beg you to remember that you are a woman,' the gentleman said in an almost threatening tone of voice. 'I demand respect for the old division of the spheres, where the higher falls to man, the lower to woman.'

'Oh, that's what you mean,' she responded, visibly relieved at having the question so clearly demarcated. 'You want to lock me into everyday realism and you won't tolerate the fact that I'm both high and low.'

'Listen, you're not on really good terms with realism,' the stranger said with concern in his voice. 'But remember that that's what brings the masses bliss and ensures that an absolutely clear and accessible world picture is upheld. What do you think the Almighty would have been without such a simplification, which arrays him in a halo and flowing clothes when that's appropriate, and a hat and topcoat under more inclement skies.'

'Well, you've got a point, it is pretty cold in here,' the woman said with a shiver. 'And here I was just about to ask if you wouldn't like to hang up your coat.'

'You do have a penchant for jesting,' said the gentleman, offended, as he put his hand to his hat to make sure it was set at the right angle. 'But don't think you can bowl me over with your talk and make me forget my errand. It's a matter of a number of persons whom you have repudiated today and pushed out into a far too early immortality. I don't understand on what grounds you reproach all these people whom I find successful, or in other ways excellent. I can confide to you, they have been my clients through all these years, and I feel almost like a father to them. Every time you've been careless or made an obvious blunder, they come to me and pour out their troubles. And I gladly forgive them.'

'Then you are more lenient than I am,' the woman said in

a tone of voice that suggested she was noting something new and surprising.

'Don't say that, don't say that, my dear lady. I am certainly no good-natured fool, and once I'm convinced of my clients' guilt, I strike hard, and turn them over to the eternal fire.'

'Then you are probably also harsher than I am,' said the woman and for a long time stared thoughtfully out into the room. 'I don't suppose I could get you to reveal your name?'

'No, kind lady, that would be quite impossible, with all the nicknames, or shall we say sobriquets, I have. Let me be content to hint that I am who I am, known under such widely differing names as His Grace and the inexorable.'

'And your livelihood?'

'Hmm, let's say judge. For the record: government authorized, even though that doesn't have such a good ring to it these days. But let's get to the point: Before I came into the hall, I'd been standing off on the horizon for a while, out of sight, listening to your proceedings with growing concern. Good heavens, such moralizing, and five hundred years after the Reformation settled the question out of hand and abolished good deeds. All these exclamations you resort to when you see you're in a fix and can't get anywhere with human nature. How was it now, oh yes: 'make it good again', 'give her a roof over her head', 'take her into your employ', 'write something nice about her', 'it's still not too late', and so on and so forth in the same key, nonstop. Permit me to ask, what in heaven's name is the purpose of all this?'

'It's my way of reminding people that time is running out and that eternity is imminent.'

'And you have no great liking for this eternity, as far as I can see. If I've understood you correctly, you see it as a kind of stagnation, or accumulation of the characteristics of the times.'

'Yes, then you have understood me correctly,' the woman said quietly.

'And this happy place that you speak so warmly about all the time? If it's supposed to be this hall, then I really think you're using pretty big words. If it's not an outright illusion, then let me say with the old woman who was here earlier, that there's an ungodly draught in here.'

'That may be,' the woman said, looking around the room with a thoughtful gaze. 'But it is nonetheless the place where nothing is conclusive and everything can happen.'

'As opposed to the unknown dimension, as you call it, and which you advise so strongly against. How did you put it in that homily you gave, when I lost my patience and felt compelled to intervene: Don't expect ...'

'Don't expect anything of eternity that you don't already find here.'

'Fine, you undeniably have a gift for choosing your words. But enough of that, we'll hardly reach an agreement and we can't continue for an eternity – if you'll pardon me – discussing these kinds of ideological questions. Let me ask instead, what has become of our little heroine, whom I kept watch over during most of the day, but by sheer accident lost sight of when I had to stop and flick the ash off my cigar.'

'She's sitting right behind you,' said the woman and pointed over at the bench.

'Well, by Jove, there she is. My my, you have taken considerable pains with her, and in her best moments she bravely lives up to her role as everyone's little charmer. But I don't suppose one can say she's really plausible.'

'In any event, she's sitting over there on the bench,' the woman said. 'And during the course of the day hundreds of people have walked by and glanced at her.'

'And what words have they had for her, if I may ask? As far as I remember a bunch of worn-out phrases of the type:

'she isn't real,' 'she defies all description,' and 'all that's missing is the halo around her head.' What do you have to say to that?'

'That the proof of her existence is precisely the absence of a halo around her head.'

'And what about the allegation that she defies all description?'

'In that she shares the fate of everything that exists, and her situation is no different than yours or mine. Tell me something, though, have you never experienced that someone has doubted your existence?'

The tall gentleman suddenly drew back and was so befuddled that he dropped his cigar on the floor. While he was bent over struggling to pick it up, he mumbled a few indistinct words which, combined with his wheezing, made it sound like he was softly moaning.

'I understand it's your intent to hit me where I'm most tender,' he said after he'd straightened himself up. 'What if I were so tactless as to retaliate and counter your question?'

'Do you mean concerning my existence? Yes, you are right, that too would be an open question, in the room in which we find ourselves at this moment. I often ask myself if the woman over there on the bench isn't the only one present, and the two of us infinitely distant, evading her and refusing to lend a helping hand until the very end.'

THE BOOK

Right before nightfall two women were walking through town, talking casually about whatever came to mind.

'Such a lot of strange books being written nowadays,' one of them said suddenly. She was a capable and energetic woman, getting on in years, wearing a blue coat with a rabbit-fur collar.

'Well yes, perhaps that's so,' responded the other one, clad in neutral grey and with a less striking presence in every way.

'Well, listen to this: Just this morning I went into a bookstore to buy some napkins, and while I was waiting my turn, I sneaked a look at one of the books that was on display.'

'Was it a good book?' asked the other one, mostly to show that she was there and willing to listen.

'Oh, I really don't know what to say. I have a bad habit, you know, of flipping to the last pages of any book I get my hands on to see how it ends.'

'Was it a sad ending then, maybe?'

'No, if only it had been. But the last pages were so desolate and deserted that I was left with a very strange feeling.'

'It can't be easy for people who write books to always come up with an ending, you know,' the grey woman said apologetically. 'In the books my husband reads someone dies in every single chapter, and at the very end the hero's left standing all alone, having cleared himself enough elbow room so he can lower his gun.'

'No shots were fired in this book,' the first woman said thoughtfully. 'But otherwise it did sort of follow the same formula. It was about a band of streetwalkers who gradually fell on bad times and were cast to the four winds. Finally there was only one left, and on the last pages she was sitting outdoors on a bench in the cold of winter, probably freezing to death, as far as I could tell.'

'Yes, but wasn't it clearly explained, what happened to her?'

'No, as I said before, the entire ending was strange and hard to figure out. She was even holding a little newborn baby in her arms, and I really do believe the idea was for them to sit there until they were frozen solid.'

'And didn't anyone come by and see what was happening?'

'Yes, in the early part of the day there had been quite a few, I believe. But in the middle of rush hour the street was suddenly closed off, and after that the plot became so complicated that it was impossible to follow.'

'Had there been an accident, maybe, since the street was closed off?'

The woman who was talking sighed heavily and made several attempts to brush it off, before she felt she could continue:

'If I were to say what I believe happened, I'd say it was a day of judgement that had suddenly dawned. But it didn't take place where it's supposed to, on high, but down on the sidewalk, right by the bench where the two homeless were sitting.'

'I don't suppose they'll sell many copies of that book,' said the grey woman, shaking her head. 'You didn't let the owner of the bookstore foist it off on you, I hope, since you only went there for some measly napkins.'

'Well, you know, he did try, of course, and I was just barely able to resist. But afterwards I've been thinking there were a lot of things in that book I'd like to have a better look at. So I guess I'll have to go back and buy something or other, so I can have a better idea about what it all means.'

'But surely you don't mean it was Our Lord himself who came down to the sidewalk in the middle of rush hour and started putting people on his right hand or his left?'

'No, it was just an ordinary woman, like you and me. But she stood firm, by heaven, and let no one escape punishment. If anyone refused to mend their ways, she simply let them disappear, so the sidewalk was nearly deserted when the elegant gentleman appeared.'

'The elegant gentleman, did you say?'

'Yes, I can't explain who he was any more clearly, because he didn't go in for introductions. After a lot of undue secretiveness, it came out that he was a judge, but now I'm wondering if he wasn't even more of a bigwig. In any case he was quite a gentleman, and he blew out such quantities of smoke that he was often completely invisible. What really happened between him and the woman, I'm not able to say, except that they got into a disagreement and fell out with each other. He probably hadn't expected that she was so fearless and so articulate. In the end the only thing he could think of was to make fun of the record book and her writing implements.'

'What was wrong with them? Didn't they look like those sorts of things normally do?'

'Oh no, you know, they were no match for the printers they used where he came from. He called her eraser a sleight of hand, and he merely shrugged his shoulders at her yellow pencil. The time has long passed, he said, when it was possible to approach the truth with a Kohinor or a Faber 2. The mystery of the world will not be solved by hand, he thundered, and that was when she couldn't help herself any longer, but made the mistake of laughing.'

'Mistake?'

'Yes, you see, he was no friend of laughter, if he couldn't have it entirely on his own terms. This bubbling human sound had always troubled him, and in the mouth of a woman was quite simply insufferable. He didn't know where it would lead to, he said, if woman had really learned to laugh and the world had to do without her pious and everlasting gravity.'

'What did she have to say to that?'

'Well, she didn't have a reply to that, because just then something unexpected happened over on the bench. The young woman who was sitting there suddenly opened her eyes and looked over at the elegant gentleman. She sat like that for a good long while, blinking her eyes in astonishment, and then she identified him as the father of her child.'

'For goodness sake! So then the whole thing ended up as a

paternity suit. But I don't suppose she got anywhere with him. It's usually to no avail, you know, when one of the lowliest brings action against one of the high and mighty.'

'No, you're right about that, she didn't get anywhere with him. Even though the woman leafed back in the record book and found that it was just as the young mother had said. 'What?' he cried out in holy indignation. 'I, come in on the last train of the evening? I, who renounce the railroads and all their reprehensible trafficking and haven't set foot in this wretched city for an eternity!' And with that he lifted his hat and undoubtedly thought he had cleared his name. But at that moment the woman looked up from the book and directed her gaze at the shiny badge he was wearing in his lapel.'

'What was suspicious about that?'

'Well, you see, earlier in the day when she interrogated the others, she'd seen that they all wore a kind of emblem on their chest. When she asked them what it was, they squirmed, one after the other, saying it was the admission pass to the nurses training institute or the press club or the home owners' association or the bank management or God knows what revered and respected union. But little by little it was revealed that they belonged to a secret society, that conducted human sacrifice and had innumerable misdeeds on its conscience. On some people the badge was so tiny that it was barely visible, on others it was more conspicuous, and on the chest of the elegant gentleman it was so big that the reflection was positively blinding. When the woman wanted to know what kind of a badge it was, he burst out in a strange laughter and asked if she'd never heard about "his grace's sun". That was supposed to be some kind of elevated joke, I guess, but his laughter seemed like it would never end, and it sounded so distant and sinister that the young mother on the bench winced and lifted her arm to protect the child.'

'You don't need to tell me much more,' said the woman in

the grey coat. 'I'm not so slow that I can't figure out where it's all headed.'

'Yes, she had to delete him from the record book, all right, there was nothing else to do. But the funny thing was that when she reached out for her large eraser, the gentleman's derisive remarks stopped. 'For God's sake, keep your fingers away from that white thing over there,' he cried in a frightened voice, quickly buttoning his coat so he could make a neat exit.'

'Oh yes, he got cold feet, I imagine, as soon as he realized what she had in mind.'

'Goodness gracious, yes, he waved his arms and bellowing asked if she was out of her mind, and didn't she know who he was.'

'But she couldn't possibly know that, since he was hardly forthcoming when he introduced himself.'

'Oh, she must have had a premonition, because she looked so frightened after she'd made him disappear, that her face was unrecognizable. For a long time after he was gone, she sat staring into space with a forlorn look, almost as if she had committed a sacrilege. It wasn't so easy to understand what it was about this upstanding citizen in coat and hat that could awaken such strong feelings in her. You'd almost think he was an old acquaintance of hers – someone she'd thought highly of and had regarded in a completely different way earlier in her life.'

'And the young mother on the bench – what happened to her?'

'Well, after the father of the child had disappeared, she sat there for a while looking expectantly at the table, quite as if she believed that at the last moment everything would turn out all right. But when nothing happened, and the woman had started getting her things together, she cautiously leaned forward on the bench and said in a high voice: You promised once that you would blow on me.'

'And no sooner had the woman kept her promise and was bending over the frozen shape, than the transformation began. During all the many hours it sat motionless on the bench, it had been pitifully obscure, could nearly have been taken for dead had it not been for the motherly arms that half-blindly reached out and tended the child. Now it grew imperceptibly rounder, like when you stand gazing at the moon and see that it's no longer old pale-face, but a luminous body on a journey through space. Suddenly the young woman had stood up from the bench and was looking around with deep and radiant eyes. And as she took a firmer hold of the child and started out down the street, she turned around one last time, just in time to see the other woman hurriedly take flight and disappear infinitely far away like a nearly invisible dot in nothingness.'

'And that was it, I suppose?'

'No, wait, now comes the strangest thing of all, it makes my head spin when I try to think about it: When it started to get dark and the young mother still hadn't found shelter for the night, here come two women around a street corner, approaching her with sure steps. Well, believe it or not, but they were walking along, each of them carrying a shopping bag, talking about whatever came to mind, the one wearing a blue coat with a rabbit-fur collar, and the other one in a greyish coat with no fur.'

'Why, what are you saying, that could almost be the two of us!'

'That's exactly what I thought when I was standing in the bookstore reading about it. Mind you, I told myself it couldn't possibly be so, and that books were one thing, and reality something completely different. But I'm telling you, I felt quite a jolt in the pit of my stomach.'

'Good heavens, that must be what they mean by being completely taken in by a book.'

'But my dear, I'd just barely started leafing through it, and

I don't even know if I thought it was very good. But I'll tell you something, I'm beginning to get a sneaking suspicion that it's just the opposite of what you said.'

'What do you mean?'

'Well, that there are books that have a kind of secret opening or crack, just big enough for a person to slip away.'

Translated by Katherine Hanson

MARIE TAKVAM

Fall and rise again

Picture

The red coffee package has a picture
of a naked, dark woman
bearing coffee beans in a huge basket.
As I drain my cup I
notice an unusually bitter, salty taste
of soil and sweat and sorrow.

I drain my cup,
the same way others drain a cup,
drain it to the bottom
unless, of course, some grounds remain
where I can make out marvellous signs
and visionaries can peer and tell
of times that still lie ahead.

1980

While millions of human beings lie starving to death
I sit in a salon in a resort town having my hair dyed.
While millions of human beings lie starving to death
I fret over my nail colour, red polish or clear?
While millions of human beings are dying of hunger
I toss out bread only one day old.
While millions of refugees are dying at the borders
I jet over oceans to relax in the sun.
While millions of human beings lie ravaged by diseases
I run to the doctor for the slightest headcold or cough.
While millions of children are starving to death
our churches discuss abortion and virgin birth in the same
breath.
The dying are so far away
I can't smell the corpses, don't see the rib bones
protruding like old washboards.
While millions of human beings approach death in silence,
lying motionless at the final border,
I am talking about making things of
beauty.

A Victory in Thinking

I spend so many moments just in living
that I never get my shoelaces tied.

You talk to me of Vietnam and Cambodia, Israel
Egypt, Iran, Afghanistan, the USA, the Soviet Union, the oil
crisis,
gas, joblessness, automation, the military-industrial complex
communism, socialism, liberalism, conservatism.
Saudi Arabia.

How can I possibly find time to tie my shoes?

Don't give me more news of the world, you people!
Some day, surely, I'll find time to tie my shoes
so I no longer stumble with each hesitant
step I take.

Once Again

Once again some other being
has crept in beneath my skin
into my blood stream
out into my lips
behind my eyes.

My hands and fingers are no longer mine alone,
but guided by invisible strings
linking us.
My feet and toes refuse to walk
the paths my thoughts have paved.
My hair falls into curls
the way it thinks you would like.
Never, never will I control my life.
When I touch a hand, a warm hand close by
I am once again captive.
Even when you are away, you inhabit my mind
pull at my nerves,
and make me a puppet
in your theatre.

Please Don't Bar My Path

It is fine, I guess, if you drink the marrow out of me
and let your thoughts spurt into my belly.
But don't ever bar my path!
It's fine, I guess, for you to suck my will
from my lips
and get it to flow out of my other openings.
But don't ever bar my path!

There is plenty for all
and space inside me for your thoughts, as well.
But never bar my path!

My greatest wish is to follow the full course of my thoughts.

And thus:
Drink me, spurt into me
but never bar the path of a wanderer!

MARIE TAKVAM

The Letter from Alexandra

Montecello, December 1, 1979

Dearest!
I know of widows who have moved out of homes they had
lived in their whole lives with the man they loved.

Their sorrow rose like a tall, pure flame around them. They
tossed out the flower pots from their window sills and all their
bedding, and threw their furniture into a raging fire.

They are attempting to burn up their past.

But the blaze from my sorrow is hidden in sour, acrid
smoke. There is something shameful about the warmth that
flowed between you and me. Something shameful about my
paltry sorrow. It cannot burn tall and clear for all the world to
see. It should probably never have been kindled.

Nevertheless, it is consuming me, burning me right down to
the bone.

I had met other men before you and you had met other
women.

But your youth encountered my withering middle age and

what blazed up between us singed off the frayed edges of the nerves and blood vessels from all the broken bonds that had been my life. Can the fire between two people burn up Time?

Of course not! But it can at least trick people into believing, for a short while, that our whole past has been burned up, that nothing exists outside the moment when two people succumb to life.

Those powerful forces threw me back down to earth. Naked and freezing I realized that everything is sustained merely by our will to live and that nothing is real.

But the same forces pulled me back up toward the sunlight, cast me off again, pulled me up again and again, tossed me again and again into the cold and the darkness: that coldness called the truth that says time is a murderer.

But if Time were not in control of the universe, no life would ever be born. Time kills and Time gives birth, just as the sun rules with its unshakable, despotic power over this sickly little planet we crawl around on.

We are helpless, and you and I were helpless under the yoke of those powerful rulers TIME and SUN.

Each time life has united me with another person, I have felt like this: never have two people come together in this way before!

And I think it's true: the way our hands touched each other, the way our lips and our genitals met, never has it happened exactly that way before, never have you or I ever met another person in exactly that way before either.

The sensuous, primitive, and also exalted rituals between two lovers are alike and still quite different, the way finger-prints are. Flowing or in tangles, facing each other or half turned away in shyness--these rituals could easily be analyzed and used as distinguishing features of the two who are inter-twined with each other.

It is beautiful and at the same time grotesque, because we believe that we are free and capable of determining our own movements.

December 4, 1979

Dearest!

You are better educated than I on the subject of classical thinkers. Thus I would never dare to write down the name of the one I believe said 'I think. Therefore I am.' You would make a fool of me if I wrote Descartes and was wrong. It was surely some other philosopher.

But I will say: 'I love. Therefore I am.'

For me there is a deeper truth in that.

Can you understand what this is like for me?

If you had been here now, I would have made you under stand.

No, I won't ever mail this. I don't want to expose myself to your laughter if you should prove to be so brutal. Maybe at this very moment you are lying in bed with a beautiful young woman and if you got these lines you would read them aloud to her and say something like:

'I had a strange affair with a fifty-year-old woman this summer! It's always interesting to try something new, titillating. Just listen to this emotional drivel she writes about our rather--from my perspective, that is--sleazy relationship. I got involved due to a lack of other opportunities just then, because I was out of money. Post-graduate work. Just one loan after another.'

Don't think it impossible for me to imagine you in a situation like that.

And still I am hoping that you are just as I have made you in my hopes and desires.

Why in hell should I repress my sexuality just because I am beginning to grow old?

I must be a glutton for punishment since I can't give up the hope of a life after last summer.

But it is very difficult to remove the image from my mind's eye: a double bed in which I alternate with a young woman.

Translated by Frankie Shackelford

KARIN MOE

Sextext

The Woman Who Wanted to Write Literature

I walk into the large bookshop on Karl Johan with a resolute stride and select a distinguished assistant who no doubt has long experience and is well informed on all sides of the business, because he turns round in that special way 180 degrees straight up and down like a page being turned over.

'Would you have a fairly long, not too thick, not smooth but not rough either pen, preferably one of those with a barrel like smooth leather which doesn't slip, you see, I'm going to begin writing literature and I wondered whether it might not be possible to write from my sexually specific female situation in a concrete, material way, that is by gripping the pen with my vaginal muscles ... didn't you know it was possible, it even says so in a book, there on the left on the third shelf from the top, yes there, you can look it up ... I would have thought that a book and paper seller with an assorted book anatomy after many paper years ... so you don't believe it, I can assure you it's possible, but it's not all that easy, so I thought it must be something to do with the pen, all these male-constructed and male-produced pens, they're both too insubstantial and too rigid in a way, I'm sure you can understand that? you've got something here, you say, if I'm serious about it, well what do you think, I've taken the train into town today for the sole purpose of making a good start on my writing career, because now I have decided, on my honour, no more virginal humming and hising, now it's going to go down on paper, everything which moves in my womanmost being, that felt-tip pen you have in your hand, yes ... *Golden Axe Marker, instant dry, colour proof, weather resistant* — so it can be used outside, yes, perhaps that's not a bad idea, it might be advisable to seek some inspiration in the natural world now and again when I get stuck, but won't it be on the dry side — *instant dry* — and then that phrase about the Golden Axe, I think I can say that's not my style, sunset over the stack of logs, that wasn't exactly what I would most like to write about, I'd rather write something warlike about Achilla rushing to the attack with a gleaming axe, oh no please, just stay where you are, I haven't begun to write yet, but think what an important role you can play in my life, there will certainly be a note in my biography about bookseller X sine qua non ... I hope for your sake that you haven't got any skeletons in the cupboard, black market dealings or something on the side, you never know, there would have to be something psychoanalytic about my formal literary vaginalism with a background like that, *gefundenes Fressen* so to speak, that pen there, yes, I really must ask your advice: do you think perhaps that you ... oh no, there's that little difference, isn't there, do you have a changing room by the way? terrible how impractical the arrangements in these bookshops are, really it's verging on discrimination against women, it's not surprising literature is male dominated when the foundation is not properly prepared, you suggest a set of charcoal sticks, it's not enough that I'm going in for hard labour, you want me to look like a chimney sweep as well, a dirt bonus, that's quite an idea, you're sharper at the edges than you look and then I need some large sheets of paper, don't give me those stingy A-4 slips, you only just get started on expressing yourself when the paper runs out, yards and yards of brown paper, wrap it up for me and then an extra large eraser, you don't become a writer overnight, many many thanks, you've saved my literary career!'

The disorientated bookseller turns the page 180 degrees towards his bookshelves and wonders how there's going to be room for the new women's writing.

Women Bleeding

The tram scrapes into motion along steel-stretched tracks, crawls slitheringly around the network of streets and snuffles along between other travelling folk, it's going downhill for those who are sitting and standing on their way each to their own. I always have the tram in my stomach when I'm travelling by tram, the hollow sounds and the sideways heave at the corners, the jerking motion when the colossus brakes squealing at a red light and leaves you behind with a hollow in the pit of your stomach. Do you think that is why I always think about women bleeding when I'm travelling by tram? Talk to me bleeding women! who are travelling on the tram with me like so many islands around me as if it is not the case that every sixth woman among us could run the tram floor red with women's blood in crimson-spattered streams which lead from one to the other with pulsating movements. And I feel that they are touching me, the bleeding women, touching my hand which writes the islands together along a network of girls from *Wenche* who is a long-legged Levi girl standing with clenched thighs and concentrating uncertain as to whether she has got the tampon properly in place, how is it constructed inside there, can you see anything, she thinks, don't be stupid, but what about that couple of spots which otherwise never, besides she's wearing a long jacket today, how many Tampax are there left in her bag, will it be enough, just think if it leaked and *Signe* who is leaning heavily against the seat back aching and shivering in her fur-edged winter coat with one hand against her stomach holding her leather bag and wanting to hold back and calm the smouldering ache which sinks downwards, spreading a bloated thought, is this the last time, the doctor had said that each coming month now, then it would be a new time, no longer to have your own monthly times to connect events to, no longer to be fertile, to stop buying sanitary towels and renewing your prescription for painkillers, stop being a woman in that way, stop being a woman? was it now she was finally going to put an end to that which was already ended and yet it is still trickling dangerously in her and *Bitten*, Jesus how good it is to be bleeding! to feel that all the knots in her body are slackening and releasing purifying pains, not just because the egg and remains of sperm are on their way out and she is just herself in her own body, four days late and a kid, now and with him, it would never have worked, she feels it with every softening fibre of her body, with just as many luke-warm drops dribbling sweetly to *Kari* who is taut like a string, it's coming in clots, something warm and alive, coagulating between her legs, she feels it sticking ominously to her clothes, Jesus Christ, no-one had told her that's what it would be like after the abortion, that she would be pumped out and pumped out until the white gleam of her skin glowed blue like soured milk, bloody and bloodless at the same time, always having to get back to normal again, replace what's lost, chew iron and chomp parsley, having to be diverted into biological sidings and interrupt whatever she was involved in, vegetating in a pool of blood, she could get so anaemically furious and now it's essential to get up cautiously, walk without parting her legs, every slightest movement and get off the tram before it soaks through and to *Randi* who has her period and it's quite OK and to *Mariken* who is a budding new woman who has dipped her finger red in her own blood, touched it with her lips and tasted a warm sweet-sour liquid which stayed stinging fresh in her nostrils, this is me too which lives inside me and moves with the moon in cosmic circles, she had asked her grandmother who was a white-haired aura of security around her what it had been like for her to be menstruating who had knitted her own rags, rinsed off the blood in cold water and boiled the cotton cloths for the next time, fresh smelling of air and sunshine, that was what it was like for her who is near and close to Mariken and all that strangeness which trembles and creeps along to *Katja*, and she is sick and tired of this nauseating dribbling, if only she could be let off bleeding in this clammy feminine mystique, but there's always someone who has their period in a heavy tone of voice, is indisposed in a discrete fashion, has the curse and is not with it, there are translucent hands caressing a brow with all the history of women's suffering in the touch of a pale hand, aching swollen bellies squeeze out blood for the unborn female conspiracy, there is fate in every grim drop which exudes onwards to *Jofrid* who can share her blood with the man she loves so that it it is smeared gleaming and glowing on white limbs and is a part of everything which runs together and splits their bodies in a large red heart, it remains still quivering in her blood's pulse on the way to *Ada*, two days ago she swallowed the last p-pill in that sachet and the physiological process gets under way controlled by hormone intake so that the whole thing is taken care of in three days, she is the same afterwards as before, even if there are still a couple of days left without the chemicals which regulate the flow and over to *Ruth* who is bloated to bursting point after seven hours at the till in the noise and fuss from so many irrelevant figures that she can't scream at can't you see idiot that I'm aching and hurting and bleeding, but she endures without a good warm hand in the small of her back until the tram home and here at least it is warm because it's crowded in the tram and our bodies, women bleeding, touch each other and hold each other up and here and there I can see men, who are bloodtight, timeless and spacefilling.

Wordskill

It's called structural violence and is words between
us which mean that

IT'S NOT ME behind the fist which thumps away
at you bloody kid I should never have had you yell
just yell when my nails sink into your soft skin
without resistance lie still don't look at me like that
howl just howl I'll teach you for not getting a place
at the creche I couldn't get a loan for a mortgage or a
training course just gasp till you're blue in the face a wretch
and a brute that's what you are fifty pounds just for a child-
minder
and then there's the pram the nappies the food I haven't anything
left you're sucking the last dregs out of me biting and chewing
my
sore nipples little idiot I've long ago been
sucked dry and you cling on like a leech just to
get out away see people for the hours when I'm washing
stairs and slaving breaking my back for your sake
all for your fucking sake I'm all you've got don't look at
me like that ugly as sin you are helpless weakling I'm
going to smash that black bawling hole take that
and that I'll silence you you can't make your father
pay he doesn't want to have you he doesn't want to see you
not even your wonderful grandparents can I get
just my heel on your soft baby hand

Rehabilitation anno domino 1980

Get yourself down from that cross!

Mary and Magdalene and Guri are
at a meeting of the Palestine committee

Pull out your own nails!

Women no longer give
priority to stinking men's bones

Out of your wrappings on the third day!

There's plenty to do here Begin
with a rusty sermon for the
lilies on Hyde Park Corner
They have need of you now
Can you turn oil into clean sea
and five drilling rigs into one living fish

More jobs for women

Through wide blue view over the smoke from the metal factory, a new working day comes seeping in behind the typewriter. I use living daylight and pull down the blinds the days the sun shines too brightly in Oslo fjord. The pattern on the hessian in front of the window is full of golddust and knots. Texts for reading aloud stand on the window sill. Beside them a roll of drawing paper, paper clips and a bowl of handpainted beachstones: *Body and Language in Psycho-analytical Theory*, the essay issue of *Bazar, The First Newspaper on the Lofoten Mountains*, News from Korsvoll Sports Club, *The Kvinherad Cake*. All is ready with the day's inspiration. Leaf, look, follow a couple of lines, think black-on-white arrangement, let one word or other seep in: EENY MEENY MISCHIEF ... My eyes drift out seawards and see before me fisherwomen in Bekkjarvik. Us kids behind the salt barrels in snowsuits, defiant and well padded with caramels: 'Been up to your mischief again, haven't you. Filthy dirty. Get outa here. You too, small fry!' Sit there motionless staring holes in a thought: something happens to language when you learn to walk and can get at a distance. Girls walk earlier than boys and use language earlier. It's a halting advance which turns into arrears. In literature too. I feel it when I write. How dangerous it is to talk before your body can endure distance and self. I'm big now and scared to death of writing even if it's as good as wild strawberries for inner city lasses on holiday in Telemark. What isn't dangerous is to imitate, slide in and out of people's ears, be clever in that other language which can be learnt to your fingertips. No-one speaks it like a well-brought-up little girl in white cotton socks. And dreams act crazy around other signs, bloody, jagged, ice-red and tiptoe around during the day: 'Auntie Peli, please can I be allowed to say a bad word you've

never heard before ... ' No. I have a log book which explains
the arrears: 'It's time you learnt not to make a mess of your
exercise book. Look at Laila.' 'Oh no, not you. No, we don't
want to have to call for the doctor. Give Lars the hammer.'
'Button your lip for ten seconds and finish sewing your pin-
cushion.' 'You're to do that washing up, never mind pulling a
face, what an awkward kid.' Language just goes on and on.
From us. I understood. They are over him and he is over you
and you are over me. And I am over the kittens. They're going
to get it. But they are sweet as well. The problem is that we're
so alive. That's what we let ourselves die of. I believed two
things when I was five: that I could spray pudding all over
(that was correct!) and that I had no skin on my face. But
blood, flesh and bone. We let ourselves die of being so alive
before we can write a single word. Set the table. Clear it.
Clean the loo. Clean the loo. Tidy up. They are sweet as well,
mine are. I have cleared up my pine table and covered it with
dictionaries: Ivar Aasen's Norwegian Dictionary, Alf Helle-
vik's little yellow one, Raknes with a brown spine and gold
letters: NORWEGIAN — FRENCH. That's how I surround
myself with men in my shapes: between covers. Women's nets
bob about on the surface, if I simply go out into the passage
with the rubbish and meet the caretaker. Yet in the writing
room a fictional male liberation reigns: everything I get written
has to go through the hands, lungs, stomachs, skulls of men
before I can get it between my covers. Hi, Mr Publisher's
Consultant! Hello, Mr Critic! You who are sitting on experience — I hope you had a good fuck last night, got your melitta
coffee and sandwiches with cured ham and sprig of parsley and
greaseproof paper with a lipstick kiss on. I need your care,
girls, to get my book published! Personally I work best on an
empty stomach. Silence. Time. Time. Time. Time. Time.
Time. Time. That is my material. Incoherent, unconnected,
devoured time. It is a part of all I write that the writing time is

measured. To the hour. To the minute. Like other women I am timed to perpetuate life, wash the dirt off it, warm it, talk to it, drive it to sports practice, put food into it, clothe it, make just about sure it's not run over, deprived of creative fantasy in a classroom, bullied by politicians at the hands of a child, I'm gasping for air for sheer life here I've dug out a square metre to write in. That is my material. Together with 80 gram white paper for the typewriter and a rough book for scribbling. Mostly I work straight down through the keys, then it's least up to my body to jump aside when it skids off the track on a bend or gets hung up on a spike. Handwriting is not fine enough, doesn't go fast enough, it's not loops I want to form with my hands, I'd rather knit string vests. The trembling of my hands just deposits itself on top of the language when it's handwritten. They become just mine and stop me writing. I want to create a trembling in conventions, in defiance or despite the signs. Straight up and down. The same for all. An old body playing an embryo for new colours, smells, movements, notes and other social forms. Think of all that has to go down in black experience on white! Think I'd better help it on a bit with red paper. Noisy red paper. With traces of the working transition from tree trunks and branches to paper. It must be furrowed paper which shows that it has been through the hands of refining workers with aching backs. That I have only written that which lies there by the language machine, the setter has seen it, the binder has trimmed it, the warehouse labourer has stacked it on the lorry, Atle Sande has driven it and the bookshop assistant put it in place on the shelves, you have bought it, put it on the bedside table and thought that you would have done yours differently. My material full of matter. Not without connections with a vase in the shape of a carafe. Wide at the bottom and narrow at the top with yellow dried flowers drooping over uneven glazing the colour of soil. Or the brown varnished woodgrain on the windowsill. The material is the urge to write. It gets hold of language with its materialness and points: if I can, you can! And the material can also be honey on your finger, Gregorian male droning, a strip of weaving in your fist, blood on loo paper, official reports, a dictionary page, concrete feelings, an ache in the guts, the harmonantiques catalogue: a woman's smile, the twitch of the jaws, the crinkling of the eye, the attitude of hips and breast which understands all, the sound of hot compress-words and language which froths. Then it starts to roll. The first word on paper is a blow. What do you want and where have you been and what do you want with me who have streams of other words as long as metre measures in Manhattan? Further on, that which turns up is kicked into being by what is already there, not that necessarily, a word or a line can slowly belch forth and sweep away what has been built up rewriting after rewriting with smooth spurts inbetween. It is a monster of a form which all censorious bodies lay violent hands on: a bastard between Old Nick and the Virgin Mary. Consultants writhe on their chairs. The norms are waiting in the bottom drawer. Let them go. Let them wait. At the end of a text it's pure carpentry. It either has to be a three-syllable nail or nothing, a screw with vowels this wide, this many together, with strong main verbs. If there are more hooks than the text can stand, then out with the pliers and straight into the material toolbox. If it all stands still, for example in the depiction of a used washing-up brush: Go. Hop. But not over to something else. Clear room on the table for a game of patience (a tip from Torborg Nedreaas, whom I never met at Leirvik, but I had a stunning uncle.) Other text stiffeners are the notice-board for MCP criticism. Male chauvinist pig gives manpigprick-critic. There we have just now (excited?) ah yes, Odd Solumsmoen with his pathetic trash about C. Løveid in the brochure New Norwegian Books 1977 with seed money from the Cultural Council. Beside it hangs a grownup strip of juicy Norwegian curses and the week's battle verse from Sylvia Plath's Lady Lazarus: 'Out of the ash/ I rise with my red hair/ and I eat men like air.' More inspiration are the rejection slips. This one here: 'Thanks for the short text. It is of course making quite a neat point, but there are also certain things which are quite difficult to get hold of. And the totality which comes across is somewhat thin. Yours sincerely.' Men with sad eyes. The totality, to hell with that. Hi there text, onwards and upwards to the next editor. Great to have texts out and up to mischief. Going to pick up the post can be as important as changing tampons. On the tip of the carry-on-lance there may be some write-on pointer: 'All right, all right — I surrender. Your small corrections made little difference either way, but being the seriously (!) well-meaning man (!) I am, I went into the ring with your text again, and again, and in the end I was quite charmed by what I even from the beginning thought was good about it.' The exclamation marks are his. As a humble textworker I have great sympathy for the hard work behind the editor's salary: 'Your text is bloody difficult to read! Here we've been sitting, two men working together, slaving away at it. Couldn't you "lighten" it a bit?' Textual lightening is no doubt interesting. As far as I'm concerned, it's textual slavery. Textual lightening is for those who can do it. If the lance doesn't help, I have a folder of accompanying letters to send in with texts. When I leaf through that, I have to laugh. It isn't nice. But then I'm soon ready to start writing again. In this folder are the sulking-sneaking-clawing-pointing-alluring-menacing formulae. From: 'Here is a text best wishes.' To: 'Take it or leave it to the rival review.' Others: 'As Roland Barthes says ...' 'The attached poem is in praise of man ...' 'If you can't explain why you're not accepting this text, then print it.' And many more. Anyone who gets stuck can ring me on 02 23 71 24. If my texts get lost, someone could write a doctorate on a reconstruction of the source texts based on submission-refusal-quarrel-meta and other writings, a little roundabout empiricism about specifically female expressions in the 70s and a pinch of literary sociology regarding the world-view of a Sunnhordlending of average height born by Caesarean in a clinic near Skien and brought up on Lofoten cod and Bergen herring and first generation civil servant ideology from Fitjar-sjødn well supported by Elvis, Rocambole and the magazine Texas, launched from Sogn student hostel, married, maintained, divorced and paid by social democratic Norway. Right. Off you go. My mother has still not got her poems published. Scrawl two words on the typewriter ball: WOMAN. WORK. And don't give up. I look forward to seeing it.

Karin Moe

Homo preludens

Should have liked a rattling good expression for the male organ
Recreate the purplish-brown experience Give a jiggling impression
of his crotch's pride which has laid earth and heaven at his balls
I haven't one myself so I must find someone who has or better
several so they can squabble about who is extra rattling good But first I must solve the compositional: the male
organ must be exposed and what is he wearing Tshirt and sharp
                                                          crease?

Skintight cords? Overalls? Inside? Outside? Day? Night?
Uggdalseidet? Marakesh? (The setting, my girl!) And then comes
the essential creative writers stare straight at the groin of the
guy: Why does he open his flies? (The motive, my girl!) Apart
from that time five or six crazy Canadians I never saw
male organs thighs just like that and parading for hungry
typewriters And what is he to do with his trousers around his
ankles? (The plot, my girl!) How? (The form, my girl!)
Go to the loo prosaically? Slip someone a quick one epically? To
Elise lyrically? Eject sperm expressionisprickly ... That it should
be so fiendishly to toss off a little piece about the male organ's
splendour, but what the hell here goes Let's say he was standing
                                                there (You must

in truth's name be allowed to pretend in literature!) Standing
there for Christ's sake Oh wow Stripped Paralysed Ready for creation
So what? Can't squeeze him out of the tube of paint and spread
him over the canvas Can't etch him in copper Cast him
in steel Don't have granite to hew at him with Wool to spin
him with Heavenly strings to play him on Earth to grow him
in No combine harvesters to tickle him with

Words are all I have

One long and two round

                                    Translated by Janet Garton

MARI OSMUNDSEN

Seven minutes to six

He had buttoned up his overcoat and put on his gloves in good time before the train stopped. Now he stood up and met his reflection in the dark window pane. They were like mirrors, these windows, as soon as it grew dark outside. Normally he avoided looking in that direction, but he had forgotten to be careful for a moment. And there he stood in the window: lean and broad-shouldered, but with an unhealthy looking green complexion. I'm not like that, he said to himself. It's this bloody lighting – it makes everybody look ill. It left him with a slight feeling of unease which did not lose its hold over him until he stepped out on to the platform and felt the sharp December air on his face.

It was still only half past four. It was too early. He bought a newspaper and went into the railway restaurant and ordered a meal. The place was full. He found himself a place at a table for four where three of the places were already occupied. He did not look at the people already sitting there. The noise in the restaurant did not worry him. These sounds meant nothing to him. There was nobody here of any concern to him. He ate his stew and potatoes feeling relaxed, relieved.

There were no noisy kids at table. None of those looks that bored through the newspaper and into his brain. Good.

The streets were full of grey dun-coloured pre-Christmas slush. What was it Ragnhild had said? *'White Christmas – so nice for the children!'* His boots were of suede leather. They were not quite water-tight. He could feel the dirty water seeping through. It was a damned nuisance that he could not use his car any more. But he was a cautious man, and he could not arrive home with the car all daubed with paint. Ragnhild doubtless had her own thoughts. As long as she kept them to herself, he wasn't worried. He wanted no discussion about this matter.

It was her fault, he thought. If it wasn't her period, then it was a headache. If she didn't have a headache, then she was too tired. *Tired!* From staying at home, in that new flat she had wanted for years, looking after her own children!

'I never get out,' she complained one evening. Out? Who was stopping her from putting the little boy in a pushchair and dressing up the little girl and going out? Not him, at any rate. He wasn't one of those who kept their wives cooped up. She lacked initiative, that's what it was.

Didn't have enough initiative to bring up the children properly. The boy clinging to her and whingeing for no reason. The girl getting more and more wild and undisciplined. And Ragnhild sitting there powerless and not lifting a hand to stop it. Letting herself being called an old bag and things even worse without answering back. He'd have to take a hand there soon. That wasn't the way he wanted his children to be.

No. He couldn't bear thinking about it.

A young girl was walking just in front of him. A good-looking girl with long brown hair falling in curls over her shoulders. He felt a vague excitement as he followed along behind her. There was a young man walking beside her holding her hand. The girl was wearing shiny black boots, with high heels. Her hips swayed with every step she took.

Black leather. Just like in that film of Maere's.

Pretty mean it was – that nickname the lads had given to Maere: *the Old Mare*. Inevitable, perhaps, with a name like that and those big yellow teeth. All the same, Maere was a decent sort. He had shared his bottles and his videos with anyone who had come his way. He was no old mare – not Maere. A bit off-beat, perhaps; a bit odd in the way that old bachelors often are, but genuine and decent. There was never any nonsense about Maere.

The girl with the black boots turned off at a street corner, and he lost sight of her.

His wife had kept going on about how she would like a video. She was quick enough to complain if he worked overtime, but she would always accept the money. There was never enough of that. Video? When the new flat took every penny of his salary and his overtime pay? Bloody hell!

Anyway he didn't want anything of that kind in his house. He knew all about the filth that was on the market. And with two children, what was she thinking about?

All the same, she was a good lass was Ragnhild – he had to admit it. And she was also a good cook. But she was too ready to take things nice and easy, that was it. All she wanted was to settle the children in front of the TV so that she could sit there in peace with a bag of crisps and read magazines. Sit back and grow fat and lazy and never find contentment. She never thought about what *he* needed. Every time it was the same old routine. She never wanted to try anything new.

One evening he had made a suggestion. He wondered whether they might order one or two bits and pieces from a mail order firm. Not whips or anything like that, just a few leather goods, garments, straps. You could even get handcuffs. It was just because he had begun to think about them and fancied trying them out. Just to see what it was like. Just to bring a little variety into their lives. Something different, something new.

Then Ragnhild had *looked* at him and said 'no'. Nothing more than that, but in such a way that he understood it was hopeless to get her to go along with that idea. Never ever. Full stop.

Christ! Here he was putting before her his innermost thoughts, and why? Because he was fond of the girl, imagined she could be relied on. Wanted them to have a good time again, the way it had been before. And what does she answer?

No!

So she can blame herself for what happens.

Silly old mare, he thought and clenched his gloved hand in his coat pocket.

*

May-Britt stopped in front of a shop window selling perfumes and looked in at the extravagance. No reindeers, but a whole lot of Christmas goblins. Scarlet hearts, plastic baubles and decorations, soaps, perfumes, adverts for a new kind of eye-shadow. The model was a dream in mink and gold. In front of the placard was a board with cheap metal clips. That's how it is: all the things they attract us with, and the things they offer us. What was she doing standing here?

Then she saw it: English soap, exactly the kind Annemor was so fond of. May-Britt gave a little smile and went in.

It was crowded in there: pre-Christmas chaos. Parcels and bags and bodies, wet topcoats, patient harassed looks, three shop girls scurrying round behind the counter ringing up figures on the till. May-Britt waited till it was her turn. It took time, but there was no hurry. She was early.

She said what she wanted, then added: 'It's a present', so low that the busy assistant behind the counter didn't hear, or pretended she didn't. May-Britt was handed the parcel without any wrapping or ribbon. Even though it was an expensive soap.

She paid and made her way out.

English soap: 'Fern', it said on the wrapping. Anne had said that it meant something like 'bracken'. May-Britt didn't think it smelled of bracken – it smelled good, it smelled of soap. English soap: something light, pure. Something young and innocent. The very thing for her daughter.

A modest present, perhaps. But then she couldn't give the girl cash, or anything that might be turned into cash. A mother must surely be able to give her child a little something for Christmas. Regardless of what has become of the child other-wise and how angry and desperate you are ...

It was always the fault of the mothers.

But what could she have done differently, thought May-Britt. She couldn't have done any more. And there was nobody willing to help her, either. What could she have done!

It was Anne's own choice. She couldn't lock the child in. Actually, she had tried that. She had tried everything. When a child refuses to come home, when a child seems set on de-stroying her life, what can a mother do to prevent it? When a mother scolds and pleads and the child stands in the doorway with that hard, distant look and that scornful laugh before she slams the door behind her and disappears? When the social services have 'no resources' and the doctor thinks the girl is lacking in 'motivation'? When the parson sits there behind his desk and says that 'the home environment is of decisive impor-tance'?

Bloody hell, thought May-Britt bitterly.

But it was obvious she should have managed things differ-ently. She should have stayed at home more. She shouldn't have let Anne see her father drunk three or four times a week. She should never have gone out and left them to themselves.

She should have barred the door to him and steeled herself and sent him packing. And when she had finally managed to throw him out, she should have been at home with her daughter, always. She shouldn't have gone out drinking and having a good time with Eddie. She should have pulled herself together and used her hard-earned cash for something other than frivolous pleasures. Absolutely.

It was too late. She had got things under control at last, but it was too late.

Seventeen, such a fair and lovely girl, a good girl.

What had gone wrong!

May-Britt realized she had come to a stop on the pavement. She was standing there with her parcel of soap in her hand. People pushed against her and hurried past. She flushed and quickly put the parcel in her carrier bag. The clock on the tower on the other side of the market place showed half past five. She crossed over with slow steps.

Of course it didn't matter if she got there too early. It wasn't even certain that Anne would turn up. She could buy herself a cup of coffee and a roll or two, take stock of things. She was in fact hungry.

She went into Glasmagasin, the big department store, and found herself a window seat in the ground floor cafeteria. What luck, right in the middle of the Christmas rush. She remained sitting there with her coat half-unbuttoned and two rolls on the plate in front of her. She lit a cigarette and kept watch. The coffee in her cup grew cold.

If only Anne would come now.

*

Kajsa thought how exciting it was to shop for Christmas presents. She had been saving up her pocket money all autumn and Mamma had given her fifty kroner before leaving. Leif had weighed in with a couple of tenners. And Pappa would surely fork out something when she met him that evening, so it wouldn't matter if she spent what she had now. The streets were full of colour. Everywhere there was music, people, lights. Four days to Christmas Eve.

She had been to Steen and Strøm's and taken the escalator right up to the top. She had bought herself a lemonade in the cafeteria, paid for it herself, found herself a seat at a table. Afterwards she had bought some perfume for Mamma down on the ground floor.

She had called in at a stationer's and bought a notebook for Leif, a kind of pocket diary. She hoped nobody else had thought of that. It was perhaps a bit of a boring present, but she couldn't think of anything else. And Leif liked things that were useful, so a pocket diary seemed right. Actually that was the one thing wrong with Leif: he was a bit too useful, so to speak. A bit too boring. Otherwise at bottom he was all right. She quite liked him. Mamma could easily have found herself a worse type than Leif.

She had saved the most exciting presents till last: the one for Pappa, and the one for Siri. She was looking forward most to buying Siri's. She didn't know what she was going to give her new baby sister, only that it would have to be something soft and woolly, a teddy bear or a furry animal. She would have to go into a toy shop and look. But first she would have to find a shop that sold wallets, for that was what she had thought of giving her father: a proper expensive wallet, in real leather. The old one was worn-out and scruffy.

Kajsa crossed the street carefully and unhurriedly on the green light.

Formerly she used to wait until some of the others walked across and then she would join them, without paying attention to the lights. She had long ago given up such childish behaviour. If Mamma could have seen her now, she would have known not to worry herself! Kajsa pulled a wry face. As if she was still a mere child. If the truth be known, it was only two months to her thirteenth birthday.

A teenager!

'But will you find your way to his office, Kajsa? Are you quite sure you know the way?'

'Of course, don't fuss. I've been to Pappa's office a million times, at least.'

'Yes, but then you were with Pappa.'

'That's what you think! Pappa doesn't fuss over me the way you do, you know. He knows that I can look after myself. I've gone out to the shops on my own while he was working and found my own way back. What's difficult about that?'

'But Kajsa, with Christmas coming everything is so busy. It's no fun for you to go shopping downtown at a time like this.'

'It's not for you to decide what *I* think is fun, I have to say. You mustn't coddle me like this,' Kajsa had said. 'You only do it because we've got Siri now and you think I'm jealous, which I'm not.'

At which Mamma had laughed and stopped fussing.

Kajsa smiled at the thought. Mamma was all right. But Kajsa was no longer a child, nor was she sorry at having got a sister either. She who had always wanted a sister!

It had obviously been nicest when they had had Pappa as their father. But they were divorced, so that was that. And actually there weren't any such things as whole or half brothers and sisters, Leif had said. Kajsa thought this was well put. Siri was her sister, and a fuller sister than Siri one couldn't imagine.

Perhaps some kind of soft rag doll, or a monkey that could put its thumb in its mouth?

There they had wallets! Kajsa stopped at a window and looked in eagerly. Gosh, but they were expensive. They cost over a hundred kroner. Should she buy one all the same? Or should she buy the present for Siri first – for she would surely get some money when she got to Pappa's office. And then she could pop out tomorrow and buy him a wallet. It seemed a bit stupid. As if she was getting money which she was giving back as a present. But Pappa surely wasn't concerned about that.

He had promised her a pizza that evening. It was great that Pappa could get Sweden on his TV – they couldn't get it at home. So long as he hadn't bought such an enormous block of chocolate! For Kajsa couldn't resist chocolate if it was put in front of her, even though it brought her out in pimples almost as soon as she had eaten it. She really *must* stop this kind of childish gluttony.

The present for Siri was the most important. Kajsa resolutely turned her back on the shop window with the wallets in it and continued on down the street. The Glasmagasin Store, perhaps? They had a toy department there. She had lots of time, for Pappa was working until seven today, and the shops shut at seven, and the time now was only ten to six.

How marvellous to be in town on one's own just before Christmas!

'What will you do if you get lost, Kajsa?' That was Mamma, with anxiety in her voice, a couple of hours earlier, just as Kajsa was going out of the door.

'You *must* stop this, Mamma!' Kajsa had answered, for she had become rather irritated. 'I'm not a silly little child any longer, you know!'

Kajsa sighed as she strolled along the pavement in her fine red high boots, keeping tight hold of her red shopping bag. The boots she had got from Pappa, but she had chosen them herself. Mamma had bought her her bag. Mamma was all right – just a bit hopeless when she got started on this fussing of hers. She really didn't seem to want to accept that Kajsa would soon be an adult.

'What will you do if you get lost ... ?'

Ask the way, what else! I'm not going to get lost, you know that. But even if I do, there's always somebody I can ask. Like some old lady, for instance. Or somebody in a shop. Or that man coming towards me on the pavement with a fur collar on his coat and a brown paper parcel under his arm – I could quite nicely ask him the way ...

*

Of course they like it, he thought. Some of them are nothing more than nymphomaniacs. And the others just think it's a nice way of earning money. Christ, it must be a super job, independent, tax-free. He wouldn't mind a job like that himself. They like it. They also like it from behind. And several times a day. Why in God's name had he married a woman who was more or less frigid?

He was well equipped. Ragnhild should have been pleased with what she got.

His arousal grew as he walked round the streets. He didn't recognize any of them. Perhaps he was on the job a bit early. Surely the girls hadn't taken a Christmas holiday ... ? There must be good money to be earned at this time, with all these people in town now.

Perhaps he should take a walk over to the Market Place. He'd had a bite over there before.

You needed to be a bit careful there. They weren't all that good. He liked the very youngest girls best. But some of them wouldn't even suck, and he could always toss himself off without any extra help, thank you very much. Once he'd picked up one who got cold feet when it came to the point and blamed it on her menstruation, even though she had hardly started to grow tits. The girl hadn't been more than thirteen or fourteen, but she claimed that she'd already started her periods.

Good God. He got furious, and told her to get lost. This was at the time he was still using his car. He had driven deep into the woods with that girl, and then she wouldn't. She'd just stood there and screamed at him! She should have been glad that he wasn't one of those who just took what they wanted, and had done with it. It was best when they were willing.

But actually they all wanted it, all of them. They liked being forced a little. He liked it too. Excitement grew in him. He seriously thought he might soon buy those handcuffs. He knew of a shop where they had things like that. He had been there and bought various magazines which he kept in a cupboard at work. He used to swap things with Maere.

Ragnhild used to call them *filth* and wouldn't have them in the house – as though it could harm anybody to read it in a magazine. As though he could harm anybody by sitting there with a sheet of paper in front of him. When it came to sex and that sort of thing, the woman had become quite scatty.

Really though, apart from that, she was quite nice. And then there were the kids, they might come across the magazines; things like that wouldn't be good for them. Seen in that light she was doubtless right.

He knew which hotel he was going to use. He had looked in and booked a room in advance. He remembered the last time he had been there, nearly six weeks ago, it must be. Christ, could it really be as long as that? Six weeks. Ragnhild hadn't exactly been in a loving mood in recent weeks either.

The previous time. That had been a good one. He had had her in his room for three hours, had her both from the front and from behind and then she had sucked him off when he had begun to droop. He could almost believe the girl felt sorry when she had to leave. He doubted whether every client was as well equipped as he was. And of course he had read up quite a bit, and he knew how they wanted it. If he caught sight of that girl, he'd have her. He felt pretty sure he'd recognize her again. She'd had long auburn hair. She was a bit expensive. But if that's the way it is, so be it, he thought. The whole of the Christmas holidays lay ahead, endlessly boring. Behind him lay the cold grey autumn, with all its grind, its harassment, its overtime. He surely deserved a little bit of fun. He had a weakness for long hair.

Should have had a rope, he thought. On an impulse he went into an ironmonger's and bought one: eight metres of blue nylon, cut into two lengths. And if that young puppy of a shop assistant gaped at him as he left, he could bloody well go on gaping.

He stood on the pavement with the brown paper parcel under his arm and his arousal grew making it hard for him to walk.

From behind. With each of her hands lashed to a bedpost, and her feet to the posts at the bottom of the bed. Yes.

He quickened his pace, turned up his fur collar to cover his ears and walked rapidly up the main street. Past the church railings, to the market place.

On the pavement outside Glasmagasin a young girl was walking towards him. Was it or was it not ... ? At all events she had long brown hair, tight-fitting jeans, high red boots. He saw when he got nearer that she was young, barely fourteen perhaps. A real Lolita type. Was it ... ?

He wasn't sure, but there was a resemblance. And when she looked up and met his glance and smiled, he asked her if she felt like earning a few hundred kroner. But he must have made a mistake, because she took fright, or pretended to. Her eyes grew wide, her little mouth opened, then she turned abruptly and dashed off in the direction she had come.

He looked about him in confusion. Two elderly women were standing waiting for the tram a little further along the pavement. Behind him a man was walking an Alsatian dog on a lead. The clock in the tower showed seven minutes to six.

The shops were full of white Christmas, all glitter and show. The window beside him faced on to Glasmagasin's cafeteria. Some middle-aged woman at the nearest table glared at him with a look he found difficult to interpret. Three young lads came slouching round the corner with their hands in their pockets. Was it the Alsatian dog which had frightened the young girl? That was it, of course. She was frightened of dogs. He shrugged his shoulders and continued along in the same direction the girl had run.

He caught another glimpse of the woman inside the café. She had half risen from her chair and her mouth formed a red-lacquered O. It looked almost as though she was thinking of jumping right through the window pane and running after him.

Women, he thought. They must have a screw loose.

*

May-Britt opened her handbag and took out her pocket mirror. In it she saw reflected her own tired, lined face. She was only forty-four, but looked older. Aged. Impatiently she raked around in her handbag till she found her lipstick. A bit of colour. There, that was better. She shut her bag, glanced at her watch. It was ten to. Would Anne come, or wouldn't she?

When had it actually started?

She remembered the first time the young girl had come in drunk. She wasn't much more than thirteen. But it must have begun before then. May-Britt recalled how Anne had spewed up over the carpet in the entrance. She remembered the sickening smell and the feeling of shock. It had been a turning point. For May-Britt it marked the beginning of that protracted struggle, the struggle to get on her feet again and get her life in some sort of order. And Anne? May-Britt did not know, but that episode in the entrance might have served as a declaration of war. Afterwards everything had gone wrong. But it must have begun earlier. For Anne it must have begun much earlier.

May-Britt shrugged and lit a new cigarette from the old one. Wasn't the girl coming? She peered gloomily out at all the Christmas activity and at the grey slush of the market place. A Black Maria swept silently and menacingly along the road. Her stomach knotted. For all she knew it could be her child they were hunting for.

How old had Anne been when her father had finally been shown the door? Ten, perhaps eleven? After that came the years with Eddie. That hadn't gone so well, either. But May-Britt could not really understand that, for she had never wholly lost her grip. She had always got to work. She had made sure that there had been a hot meal every day. She recalled small intimate moments spent over homework and clothes that needed mending. It *couldn't* be just her fault.

It's always the mothers who get the blame.

Was that Anne coming over there? May-Britt leaned closer to the cold window pane and looked. No, it wasn't Anne. Anne was a bit taller, and fair-haired. The girl on the pavement had long brown curly hair and couldn't be more than fourteen. A man approached her from the other direction. He stopped right outside the window and said something to the girl. May-Britt saw his lips move, and she saw the expression on the girl's face. Then the girl turned abruptly and ran. Dear God, thought May-Britt in terror, she was just a child, perhaps no more than twelve. *And right in the middle of town, four days before Christmas, dear God!* The man stood a moment silently on the pavement. She could have stretched out an arm and seized him by the shoulder if the window pane had not been between them. He looked round uneasily, and for a moment their glances met. She read something there which terrified her. Without thinking, she rose to her feet. She clasped her hands.

'You murderer,' she whispered.

Then the moment was past. He adjusted his coat collar and

began walking. He vanished from her line of vision. Behind him came a man with a dog. The clock showed seven minutes to six. The three women at the neighbouring table got to their feet and began collecting up their coats and their shopping bags. One of them gave May-Britt a funny look. May-Britt flushed and sank back on her chair again. What was she up to, making herself a laughing stock in front of the entire café like this! It must be her nerves, she decided. For nothing had happened. Just that that little girl had reminded her of Anne. Actually she wasn't like her at all.

Nothing had happened.

Wouldn't Annemor come soon?

*

Kajsa saw that the man with the fur collar had caught her eye. It looked as though he was thinking of saying something to her. She stopped in front of him. Perhaps he had lost his way, she thought. Perhaps he didn't know his way about the town and wanted to ask for directions. Nothing wrong with that, she thought, to help an older man to find his way. Perhaps he wanted to take the Underground? She knew very well where the nearest Underground station was. Kajsa smiled at him.

'Would you like to earn a few hundred kroner?' the man whispered.

For a moment she stood stock still.

His eyes were hard, sharp, grey or blue. She recorded nothing of his face, only something of the expression which stuck to her, like glue or chewing gum, something disgusting that attached itself to her and fouled her. There was something about a rope, a blue rope. Something nasty. His eyes did not waver. It was as though he came nearer, she could not breathe. Then he blinked.

Kajsa turned and ran.

She did not know whether he was following her. She turned off into a side street; down another. Her legs were on fire. She stumbled, caught her balance again, ran. Ran. Her new boots with their high heels were hurting. She was sweating in her padded jacket and her face was wet. She did not know whether it was snow or sweat or whether perhaps she was crying. She pushed past people on the pavement, gasping for breath, not knowing where she was any more. Running.

Finally she had to stop. She flattened herself against the wall and looked round. No, she could not see him. There was a doorway nearby. She slunk into a dark courtyard. There were a few dustbins in there. She slipped behind them. She had run away from him. He couldn't find her now, could he? She'd got the stitch and she bent double the way her school teacher had shown her. Taken a deep breath. Broke wind. That helped.

It was dark in that courtyard. She heard the cars driving past, driving past. A little way down the street she heard a motorbike start up, or perhaps it was something else. Kajsa couldn't stop herself trembling.

She sat crouched behind the rubbish bins. Safe. Safe now. Wasn't she?

It had started to snow.

*

Should really have taken himself an Indonesian girl, he thought. He had heard of people who had married girls from down there. Hot stuff and willing in bed, that's for sure, and nice in other respects too. Grateful for everything that came their way. That would have been something, he thought. The women here at home were a pain in the butt in his view.

He detested these mincing little tarts, all knotted up and feeling that sex was something to be ashamed of. Primping themselves out with tight jeans and scent in all sorts of places, that was OK; but as soon as you were on the job, they played all innocent. What they needed was to be given a good hard fuck, the whole chicken-brained lot of them. That would give them something to think about.

It was a bloody nuisance he couldn't use his car any longer. Maybe he could take a chance again soon. There hadn't been many of these protest actions for some time, from what he had heard. Imagine daubing other people's cars with paint in that way – sheer vandalism. If ever he got his hands on one of these red-stockings, she'd learn what's what.

He gave himself a moment or two to relish the thought.

I reckon I'd prefer a regular whore, he thought. You know what you are getting then. And the girl knows it. Frankly and honestly, no pretending in that situation. As if everybody didn't have their sexual impulses! It's their own choice after all, he thought.

He had now come up to Karl Johan Street. On the corner by David Andersen's stood a girl he'd seen before, a blond, a little older than he preferred. But what the hell – at least this time he could be sure. He went across and asked, but she claimed she had an appointment. Somebody she had to talk to. Talk. Did she expect him to believe that, he said. Come on. I'll pay a decent price. I have a hotel room. She had to keep her appointment, she said. She was already late. But if he liked, she could come up to his room in half an hour. He hesitated, but then went along with the idea and gave her the address and room number.

Smart girl, he thought and he gripped his parcel tighter under his arm. Should have had a half-bottle, then he could have helped himself to a drink first. But that was of no real concern. He could go out afterwards and have a beer or two instead.

Though actually he didn't need it.

*

The time was ten past six and May-Britt sat with a hard lump in her throat. She knew Anne would not be coming now. Either she came on time, preferably a little before she was due, or not at all.

The cafeteria shut at seven today. She could sit there till it closed. She had nothing better to do anyway.

When she looked up, Anne was standing at her table.

It really was Anne: that long fair hair, those dark-blue eyes, those chubby hands. She had on a grey fur coat which May-Britt had not seen before; and her face looked older than May-Britt remembered, even though it was only a couple of weeks since they had last spoken. But it was always like that. This child of hers always looked like a stranger to her, and May-Britt never managed to come to terms with it, never succeeded in accepting that this unfamiliar, severe-looking adult person standing there was her own daughter.

'Hi, Mamma!' said Anne.

'So there you are,' said May-Britt, making her voice sound welcoming. She talked and smiled and moved over, and told herself that she must not – *must not* – start scolding or nagging now, not this time. Now she had to keep calm. Nice and calm.

'I almost didn't think you were coming,' she said. 'There's nice you are looking. What a lovely coat you've got. Is that real fur?'

'Blue fox,' Anne said. 'It's not mine. I've just borrowed it.'

May-Britt swallowed and did not ask who was lending blue fox fur coats to her daughter. 'Are you hungry?' she asked instead. 'Would you like a coffee? A smoke?'

'A coffee would be all right,' said Anne. 'What kind of fags have you got? The usual menthol rubbish? No thanks.'

May-Britt fetched the coffee from the counter. She only took her purse with her, not her handbag. When she got back to the table by the window, Anne was sitting there quite openly going through her handbag.

'You can save yourself the trouble,' said May-Britt and she heard how forced and bitter her voice sounded. 'I haven't any cash or a cheque book with me.'

'You never know,' said Anne calmly and put the handbag back on the table. 'But you could manage a hundred?'

May-Britt shook her head. 'It's no use, Anne,' she said wearily. 'I've hardly any money on me.'

'You old bitch,' said Anne.

May-Britt lit herself a cigarette and saw how her fingers trembled. She waited until she felt her voice was steady before she said: 'That's just fine, Annikin. You can sit there if you like and call your mother a bitch. But have you looked at yourself recently? Have you seen yourself in the mirror? Can you imagine what you're going to look like when you are as old as I am. Can you, Anne? Can you?'

'Stop yelling like that,' said Anne. 'If you yell at me, I'm going.'

May-Britt kept silent.

'I've got to have money,' said Anne.

May-Britt said nothing.

'Do you hear what I say! *I've got to have money!*' said Anne and leaned forward and looked her full in the face. 'I'm sorry, I didn't mean to call you a bitch. But *I've got to have money!*'

May-Britt silently shook her head.

'Do you know what I'll do, then?' said Anne, and her voice was low and menacing. 'If you don't give me something, do you know what I'll do? I'll tell you what I'll do, Mamma. I'll go straight from here to a hotel room I know of. An old swine is sitting there waiting for me. And I'll lie down and open my legs and shut my eyes and think of something else. And when he's had enough, I'll get three hundred kroner if I can keep him going long enough. So what do you think? Shall I do that, Mamma? Shall I?'

'Stop it,' May-Britt whispered.

'No,' said Anne. 'I think you ought to know how things are. But I don't expect you want to hear about it, do you?'

'How can you choose a life like that,' said May-Britt.

'Choose?' said Anne and laughed. 'You don't really understand what goes on, do you, Mumsie?'

She stood up and tied her scarf more firmly round her neck.

'Anne,' pleaded May-Britt. 'Don't go. Couldn't you come and see us at home? On Christmas Eve. Couldn't you come?'

'Never in this world,' replied the girl who stood there and called her Mamma. 'Not even if you paid me for it. That's the one thing on earth I wouldn't do even for money. No! Now you are rid of me. And that's the way it's got to be. For that's what you always wanted, wasn't it?'

'No,' cried May-Britt. 'No! It's not true!'

'Oh yes it is,' said Anne. 'You could chuck Pappa out, and actually you would have been glad to chuck me out after him. But that you couldn't do, so you forgot me instead. That's the absolute truth, for that's exactly how things were. Now I'm going,' said Anne.

'Wait,' said May-Britt dully. 'Wait, I've got something for you!' She began desperately to rake about in her handbag; then she remembered that she'd put the packet down in her shopping bag instead. She lifted the shopping bag from the floor and fumbled in it.

'So, you did have some money after all,' said Anne.

'No,' said May-Britt. She wasn't able to say any more, not even 'Happy Christmas' or anything like that, but just laid the packet of soap on the table. She put her head in her hands and hoped that people wouldn't notice her sitting there weeping.

When she looked up, Anne was gone.

The packet of soap was also gone.

*

Kajsa remained sitting behind the dustbins until she began to freeze. She wasn't so frightened any more. She was still trembling but that was probably because it was so cold. Perhaps it hadn't really been all that dangerous, she thought. Perhaps she had mistaken what the man had meant when he asked if she wanted to earn a few hundred kroner. She did know a little about these things, because she had talked to her mother about them; and sometimes there would be a bit in the papers about girls who had been assaulted. Sometimes they had gone missing. There had been some girls earlier that autumn, and something about one of them who was only six years old. But that wasn't here in town.

She had clearly made a bit of a fool of herself, thought Kajsa. Just think if he'd meant something entirely different? Perhaps he'd only wanted her to carry his parcel for him. It had been right in the middle of town, and lots of people about. It was childish of her to be so frightened.

She got up, hitched her bag over her shoulder, went cautiously out to the gate and looked out at the street.

No people. She did not know where she was, but that didn't worry her. She would surely always meet somebody she could ask the way of. Some old ladies. Old ladies weren't dangerous. If she saw an old lady she would ask her.

There had been something in his eyes ...

But she mustn't think about that. She must never think about it ever again. She shut her mind to the memory, and it was just as though a clock had stopped within her. It stood at seven minutes to six, and time could never be the same.

When she got to the end of the road, she recognized where she was. She wasn't very far from Pappa's office and it was still only half past six. There was nothing to fear. Now she would go straight up to Pappa. She would tell him about the man and ask what he thought about it – whether she'd been silly to be so frightened, or what. She would rather buy the Christmas presents tomorrow.

She ran up all the stairs, for suddenly she had no desire to take the lift.

She stood a moment in front of his office door and drew breath, then she knocked and went in. Calmly, quite calmly and as normal. He was sitting at his desk, bent over his papers. He straightened up as she came in and glanced at her from behind his glasses with his gentle and familiar look. But why had she never noticed how helpless he looked?

'Hi, Kajsa!' said Pappa.

The words she meant to say somehow vanished leaving a small empty space in her head.

'Everything all right?' Pappa asked. 'Have you done all your shopping? Had a nice time?'

'Yes. Everything's fine,' Kajsa replied. She let her bag fall to the floor with a thud. Then she went and stood with her back to the window so she didn't have to look out.

'Everything's fine,' she repeated and smiled at him.

Translated by James McFarlane

GERD BRANTENBERG

Embrace

Chapter 25

Irene discovers that she has finally been given some breathing space in the few months which have passed since Christmas. She is free from Torgeir's jealousy, free from her own passions. And in this breathing space the dream begins.

It's nothing new that Irene longs to be elsewhere. She has longed to be elsewhere many times, even before Aud. But for the first time the longing isn't like a distant beating of wings she doesn't know how to reach. This time it has a shape and it's right before her eyes. 'I want to study law.'

She begins systematically to look into the possibilities and the syllabus. Recently the first year of law has been offered at the college in town. And after that? Well, then she would have to go to Oslo, if she got that far. But for now she is concentrating on this. In secret and with a feeling of awe she gets hold of some of the text books for the first year. She leaves them in her locker at work. Reads during her breaks, burning with excitement at the heavy chapters. Knoph's 'Introduction to Norwegian Law'.

In the beginning she isn't quite sure why Torgeir absolutely must not know about this. It's an intuition. For the time being her plan is just a dream whose chances of becoming reality are dependent upon nobody being consciously aware of it. Not demolishing it with words – with objections and bitterness. And not with jubilation or expectations either. It has to be totally ready before it comes out. Like a foetus, Irene thinks. Yes, it's strange. It's like a secret pregnancy. Hidden underneath loose clothes and courage. When the child arrived, even the most unwanted child – nobody could deny its existence.

Irene reads. And there between the letters on the pages is Aud. In the chapters about Norwegian law and everywhere. As if Aud lived there and knew everything. Very slowly the time with her becomes alive once more.

A new life. I knew it. I have always known it, I said it to myself from the first moment. It's nothing new that women are lovely. But I forgot my discovery. Or perhaps I didn't understand what it meant? I didn't manage to decipher my body's tender, sensitive reactions. Only in a free relationship to another woman will I be able to live out MYSELF!

But then she had been so sadly disappointed. She had felt pressured – yes, almost abused by her new frantically desperate female lover. Not at all as she had imagined.

But now she is thinking through everything again.

She starts to write to her. Long letters she doesn't dare send, but whose content she reads and moderates. She is surprised at these letters – it's like meeting herself on the page. What have I done?

At last she furnishes the room in the cellar which she has talked about for years. Torgeir is enthusiastic. He helps her. Puts up shelves and hangs lamps. She also gets a little paraffin lamp as a decoration. She's always wanted one of those. They fetch a wicker chair down from the loft. Astrid gives her a rug to hang on the wall as a present. When she has finally installed herself, Torgeir brings her a tray of coffee. 'Thanks Torgeir. I'll sort myself out now.' He is sweet to her. He's making up for a wrong he won't admit he's committed. He's so easy to see through.

She sits here well into the nights. Reading family law and thinking of her future. She has the books in a drawer. First year in Trondheim. Then to Oslo. To Oslo! She need not think that far. One step at a time.

Finally, she also starts work on the book about domestic violence. She gets out the tapes on which Jorunn Bergersen has recorded interviews with abused women. She has had them lying around for a long time. She sits and listens to the low-voiced testimonies. Plays and transcribes, plays and transcribes. It was a laborious way of working but it was more precise. Besides, this way she had the chance to include the spoken language. But she had to edit it as they tended to repeat themselves quite often. That wasn't really so strange. It was the same events and threats which were repeated. 'You bloody cunt. You bloody whore. If you look at him one more time then I'll decorate your face. Decorate your face. So nobody will recognize you. Who do you think you are? What do you think you're doing, you cow!? Going along wriggling your ass! I'm telling you, I'll teach you to wriggle your ass, I will! I'll wriggle your ass so much that you won't be able to wriggle it for five weeks.' 'And then he kicked me,' says a quiet, slightly husky voice. 'Where?' It's Jorunn. A slight pause. 'Everywhere. My backside, my back, my stomach. I lay on the floor. Afterwards when he had quietened down I went to the Accident Unit. I was black and blue all over and had broken three ribs. They couldn't do anything about that.' 'And then?' 'Yes, then I went home again and was scared to death. I thought he'd punish me because I'd run away. But when I got home he'd fallen asleep, luckily, and the day after butter wouldn't melt in his mouth.'

How could anybody endure such a prison? The women on the tapes had endured it for a year, for ten, for twenty, even for forty. How could it carry on – without the authorities intervening? When they intervened in all kinds of little tiffs in the street? She's shocked. She had known that it was bad. But she only understood how awful it was now that she heard the women's own voices.

She was overwhelmed by what she heard. She told Torgeir one evening. 'This abuse, it's torture pure and simple!' 'Yes,' said Torgeir. 'I don't know why those women stay in their marriages for so long. A woman who's beaten by her husband ought to get a divorce.'

With that the conversation was over as far as he was concerned. He continued reading an article about §68 in the French penal code which had been preoccupying him recently.

No it wasn't that easy. Irene knew that. But he didn't want to know about it. She'd noticed that before. She called Jorunn.

'Oh, those marriages – it's the biggest disgrace in Norwegian history since the Gestapo left the country,' said Jorunn.

Irene thought of the tyranny she herself had been subjected to. A mild form of tyranny compared to this. Nevertheless enough to curb her. But it was different. Because she stayed married to Torgeir not because of force, but because of what they had in common. She still looked at it that way. But her belief in the equality in their relationship, that had crumbled. She reproaches him more and more in her thoughts because he wasn't able to talk properly with her about what had happened. Because after a very short time he had just categorically demanded that she should choose. It was almost as if she had set off an alarm in his head which caused a kind of madness. She didn't really recognize him when he was like this. Yes, he could be hot-headed. He hadn't come through his marriage without coming to blows either. But that he could be so beside himself – she hadn't known that before the day she told him about Aud.

Aud knew nothing of what had happened then. Indeed, Aud had shown little imagination in general, little desire to understand her situation. Just gone on about her own needs. Just thought of herself. Irene felt bitter towards her for that.

But as soon as the pressure eased and she was no longer pushed from two sides, it was the feeling of longing and renunciation which nevertheless surfaced. The wish for reconciliation. Yes, more than that.

Irene had sent her small cards. But she hadn't had any reply. Cards with women in costumes from the last century. Erotic circles in the air. But no. Was she still angry? Did she still hate her – like she'd written on that note she got before Christmas?

Irene writes a letter and asks. She says that she thinks a lot about what happened that time, and asks Aud to reply if she can.

Then Aud writes. 'Irene? I didn't mean to say I hated you that time. I tried to hate you, but I didn't manage it. You ought to have been hated though. I wrote it, but it wasn't true.' 'I was pretty much immune then, I think,' Irene writes back. 'When I read your letter now, it dawns on me that the words didn't seep in. They just stood there, dead, on a slip of paper. I can't remember what I was thinking. I can remember almost nothing of that period. It's just as if it is falling away from me into an abyss, and a bridge is being formed between our first meetings and now.' 'But we mustn't forget why things went wrong,' writes Aud. 'If we suppress it now, we'll never learn anything from it. I don't know if I can ever forgive you for the note you wrote. I am trying. But it comes back again and again, like a toothache.' 'But I don't remember,' writes Irene. 'There is a period which is almost a blank for me. I don't know whether Torgeir forced me or if it's something I dreamt.'

'Forced you? You wrote in your last letter that perhaps he forced you. How? By saying that he'd take Rulle from you in the courts?' 'No, I don't mean that. Yes, he forced me with that threat too, of course. But what I wrote in my last letter, I meant quite concretely. I dreamt that he stood over me and dictated the note. That cruel note I sent you. I can't even remember what was on it. Or maybe it wasn't a dream?' 'Dear Aud! There is no reason for there to be any contact between us any longer. Irene.' 'Now that I see those words, in black and white, which you write that I wrote that time, then I well remember what I was thinking. I was thinking that I had to live his life. He asked me to choose between you and him. And I thought it wasn't a choice between Aud and Torgeir, but between him and me. So I chose him. And I had to choose him on account of the child. That's how I think I was thinking. There was no choice. I was exhausted.' 'You asked in your last letter why I was so tired. Did I have so much more to do than other people? Oh dear. Why have you always been so jealous of what I have to do?' 'It's not what you have to do I was jealous of. But your way of organizing your life around it. Your life is so totally busy. No room for surprises. No room.' 'By the way I have got a room. Quite literally. I have got a room set up down in the cellar. We've talked about it for many years. And at last it's come into being. I can sit and write to you down here. Totally undisturbed. Your letters make me so happy. Even though much of what you write is difficult for me. No, what I meant when I wrote that I was 'exhausted' a while ago was basically that I just cracked. After you forced me to tell Torgeir about us, I cracked. Why did you force me to do that? That was the cause of the whole problem. And I've never understood that.' 'Dear Irene! I think about you so much. I really look forward to getting your letters. And I think it's great to hear that you've got a room in the cellar. I got a new letter from you today, right after I sent the last one. You say I forced you to tell. But it wasn't really an order! I've reproached myself for what I said that time. But you needn't have told him. In spite of everything it was your responsibility too. Why did you tell?' 'You answer me with a new question. I told Torgeir because I was afraid of losing you. Maybe that was what your entry into my life meant. That it dawned on me that I *didn't* have any room for myself. And you did! And when I wanted to stretch my arms out for you, there was no room.' 'No, that was really what I thought was so awful. Being together with you gave me a feeling of participating in life itself. To be shut out from that – the opposite ... '

Irene is sitting in her study reading these lines from Aud's last letter again and again. Their communications are very short. They're trying to peel off layer after layer in each other. Many times the correspondence is totally unsynchronized, as many of the letters are en route at the same time. They are also writing more and more frequently. After a while they may get up to three letters between each time they get an answer to what they last wrote. Irene becomes totally absorbed by it. She notices that she is now living her life almost more through these letters than she did before through their meetings and the arrangement of them. It is both a calmer and more upsetting way of life. She still has to hide what's happening inside her, but that's easier now she has the room.

Irene reads the letter again. Why had being together given Aud a feeling of 'participating in life itself'? Wasn't she in it otherwise then? She had all of her activities, a job she liked and her group 'The Gossip Mongers'. Wasn't she in them? Or was it that she seemed to be so together, so much in control on the surface, but then inside there was something that always troubled her? Fear? Depression? Loneliness? She didn't really know Aud. That was what was wrong. She hadn't known what she was getting into that time. When I heard her voice behind me in the night and I just turned and went to her ... I couldn't do anything else.

And I can't and don't want to do anything else now either!

Suddenly Irene realizes why Aud forced her that time. 'It was because I didn't welcome her with open arms.'

She is taken a little aback by the thought. Doesn't know what it means at first. 'But I did really want to welcome her with open arms. There was nothing I wanted more. I just couldn't do it, because there wasn't room for it in my life.'

But there can be! She thinks. I can make room for Aud in my life if I want to.

And at last she clearly sees that this is what made Aud feel desperate. This fear of being pushed away ... Had she been pushed away before? Irene was wondering. What about those women who had come into her father's life after her mother was dead? Had *they* welcomed her with open arms? ... She didn't know enough about it. She had to ask her about it sometime.

At last Irene sees that it was an appeal Aud had come to her with that time. Not an order. Oh, how much injustice she had done to her in her thoughts since then! She had let all her hopes of a better world between women, all her belief in the strongest feminists who lived in free, equal relationships be crushed because of this single hasty action. If Aud could force her like that, then it was all just an illusion.

And Torgeir? He had forced her too, and his force had been real. A totally physical presence, with all the machinery of the law to fall back on. Nevertheless she had judged Aud so much harsher than him. Why?

'Because the threat from Aud was greater inside me,' she thought. 'It was there her force towards me was born. Here inside. Where I loved her. It was this that she had to pay for.'

Irene falls to her knees. – Yes, she falls before the narrow bench in her small study and clasps her hands together. 'Forgive me!' she says out loud. 'Forgive me for acting so desperately and crazily as a result. Can you? Will you ever be able to?'

She gets up and finds her note pad. She sits and writes a long letter well into the night. She begins writing long letters in her thoughts. Aud doesn't answer everything. She doesn't respond as openly to her declarations of love either – which she from time to time and eventually never can stop uttering on the page. 'My love! – ' Nevertheless she feels that Aud is there, and that she can allow herself this, something she very rarely has done in her life – to enlarge upon her inner self. She did not exactly know why she could trust Aud in this respect. She just had a constant feeling of Aud's presence in her. And she knew it was this spark of life which would carry her further in the world.

But as time went by and Aud still answered reservedly and briefly, it seemed to Irene that she had lost a great chance. Life had given her this one chance to finally develop a decent loving relationship with another person. A relationship based on equality and respect.

Was it too late? Would Aud still let herself be called back? Or would she cut off any possibility of love between them in the future? And was she now keeping the correspondence going only for decency's sake?

With sadness Irene thinks back to that moment when they were sitting there in the corner sofa in Fjærvik and simultaneously came up with the idea that equality will only be achieved in a matriarchy. An apparent self-contradiction. Authority and care combined; only that could lead forward. Between two people as well as in the world ...

Chapter 26

Irene hears the telephone ringing up in the house. At once she knows it's Aud. Telepathy exists. They had ascertained that before. Tremors of joy shoot through her. Luckily Torgeir is out. She dashes out of the cellar and runs up to the bedroom where the telephone is and picks up the receiver. The dull melancholic sound of the dialling tone greets her.

She goes out to the kitchen and stands a little puzzled. What was it she was going to do? Peel potatoes? Absent-mindedly she gets out the bag from the refrigerator, stands at the sink and begins to peel. She lets the cold tap run. In the spray she sees the bald skull of Georg Strand. He sits there, thin but nevertheless large, with that shiny head and the pale, dishevelled eyebrows, moist eyes, sharp and a little protruding, as if all that is left of this once so vital actor is thoughts. 'Passion! Passion! You could die of it. But when it dies, then the world will be extinguished.'

Irene had come to a place in the potato where there were only brown flecks, however much she peeled them out with the peeler. She was just about to cut across the whole potato to investigate its condition in cross-section when the telephone rang again. 'Oh thank God!' She dried her hands and ran to the phone.

'Hello,' said Irene warmly into the receiver.

'Yes; hello?' The sound of a strange female voice greeted her.

'Hello. Can I help you?'

'Wh ... who am I talking to?' asked the strange woman. She sounded quite young and awkward.

'You are talking to Mrs Jacobsen. May I ...'

'Oh, you are home at last!'

'Mm. May I ask who's calling?'

There was a short pause at the other end. A throat was cleared and the voice said, 'Excuse me for disturbing you, but ... am I disturbing you?'

'No', said Irene. A knot of irritation began to grow in her chest. 'What do you want?'

'I am ... yes, I am ... ' Again there was a short pause. It was as if the woman at the other end really had to pull herself together.

'Mrs Jacobsen,' she said. 'What I am about to say is terribly difficult.'

'Yes, but what is it then for God's sake woman? And could you first be so kind as to say who you are!'

'I am,' said the woman, and had to evidently pull herself together again. 'I am,' she repeated after a moment's hesitation, 'Anne Hoffmeyer.'

'Anne Hoffmeyer? Are you sure that you have the right number?'

'But aren't you, aren't you Mrs Jacobsen? Mrs Irene Jacobsen?'

'Yes.'

'Yes. It's you I want to talk to. Listen Mrs Jacobsen. May I call you Irene?'

'Call me whatever you want.'

'Yes. Irene. There is something I want to tell you, and it isn't very nice. So ... But I have been thinking it over for a long time.'

After that sudden mobilization of energy, it just as suddenly went quiet.

'Hello? Mrs Hoffmeyer? Are you there?'

'Yes, hello Mrs Jacobsen. I am an acquaintance of your husband.'

The latter was said with such emphasis that it sounded as if it was the unknown Anne Hoffmeyer's only message.

'Yes?' said Irene uncertainly. 'So?'

But just as she spoke, she realized what the strange woman at the other end of the line was trying to say.

'Yes,' said Anne. 'Not only an acquaintance.'

'No?'

'No.' She paused briefly. 'We have been together for three years.'

The voice was steady now, not so uncertainly girlish as in the beginning. Irene heard it as if at a distance, as if through a funnel. She took a deep breath, controlled herself.

'Why are you telling me this? Do you want to take revenge on him?'

'No, I don't feel I have anything to avenge. I only thought it was right that you should know.' When nobody said anything Anne immediately added, and it sounded oddly like a little girl trying to be grown-up, 'I think it is best for all concerned.'

All concerned! Was she, this mixed-up young girl on the phone, this naive and intrusive Anne Hoffmeyer, concerned? Concerned – in her and Torgeir's lives? She wanted to say something sarcastic, but controlled herself again.

'I see,' she said drily. Now she sounded definitely un-friendly for the first time.

'Yes?' said Anne Hoffmeyer simply. 'I'd just like to tell you what I've been thinking. But you don't really want to listen to ... You surely hate me ... '

'No, no, go on!' Irene blurted into the receiver. 'Tell me. Tell me what you've been thinking.'

There was another short pause. It sounded as if she was lighting a cigarette.

'Yes,' she said. 'You don't know me of course, but you probably think I'm stupid.'

'I think nothing whatsoever about you.'

'Oh..hh. It's unbelievable how quickly you get an impres-sion of a person. And you probably think I am young and naive.' Irene didn't know what to say to this. 'Excuse me, but may I speak to you informally? It's OK being formal, but I get mixed up. Don't you?'

'No.' With that answer it seemed as if Anne got confused anyway. She stuttered when she continued.

'Do you know, Irene Jacobsen ... I have thought so much about you.'

'Yes, I can believe that.'

'But you know, I was actually a happy girl. I ... I mean like naturally happy. But this past six months! I have never been so out of it in all my life. Do you understand me? I have felt so desperately lonely.'

She paused a little. Irene realized that she had to pull herself together to curb the reactions which now slowly began to manifest themselves.

'I don't know if I'm in the mood to think about your loneliness,' she said.

'No. I understand. Sorry.'

Nobody said anything. 'What now?' thought Irene. 'Shall we hang up?' She noticed she began to feel quite restless. She wanted to have her thoughts and her feelings to herself. Anne Hoffmeyer woke her up by saying, 'You understand, *that* was what I was thinking. While I was feeling sorry for myself, I mean. It's not just me who is unhappy. Torgeir is making more people unhappy than just me.'

'What do you mean by that?' The question came spontaneously. But at the same time an awful feeling arose when she heard 'Torgeir' pronounced in this intimate way. Suddenly Irene realized that he shared a universe with someone else. As if Anne Hoffmeyer ascribed herself a natural right of possession over him equal to her own. 'No,' she thought. 'That's enough. I don't want to know any more about this than what he can tell me himself.'

'I know Aud Strand,' Anne said.

'What?'

'She's not doing too well at the moment either.'

Irene saw scarlet. She did not realize she had such a well of rage.

'I'm not interested in hearing your effusions about my private life, Miss Hoffmeyer! And I am completely uninterested in listening to your regrets. I will thank you to refrain from making undesired telephone calls in the future.'

With that, she slammed down the receiver.

Chapter 27

He is pacing up and down in the room and deciding not to drink. He's going to be sober for this scene. Now she has to be leaving work soon. He thinks about the bottle of red wine in the cupboard in the bookcase, of the bottle opener out there in the kitchen drawer, how easy it is to open it, pop, but no! He's going to be crystal clear. Remember everything. Everything between them. Before and now. And he was totally blameless in this last thing which happened.

He had come across the letters quite unexpectedly. He just wanted to go down into her room while she wasn't there to tighten up a leg on the little desk which he had noticed was wobbly. As he was doing this, the bottom drawer opened slightly, and as he leaned a little on the desk, it suddenly fell out. It was silly really. He should have taken the drawers out before he began. He took out the drawers and saw some paper in one and a letter jutting out from under some books. He continued with the leg. He had only glanced at the letter. It was as if he first read the sender's address only after he had looked away. He looked again. Yes. 'Aud Strand.' He snatched the envelope from the drawer. At that moment more letters appeared. All with the same despised sender, addressed to Astrid Asmundsen. So she was in league with Astrid! He had taken the letters in his hands. Rage had risen in him so quickly that he felt he could have done something crazy on the spot. With an animal-like sound he threw the letters to the floor with full force. But it was good that nobody was watching, as the effect was, to put it mildly, not very impressive. The air gently received the letters on their journey, they whirled in various lively somersaults before they finally slid elegantly to a landing on the floor.

He started to pick them up. The dates on the postmarks

bore clear witness to how long this had been going on. What should he do with them? He took them up into the living room with him. Sat with them in a neat pile in front of him on the table while he waited for her. This way she could be treated to a shock when she came in.

He opened the uppermost letter. His eye was immediately captivated by the sentence, 'But you could have decided not to tell him.' So that's what she thought! He skimmed the next section. He got so angry again that he even wanted to overturn the table that the letters were lying on.

No. This was no way to welcome her. She shouldn't manage to get the better of him this time. Much better to begin by putting on a good face. He gathered the letters together again and went down to the little room and put them back where he had found them. Then he went upstairs and waited.

No, this time he wasn't going to dissolve into sentimental tears and need comforting. She always got the upper hand of him then. He never felt as small and wretched as he did when he was in her arms. How did she do it? How did all the strength drain from him when she stood there receiving his unhappiness, his fear? He became naked then. As naked as a new-born baby. Not naked like a man. Was that how she loved him?

Or was it just a trick she used?

But now he had the better of her. Now he knew something about her that she didn't know he knew. How could she do this to him? He had told her she must choose. Nevertheless she sneaked about and lied as before. Set up a room in the cellar so she could work on that book. 'Yeah, I bet that will be some book!' thought Torgeir. But now he would put a stop to these deceitful books. He was fed up with this arrangement, which was dishonest and treacherous to the core. In one way he was almost thankful that he had come across those letters, however hateful the thought of them might be. He sat and almost revelled in the thought of how he would manage to disconcert her. She was always so much more well-balanced than him!

Standing there with her slender body and the strong sinews in her slim neck, her small, steady hands, she would hold him, look right through him and be confident. Calm, she was calm. She knew him to the innermost wretched little sliver of his soul and knew how everything was connected. But he didn't know her. She was, and she remained, mystical. Was that it? That she knew him so infinitely better than he knew her? Was that what gave her this bloody all-consuming power? Meant that she could be Home to him, which he could stay in or run from, without it mattering – while she never had to move?

They were *not* equal! However much they had worked on it and talked about it, they were not equal. They were not alike. The truth was simply that it was her who had the power. What power does a baby have? What power does a person have who is pampered and mollycoddled against the one who does the pampering and mollycoddling, and knows everything from the slightest little poop in the pants to the first spoken word? Pamper, pamper, pamper, always be with her little boy. Was that the kind of relationship they had?

It wasn't strange that he could run away and have someone on the side. It made no difference to Pamperville Cottage. It was like going on a football pitch and scoring a goal. He always came home again, and it didn't mean anything.

But why then couldn't she ever have her football pitch?

Because you can't pamper and kick a football at the same time. After all, it also needs one hundred percent commitment while it's happening. And it was incompatible with the constant care. The omnipresent. The never-ceasing. That which just *was*.

Was that how it was? Oh God, one became a captive in this! Both her and him. When all was said and done, why was it so difficult to give her what she called her 'freedom'? Because he always needed her? Even when he didn't need her, he needed to know that she was there. Just like Rulle. That was what was so exhausting about Rulle. That Rulle was in a kind of fairy-tale all the time, where mum and dad always existed. They existed for her. Their aims and opinions never affected her. He had to go into her thoughts and her world and her needs – and she exploited this to the full, especially when she was sick. Then she became smaller, like a baby under a duvet. Why couldn't he ever stand Rulle for more than half an hour at a time? She was funny and sweet and he loved her, but somehow he always had to go out and breathe. Because he could never have a single thought in peace. She owned him in a way, hook line and sinker – and spirit – as long as he was with her.

Did Irene also feel this – that he owned her and that she couldn't have any thoughts in peace? Then she was forced to play this game with him, and thus had to be sneaky and lie to him. Was *that* her freedom?

Freedom through lies and deceit.

Only she could be unfaithful, not him.

Torgeir stopped, surprised at this. He was standing in the middle of the living room and thought he had arrived at an interesting and astonishing paradox. There was no unfaithfulness in his unfaithfulness, as he never pretended to be faithful in that way. How can you be unfaithful to a promise of fidelity which was never made?

His ears picked up the click of the key in the front door. He sat down stock-still and tingled. Her noises, the chink from the hook on the coat hanger, the sliding noise from the zip on her boots, a little clearing of the throat, she was blowing her nose. 'Torgeir? Are you there?' she said. The voice was cheerful, questioning, feminine. 'I love her.' These words just surged through him, took a hold on his soul and body.

She appeared in the doorway and stood there. Her white jacket shone against her black hair. Her dark eyebrows were outlined sharply and beautifully above her eyes so the white light and the blue were bluer than he remembered. Her serious mouth was closed, her arms folded as she rested on one leg so that her hip in her black trousers protruded a little. 'She's so pretty,' thought Torgeir. 'Pretty!' For a moment his bitter thoughts disappeared.

He smiled a little smile to her, and was immediately unsure. She just kind of stood there and was beautiful.

For a moment it was as if he was seeing her for the very first time.

He stood up. He felt instantly how tall he was and that he wanted to go towards her. 'Aren't you going to ... Aren't you going to come in?' He said it as if he was inviting her into a place she had never been before, as if he wanted to excuse himself a little because it didn't perhaps look exactly as she had imagined, as if he wanted to escort her to a suitable seat and offer her whatever she wanted.

'You look strange!' she said, unfolded her arms and came towards him. She looked straight at him, stopped right before his chest and said, 'Torgeir, I'm furious with you!'

She said it with a friendly tone in her voice.

'Why?'

She didn't answer immediately.

'I don't know ... what you're talking about,' he said hesitantly. And he really didn't know. Torgeir's head went blank, empty. He was only filled with a love which now suddenly and incomprehensibly was met with hate, animosity.

'I have always known that you look after number one,' she said calmly glancing at him. 'But for some reason or other, I've always imagined that you were honest.'

'*You* dare to talk about honesty!'

'Yes. I didn't know that you were playing a double game.'

Then it dawned on him like a brilliant beam of light. He was so used to having twinges of remorse that he had become quite numbed inwardly over time. But now it was exposed, everything got mixed up in his head.

'It wasn't ... it isn't ...' he said.

'Yes! It was and it is, that's obvious, that is,' she said.

'Irene. It doesn't matter!'

'Doesn't matter? For who? For her?'

'For *us*.'

'Us?'

Irene turned away from him where they stood in the middle of the living room, right opposite each other. She walked past him and straight over to the little cupboard door in the book-case and pulled out a bottle of red wine.

She went out into the kitchen without looking at him, fetched the corkscrew and came back and opened the bottle without looking at him, got out a long-stemmed red-wine glass from the sideboard, without looking at him. Poured. Drank. Then she turned towards him and her eyes were still beautiful, even more so than before.

'So?' she said. 'Is she young and pretty then?'

Torgeir gasped out loud, theatrically sincere.

'Oh Irene! Nobody's prettier than you.'

He meant it with all his heart, and it filled all of him as he stood there.

' Oh, Torgeir. Don't put on an act. Here you are forcing me to give up a girl friend to be faithful to you, while you yourself are busy keeping a lover for years! What sort of story is this?'

'But it was serious for you!' he shouted.

'Yes, it was.'

That cut into his heart. And with the pain, the resentment rose like a flood in his blood. He felt it wash through him. This – He – Did not want – To hear – No – NO! With one blow he was thrown back into the darkness he was in before the dream had rescued him. That black avalanche of misery which only pulled him further down. He slowly turned towards her. 'Why the bloody hell are you talking in the past tense?'

'What do you mean?'

' It *was* serious for you, you say. As far as I understand it, it's still serious.'

Irene didn't answer.

'Answer then, damn it!'

'Was it a question?'

'No, it wasn't a bloody question, damn it!'

They both sat trembling, trying to find barbed thoughts to throw at each other. Irene was now more confused than Torgeir. They sized each other up.

'Do you know what happened today?' said Torgeir, feigning a narrative tone which was exaggeratedly calm and jovial. He lit a cigarette. Took his time. 'You see, I thought that I'd make myself useful,' he said. 'Not bad? Mmm? So I went down to your room and tried to get your desk to stand a little steadier. You'd complained that it was wobbly, hadn't you?'

'I didn't complain about it.'

'But it wobbles. Do you deny that?'

'No. But it's OK. You don't need to do anything about it Torgeir. Really not. I'll just get a match-box and flatten it and ...'

'It's too late.'

Irene was silent. The room was deadly still. She was deadly still inside. Thoughts full of fear shot in all directions in her head. She sat motionless.

'I was going to repair it ... THE TABLE!' Just as he said 'the table' he slapped the palm of his hand on the table they were sitting at.

'Torgeir!' she shouted. 'There will never be any go ...'

'Shut up, you piece of shit!'

'But have you read them?'

'Read them! I wouldn't touch them with a ten foot pole!'

'Torgeir, listen. You must listen to me. They are not the sort of letters you think they are.'

'Go and lie down there and masturbate over them! That's what I think!'

'Oh, Torgeir, you think ...'

'I don't know what you think I think. You promised me not to have any contact with her. And you broke that promise.'

'Yes.'

'So you admit it? And so why did you do it?'

'Because I needed it.'

'Needed it! What did you need?'

'Her.'

'What the hell do you want with that ... that ... f...'

'Stop it. What the hell do you want with Anne Hoffmeyer?'

'Absolutely nothing. She is a nonentity.'

'How can you have a relationship with somebody you think is a nonentity?'

'I don't have any relationship with her.'

'No relationship? You have been unfaithful with her for years.'

'I have not been unfaithful.'

'How can you say such a thing? What do you think you are then?'

'A dependable and loyal husband. Who has had some diversions you never knew anything about, and which haven't hurt you for an instant.'

Irene was silent. 'What you don't see,' said Torgeir, 'doesn't hurt you.'

'Yes, if that is true then shouldn't you just let me have my private correspondence in peace. That's quite some double standard. You mean to say "What Irene doesn't see won't hurt her". But Torgeir is obviously allowed to poke his nose into everything.'

Torgeir jumped up.

177

'I certainly don't bloody well understand what you want with that fat lesbian country bumpkin! What? What do you want with her? I don't bloody well understand why her letters are so vital. What do you want with them?'

Irene got up. Her eyes narrowed. Quietly and bitterly she said, 'You shouldn't think you can talk like that. You're not exactly pencil-slim yourself.'

He stayed calmly seated. 'Me? I'm a fit, well-groomed man.' He had switched to that smug, good-natured tone. But underneath she could see that he was white with rage. She realized that she was afraid of what might happen. She had the impulse to run away from him. She knew he was going to retaliate. But she held her ground.

'I don't care that she doesn't dress up and flirt around. She is herself, I tell you.'

'And me? Am I not "myself" as you say?'

'I was actually referring to myself,' said Irene. 'Not to you. *I* am not myself.'

'No, I've also thought that,' he said. 'Have you ever considered starting therapy?'

'Yes,' said Irene. 'They're my therapy let me tell you, the letters from her.'

He got up. Stared at her. Walked straight ahead, pushing her aside as he said, 'I was actually thinking of a different type of therapy.' With that he strode across the living room.

'Fucking cunt,' he thinks. At that same moment he stomps out of the room and down the stairs in a few bounds. When he gets downstairs, he jerks open the drawer, finds the letters where he has left them. He stands there with them, not knowing what to do. Now he hears Irene's voice upstairs. 'Torgeir, what are you doing?' 'What am I doing? What am I doing?' he thinks and he starts to open the letters, screw them up and throw them on the floor. One page, screw it up and throw it on the floor. One more. He stamps on them. Yet another one.

'Torgeir? Are you there?' Irene appears on the stairs. 'Here!' he says and shows her, insanely shaking the letters as he shouts. 'This is what I call therapy.' He tears open yet another letter, rips it to pieces and throws it up in the air. 'And this!' The same again. 'Torgeir. Stop it.' He brushes her aside violently. She falls to the floor with the glass of red wine which she still has in her hand. As he shoves it slips out of her hand and is broken. 'Clean it up.' He points to the mess. Points once more. 'Clean up after yourself.' He continues tearing the letters to pieces. 'Stop it Torgeir.' They hear Rulle crying up in her room on the second floor. 'Daddy,' she shouts before she can even see them, 'Stop it.' She comes down the stairs barefoot. 'Be careful here, be careful Rulle,' he says nervously hushing her up. 'There are pieces of glass. Mummy dropped a glass. See to it that you clean it up.' 'Go back to bed Rulle. Mummy will be there soon,' Irene says to her. 'Yes do as Mummy says.' 'No,' says Rulle and grabs hold of Irene's jacket. 'Do as Mummy says,' shouts Torgeir to the child and takes hold of her and carries her kicking and scream-ing up the stairs to her room. 'There; now stay here.' He slams the door shut and locks it from the outside.

When he comes back Irene is picking up pieces of the torn-up letters. 'Stop that,' he shouts. She continues. He grabs her wrist, twists and drags her up. 'Let go,' she says. He can see her face distorting. 'Let go, let go.' 'I will not bloody well let go before you let go of that disgusting woman!' And with that he hits her in the face with the back of his hand. 'There! See to it that you clean up what you've spilled, I say,' he roars. She turns around and goes up to the kitchen.

Irene fetches a bucket and a wash rag, a dustpan and brush. She starts to mop up the red wine and the pieces of glass. Torgeir continues finding more letters in the drawer, finding more of Irene's writings and throwing them on the floor. 'Mummy,' shouts Rulle through the door upstairs. They hear her little voice in the distance. 'Shut up,' Torgeir shouts up the stairs. 'Or if you really want to, you can just as well come and see. Come here Rulle. Look at your mother. Look at a lesbian tart.' They hear Rulle wildly shaking at the door handle, hammering at the door and shouting.

Irene runs up to her, wants to calm her, but realizes the door is locked. 'Torgeir,' she calls down to him. 'Where's the key?' 'Huh, that's something you don't know,' he shouts back. 'Torgeir,' she calls again. 'You have no right to do what you're doing now.' 'I bloody well have the right to do exactly as I please,' he says. Irene stands and calms Rulle through the door.

Torgeir is standing down in the cellar looking at the pile of letters. Now he hears her steps on the stairs. Then he grabs the lighter and sets them alight. Stares at the little flame. It won't burn properly. She is in the doorway. 'God. Are you crazy?' She wants to run into the room and put out the flame. 'Keep away,' he roars, barring her way. The fire is about to go out. Suddenly he catches sight of the paraffin lamp. He grabs it and pulls off the glass. 'Torgeir.' 'Shut up.' He dribbles some drops down onto the pile of letters. She rushes towards him, but at that moment a tall flame shoots up around them and in the next moment the curtains catch fire.

Now Torgeir is also forced to retreat. He grabs a cushion and begins to beat out the flames, but as he does it his hand begins to burn. It's covered in paraffin. He rushes up to the bathroom screaming and puts his hand under water. The flame flares up worse than before. Irene runs after him, tears off her jacket and throws it around Torgeir's hand. He falls to his knees. They hear Rulle calling. 'The key Torgeir. For God's sake what did you do with the key?' But Torgeir isn't in any position to think about what he did with the key. He is about to faint. 'Rulle?' says Irene. She is standing close up to the door talking in a low, calm voice. 'Darling? Listen. Now you have to do exactly as mummy says.' 'Yes?' 'We can't find the key. Now you have to get the stool and climb out of the window. I'll catch you outside the house.' 'It's too high up!' 'I know. But you have to do it anyway.' 'Yes.' Irene runs outside, positions herself under the narrow high window to Rulle's room. Immediately a little dark head appears in the chink, a hand, a foot, she is clinging to the edge. 'Can't you fetch the ladder?' asks Rulle. 'There's no time.' 'Time?' 'It's too heavy Rulle. Don't ask questions. I'll explain later. Just hold on with your hands, then let go, and I'll catch you.' Rulle climbs out, hangs from the window sill. It is still several yards down to the ground. 'Let go,' calls Irene. Rulle lets go. Irene catches her in her arms, and they tumble on the ground. 'What is it mummy? What is it?' Rulle pulls at her. Irene rushes into the house, to the telephone, dials the number. She hears Rulle calling as she comes rushing in after her. 'Mummy, what is it?' But suddenly Rulle sees the smoke which is pouring up through the stairs. She hears her mother's voice from the bedroom. 'There is a fire at 12 Birkegaten.'

In an unbelievably short time you can hear the fire engine's sirens. The ambulance is following. Like jack in the boxes people appear in the deserted streets and gather in a black mass outside Irene and Torgeir's house. 'The Jacobsens' is on fire. The Jacobsens' is on fire.' Most of them just stand there and watch, but some individuals come running in and ask if there is anything they can rescue. 'Yes,' says Irene. 'My husband.' She has just barely managed to drag him out of the bathroom. Now she is helped in carrying him outside. He is writhing in pain. The neighbour's daughter who has come out, runs back into her house. She comes running out again with a first-aid box. Several women are now bending over Torgeir examining his hand. It's an unpleasant sight. Irene holds his healthy hand. Rulle is standing there too – in her pyjamas and red padded jacket, peering at her strange-looking father. Then she notices something twinkling on the ground where he is lying – right by his pocket. The key. Before Irene has a chance to stop her, she snatches it and runs into the house. 'Rulle.' Several people call, but she's gone. Irene runs after her. Several others run after Irene. 'What's the child doing?' The crowd gasps, flustered and aghast. 'Didn't the Jacobsens have an oil heater?'

Soon afterwards they see the little girl at a window on the first floor. First she throws out a stamp album. Then a big toy doll with light plaits and a blue checked dress. It flies through the air, round and round with an unchanging smile on its face. Each time a gasp goes through the crowd. 'There comes Miranda,' a little boy calls. That had to be the doll's name. A new item is thrown out, but at that moment Rulle is seized from behind by some adults. People follow the last toy through the air. It whirls in a multi-coloured arch before it lands. It is a colourful shoe-box with a lid.

Irene rushes through the living room, wanting to sweep things away with her, but just grabs at random. Everything that she feels she wants to save is in her room. Now she runs out in an irresolute panic with an electric kettle in one hand and three books in the other.

The medics take Torgeir on a stretcher, drive him away. The fire brigade arrives. They stream in with their equipment. Irene and Rulle stand and watch. The people look at them and the fire in turn. You can't see many flames, mostly smoke. Rulle watches wide-eyed. Somebody points to the mother and daughter, but most of them know that they are the ones who live in the house. Astrid Asmundsen comes and stands with them. She puts her arms around both their shoulders. Then she begins to cry.

The rumours fly. Some say that it's unsure if the lawyer will survive. Various, low-voiced versions as to the cause of the fire are circulating. 'Shhhh,' say others. 'The lawyer's wife is standing right over there.'

In a very short time the fire is under control. One of the firemen comes over to Irene. 'Mrs Jacobsen?' he says raising his hand to his helmet, 'We managed to save the house. But there isn't much left of the room.'

*

'Mummy,' says Rulle looking up at her. 'I want to see the room.'

'No Rulle. The room is sealed off.' She herself hasn't been down there either. She knows that everything inside it is totally wrecked. But Rulle doesn't give up. Irene turns on the electric plate. Rulle has just come home from school. 'Shall we make cocoa with cream?' asks Irene. But Rulle won't be put off. 'I want to see the room.'

'Can this be right?' thinks Irene. 'No.' Irene is most inclined to believe that you should save children from shocking experiences. Beyond a certain limit, they really learned nothing from them. 'But ... ' she thought. Maybe Rulle's suppositions about how the room looked were much worse than the reality? She had misgivings. 'I want to see the room,' Rulle says again.

Irene took the little girl's firm hand in hers. They went down the stairs. She didn't know if what she was doing was right. But she broke up the barrier in front of the door, shoved it open and together they looked in at the charred remains inside.

Everything was brown or black. There was nothing left of the pile of letters on the floor. The books in a collapsed bookcase were scorched. She recognized the contours of the big picture book from Tarquinia she had bought in the autumn, made out the titles of some of her favourite books. Virginia Woolf. Sigrid Undset. Arne Garborg. The remains of the paraffin lamp could be distinguished on the floor. On the wall hung the pitiful, brittle tatters of the rug she had got from

Astrid. 'Norwegian Christmas Traditions 1848' by Tidemand. It was one Astrid had had in her living room for a long time. And after Aud had visited, the rug reminded Irene of their time together in that living room. Then she had been given it. 'And even that lovely rug!' said Rulle.

Their eyes wandered. Spontaneously Irene put her hand on Rulle's shoulder. The smell was awful. Rulle held her nose. All her papers on the desk were incinerated. He had obviously pulled out everything he could find. Her own unsent letters from January, her notes for her law studies, family law. And at last she recognized — in a melted, twisted form – the remains of seven cassettes.

'Now the women who talked on the tapes have to say all they said over again,' said Rulle. 'Do you think they'll be able to remember it?'

'Yes,' said Irene. 'I think they'll remember.'

Translated by Tanya Thresher

LISBET HIIDE

Adam the dream of lioness S, after elegant studies in Kronborg Zoo he rediscovers her

I

He's a tourist. Wandering through the streets of a strange town. Smiling. Reading street signs, amused at the ring of the foreign names on his tongue. Turns the corner of Waldendorff Street. Small white houses and low red tiled roofs. He is tall. With broad gleaming naked shoulders. Red headband. Corn-coloured hair. Bleached by the sun. Bowie blond. Muscular. Looks like Ryan O'Neill during a pause in filming A BASE-BALL STAR'S LIFE. All he needs is the kneepads. With the baseball team exhausted and panting on hard wooden benches in some changing room or other each with his Pepsi light. He grabs the camera. Snaps a green-eyed crouching cat about to pounce on a flock of birds. She snarls and arches her back elegantly at the click from the camera. A flash of green. Otherwise the roll of film is full of museum buildings, statues and museum attendants. He eats creamy-coloured soft ice and spongy warm cakes with sweet white icing. Licks his fingers and leafs through a bundle of English newspapers from the previous week. Buys a large brightly-coloured postcard of a dark-haired girl in a dazzling red bikini. It is her eyes which captivate him. Narrow. Direct. Tiger eyes. He can't think of anyone else to send it to but his mother. Writes a brief greeting with love Adam. He is just like a man should be. His body is juicy. Like a fruit. Sun Maid. Like a ripe apricot or peach where the skin is softest. Sweet as grapes. His dark juicy peach. Wet.

II

He blinks at the sun. Exposes a row of chalk-white teeth. Admires girls' backsides. Whistles softly at women he will never get to know and therefore dares to admire. Feels his well-trained body tensing. He enjoys his independence. Worships loneliness, the beloved. He no longer wants to resemble the faceless conquerors women want him to resemble. BATMAN in clinging tights dives down from the sky into a narrow New York street. Snatches the YOUNG INNOCENT SECRETARY from the bandits' clutches AT THE LAST MOMENT. 007 WITH LICENCE. Kills his women with steely charm. Cocked revolver and silver-grey temples. Constantly conquers stupid blondes between silk sheets and never tires A THANK YOU FOR SAVING MY LIFE. Bowls over half-naked women like streamlined billiard balls in a celebrated salon with dimmed lighting. Or the masked PHANTOM THE MAN WITH THE CAPE MASKED AND FACELESS. The mysterious bundle of muscles. He strolls indifferently past the kiosks' gleaming display of parted thighs and wet nipples. Where exotic girls with painted genitals stare with deep seriousness into everyone's eyes I WANT TO BE POSSESSED BY YOU. Deep red vulva. Dark ruby. Chanel lipstick. He jogs down towards the harbour. In his worn denim shorts. With a faint scent of sex. Of sweat and sperm. Large wet stains on the front of his shorts. Always a bit moist. He jogs, his naked silken thighs taut.

III

A girl is walking down the street towards him. Very tall. In an expensive worn fur, leopard. With skintight jeans. Walks like a tiger, sinewy, muscular. With open fur, naked throat. Hide and skin, perfume and juice. Just a gleaming belt around that narrow waist, in dark hide, hardly different from his own skin. When he draws in his breath, her smell knocks him out. Rank. She lopes along the street like a fine tamed wild beast. Hunting, sniffing the air. She has a broad grin, not aimed at him. Small steps. Gimlet-like heels restrict her steps. Make them artificial, rapid, mincing. On the hunt over black asphalt. Eyes with yellow gleam, pointed white teeth. Sharp filed nails. Long. Gleaming. Raw. Flowing hair, like a groomed mane. She brushes close. Her eyes shine, he tries to catch her glance. She walks on, unapproachable as an animal. He stumbles after.

IV

He is by the entrance to the zoo. Kronborg Zoo. Clasps his head, dazed. Follows the crowd. Walks in amongst the giraffes and zebras whose stripes seem blurred. Frozen kangaroos. Tame wild boars which eat from your hand. Buzzing voices, women shrieking. Retired American amazement. Silver hair, dead fox, imitation. Skyblue turquoises on white fingers. Here and there an opal. Dull skin, violet-hued. Silver. Gleaming excited heads with thinning hair. A pale lisping guide. He stands distracted in front of the wildcat enclosure. A couple of heads higher than the tourist group. Pressing close together. Whilst the guide lisps softly '... about the wild cat's superiority, the problems of taming it'. Import from West Africa. 400 kilos of living meat. With nerves sharp and quivering. The greatest hunter of the plains in an enclosure of 400 square metres. They are ordered to keep back from the wire. 'She is dangerous.'

A shiver runs through the crowd as SHE crashes through the hedge. THE SHE-CAT. A FLASH. He sees nothing but yellow, yellow streaks gleaming through the air. Blinding. THE LIONESS. She snarls, roars, golden with hissing movements. As she snatches the bloody carcass. Tears it to pieces in the air. It steams. She hisses at the crowd, which has retreated ten paces. Rolls in dung, happy. Shakes herself over the pale American women's thinning fox-fur. Adam raises his camera. As he clicks she throws herself towards him. With her full weight against the netting. Hurls herself forward time after time....

... towards the savanna. The rippling plains by the Urma river. Speeds towards Lake Rudolf. Where the sinking sun is mirrored in the leaden-grey surface. Against a background of African mountain ranges and yellow sky ... He goes up close to the netting. Whispers. She crouches for the attack. Ears painfully flattened. Soundless but for the lashing tail. She slides forwards, so near that he can lick her teeth. Senses a faint salty smell of dead flesh. 'Keep back from the fence.' He goes closer, can't help it. His heart thumps hard. As she lunges, he shrieks. She slashes his tongue with a dark tear. He feels the shock waves from her heavy body as she throws herself to the left. All escape routes closed.

... hurls herself onwards towards the plains. The savanna. The sun ...

Hears her distant roar. Is left standing with the smell of wild cat/ honey. Silk, grass, dead meat and excrement. He staggers down the street. He feels drunk. The camera lies abandoned in the grass.

V

She is standing at the tram stop. Under the street light. It is lit. The light floods down over her hair and her naked throat. The black asphalt is damp and dark. She is walking restlessly to and fro. Her fur jacket is half open. He can see the gleam of her naked moist skin beneath the street lights. Thinks: she's going to take me. She turns lazily, laughs softly. There he stands in the middle of the street in the heavy rain with a wet T-shirt and hard nipples. Wet thighs. Sun-bleached denim shorts. Bare-legged, as if stiffened in the asphalt. She arches her back, opens her mouth. Her hair billows. A faint scent of sex from the open fur. She gathers herself for the attack. A glint of orange. Her eyes narrow, focused on him. Luminous. Her hair moves, heavy and scented. He must burn himself, must touch. She lifts her arms over her head. Moves her hips in a slow rhythm. Holds his glance. He cannot move, he is in her power. Relishes. Her lips are dark. She shows her teeth, as a surge runs through him. Shakes his body. He staggers, loses his footing. In her power. YES COME! But she doesn't touch him. Not yet.

VI

The fur lies around her feet, on the wet asphalt. In the gleam of the street lights it looks alive. She steps out of it. Naked. With long white thighs, pale belly. The street lights are bathed in the asphalt. There are people hurrying past them on the pavement. A dog gives tongue. No-one seems to react. The tram clangs in the street. Glides over wet cobbles, slow and indifferent. She runs her finger over his lips whilst she slowly pulls his zip down. The whole time she holds his eyes with hers, dangerous yellow, piercing. Beads of saliva at the corners of her mouth. She takes hold of him, strokes him hard with long slim fingers. Purrs softly. Whilst her lovely thighs open smoothly. Sees her juices start to flow, wet, dripping. He flushes violently, breathes heavily and with effort. She rubs him against her slit. Spread, open, wet. Open flower. The street lights burn in the street. A drunken man lurches into him. He doesn't notice. She bends down and licks him, swallows. Her legs are taut, poised to spring. She wants more. She likes to suck, he thinks, elated. He enjoys the sight of the wide red mouth around him, shaped like a large red dahlia. Enclosing him. Drinking him. She tosses her head back, her hair crackles. She pants for breath, her teeth gleaming. She rips off his trousers. Until he catches fire, perishes. Her hair, her skin, her nakedness there in the street. Her hard grip, her imperious eyes. Her desire for him. TAKE ME TAKE ME TAKE ME he screams.

VII

She climbs up on him. Rides him. Guides his arching prick as it sways stiffly. She licks around her mouth with her salmon-pink tongue and presses it against her, into her. She sways, she climbs, mounts him. Roars, loud and golden. People don't even turn round, just hurry on. He explodes. As she screams and tears gashes in his skin. With sharp claws. Bites his forehead. Claws channels of blood, streaming wounds. Throws him to the ground, the force stuns him. As she crouches for a mighty spring. Over towards the plains, the savanna, the sun. He is left lying there, groaning, with bloody marks from sharp nails on the back of his legs, shoulders and throat.

Translated by Janet Garton

SISSEL LIE

Strange things happen when my forest burns

The glass wall swayed in the wind, the sunlight made patterns in it like little flecks over the whole surface. She sat down in front of it to let herself be drawn into the shifting patterns of light when the wall panel suddenly emitted the warning signal. Immediately the glass wall had to be made solid and opaque, and she reached out irritated for the series button to find something she could watch. 'Why do they always have to disturb me when I want to be left in peace?' The voice from the wall panel said: 'Do you want one partner or several? Do you want one partner or several?' She threw the nearest cushion at the wall panel. 'Leave me in peace,' she shouted. She would show them that she was willing to cooperate, they were entitled to be worried that she was shutting herself away in her own room. But there were so many things she had to think through, and they never let her think one thought through to the end. No normal creator or educator reacted the way she did. 'You need reactions from others,' they said to her. In order to be left in peace by the guardian who watched her through the wall panel, she could create a mind image which his glance could not penetrate. But they were right, to concentrate enough psychic energy to create without stimulus from others was almost impossible. And chemical stimulus made the pictures the wrong colours, she shivered at the thought of pink soldiers and blue guardians.

Teaching did not inspire her any longer. The pupils' mind images had become so weak and difficult to pick up that she had stopped believing that it was possible to teach even the simplest techniques. It had been exciting to develop new methods, new caresses and positions. Now she saw the partners in her pupil group as parasites on her own creative ability, they used her up, and she was not developing any longer. The joint committee spied on her unceasingly through the wall panel after they had begun to suspect that she was opting out. At first she had amused herself by blocking their vision with colourful mind images, then after she had had problems with psychic energy, she let them stare.

She knew who was watching her most of the time. He had been planted in a beginners' group, some of the partners must have reported to the joint committee that she was creating too little and giving herself over to pleasure too much. She had immediately disliked skin contact with him, it felt cold and clammy. He was a guardian, the round, hard muscles in his upper arms made him resemble the enemy in the streets. She had never had any of the enemy in her groups, they were known to be aggressive and uncreative. Guardians were not creators either, he never had mind images, and sent unfriendly thoughts towards her the whole time, so that she almost let them take control over her. The struggle between them had given her good opportunities for performing. She could not abandon herself to a man who used techniques of control against her, at the same time as she could not stop her body reacting to him. This led to a concentration of energy which exploded in the most astounding images.

The wall panel signalled that she could make the glass wall transparent again, but not porous, as there was still a lack of oxygen outside. She played through one of the series they had made whilst he was present, he was lying in the midst of a group of playful youngsters, heavy and sullen. She had wondered why they sent him, when he had all the characteristic features of a guardian, the muscles, the narrow eyes, the sallow skin. The joint committee wanted to make it clear to her that she was under observation, they wanted to frighten her into creating. She smiled a little at the thought. She had really not liked him, he corrected her when she demonstrated caresses and positions, he became furious when she lost control together with one of the others in the group so that a mind image was distorted. He scoffed at her when she became ardent and tender in her teaching. 'You can't create without desire,' she defended herself. 'It is your task to teach the groups control and concentration of psychic energy. You have no right to destroy their future by teaching them your aberrations,' he said darkly.

It was no simple process she was supposed to teach them. They ought to have learnt control before they came to her, but their general education left much to be desired. They rarely managed to call forth images when they were beginners, even after intense excitement and a controlled climax. It was a difficult moment when the mind image had to be transferred from the consciousness to the wall panel, and then fixed into pictures and series. Absolute control of the senses was essential, an orgasm made the picture dissolve before it was fixed or made the transfer impossible, depending on at what point of the creative process it happened. She herself was a specialist in pictures of the forgotten past, of everything which had once existed, and there was great interest in her teaching and production. But there were few who were willing to give themselves over to this process as totally as she was, most of them gave up before they had learnt what was necessary.

She had been one of the few who had access to the archives. It was there that the documents from the past which were not registered in official series were to be found. It had been a privilege, those long journeys down under the earth, to visit those large screens. She could see into the archives and manipulate the documents with the help of robots. In front of the screens she had found peace to think, questions took form to which she had longed to find the answer; but they were also busy times, she had to find material which produced good mind images, so that the joint committee could see that it was useful for her to have access.

Something unusual had happened to her the last time she was there. Instead of withdrawing again after putting out the documents, some of the robots had taken hold of the hands which she stretched out towards them through the gloves set into the holes in the wall. They caressed her palms skilfully and for a long time. Despite the fact that she knew very well that they were not constructed for transmitting thoughts, she had a feeling that they wanted her to create something. There was no law which forbad creative activity in the archives, and she let herself be stimulated by the caresses through the material of the gloves and showed them a picture on the enormous wall panel of one of the greenhouses outside the centre which she herself often saw in dreams. The sun was shining down through the open roofs, and the golden enemies were gathering tomatoes and cucumbers in the thick forest of plants.

To her surprise, the robots did not stand still behind the screen, staring. If she had not known better, she would have believed that it was love-play they were dancing. It was idiotic to think that robots were longing for sunshine and green plants down there in the special atmosphere which was required for the preservation of documents, but it was nevertheless strange how preoccupied they were with each other. She had to remind herself that there were no human faces behind the metal masks, simply wires and switches. Soon the sirens started up, and members of the guard began to stream out of the lifts; her mind image had blocked the guardians' overview of the hall. She had time to wonder why they needed so many guards to keep an eye on a group of robots constructed for work in the archives; surely it was not her they were afraid of? Then she was pushed into a lift and taken back above ground. It was just after that that the guardian appeared in her group, and she had never returned to the bluish-grey light in front of the screens; she no longer had security clearance. She did not like to think about the robots' entwined bodies as they lay there frozen whilst the guards yelled.

The guardian had been a reminder that she should not give herself over to pleasure too often, her body took over and broke down the controls sometimes even when she wanted to prevent orgasm. After he became a member of the group she worked together with him quite a lot, so that she could avoid being carried away by sensual pleasure. Unfortunately he found other things to accuse her of. Once, when the wall panel emitted the warning signal, she was so absorbed by the process of creation that she did not operate the blackout quickly enough. Everyone knew it was warfare they were not supposed to see, and they were relieved to escape the sight of the red soldiers surging past. In the days when it was part of the educational process to watch the enemy being defeated, many people had had problems with their deep breathing and their communication with the subconscious. The camps were crowded with people who could not control their emotions and fainted at the sight of blood. In the end the joint committee had found it necessary to decree that the battles should not be accessible to viewing. The inaccessibility had to be absolute;

there were severe punishments for those who saw the smallest detail of what was happening outside.

It was the series with the group; she watched with satisfaction a massive construction made out of square stones which she had created, a kind of habitation from the past of enormous dimensions. It was obvious that people at that time lived in large groups, not singly as now. She shuddered at the thought of having other people close to her at night. He had not been a member of the group when she made this image, it was before someone had informed that she was offering the group pleasure without control, and he had appeared as a partner. The wall panel chattered: 'Do you want one partner or several? Do you want one partner or several?' in order to demonstrate that the series had finished. 'Not just any partner!' she thought suddenly and felt the narrow, black eyes on her, he had surely discovered that long ago. 'The teaching of spontaneity without control is enemy activity,' he had repeated, but he had never mentioned the fact that it was forbidden to be fixated on a special partner, even though that was just as threatening for the system.

'Can you give anyone a really friendly smile?' she asked the wall panel. The smile he had smiled at her when he bit or caressed with his dark red pointed nails had been just as menacing as when he hit out, with his eyes like slits and his teeth bared. He knew something about her which could destroy her, but he had not reported it, otherwise she would be sitting in isolation in one of the camps with a new guardian. She loaded the next series, and squirmed as she saw herself on the panel. She was demonstrating a difficult exercise together with him and another partner, and the hunger for just that body was unbearable. It was the muscles in his upper arms which had clinched it. How could an ordinary guardian develop a body so marked by sunshine and physical work? He resembled the enemy, he was just as strong and well-built as they were, perhaps just as aggressive too. But he was not a rebel. The enemy kept on protesting about the working conditions in the greenhouses and marching on the centre, until they were driven back by the red soldiers. Whilst he sat there invisible, staring at her as if she were the enemy. She lay down in the warm rocking mattress for comfort, downy arms held her tight. Now that she knew what was wrong with her, her desire could not be repressed.

She turned the red switch, and the group came out of the panel in three-dimensional life-size; it was painful to see herself in activity, it was so long since she had had a partner. She pressed the communication button and said to the panel: 'You are the one I want.' The series disappeared, and the image of him came out into the room towards her. 'You'll be interned in a camp soon, if you can't behave like other people,' he said crossly. 'It's you I want,' she repeated. 'Irresponsible people cannot walk around freely in the centre,' he said, unmoved by her provocative gestures. 'What kind of a system would we have if we all just kept to one partner?' he said scornfully before he disappeared. 'Come,' she said to the empty wall panel and undressed with languid movements whilst she waited. The wall panel gave no answer, she let herself be rocked again and felt how easy it was to gather psychic energy. The sunlight made patterns of flecks on the glass wall, and she wondered whether it was possible to teach him pleasure. As long as he was her guardian, no-one could discover her fixation.

He had red soldiers with him when he came, and he was more frightened than she had expected. She parried his attempt to control her thoughts with hatred, and returned feelings of tenderness and laughter. That provoked him exceedingly, and for the first time she realized that his hard and tensed muscles were a signal that he had problems with control. 'I would like a partner before we leave,' she said submissively. Everyone had a right to hygienic intercourse in order to drain off their energy before they were isolated in the camps. Even though creators normally used the sexual act for their image production, he could not refuse her an orgasm now. He turned towards a red soldier, hesitated, and decided to perform it himself. The muscles in his face were stiff. 'You are afraid you'll lose control, you're just as fixated as I am,' she thought, and grasped his upper arms. Again it occurred to her that he resembled the enemy, she thought of the image of the greenhouses she had created in the archive hall. 'Can we manage to follow the enemy back after an attack?' she thought. For a nasty moment another thought took over; she saw them both enclosed behind metal masks and stiff costumes in the archives, was that the punishment? She pushed the thought away and said in her educator's voice: 'There are still things I can teach you.' She felt that he stiffened and had an impulse to brush her aside and go, but then he pushed her roughly against the wall panel and opened his cloak around her.

She controlled the excitement, and the mind image took form around them with tree trunks and birds. This was not the moment when her senses could take charge, she let the forest come alive beneath the sunlight and felt the sweat from the effort making her body sticky against his. 'Don't you know that I am the best at recreating the forgotten past,' she whispered to her opponent, who was restless and unfocused 'This is how the forests looked.' She added flowers and ivy climbing up the trunks. She could not easily decipher his thoughts, they were unclear and chaotic, and certainly not friendly. She chose a cliché from the symbolic language of ancient times, and let the flames crackle up through the leaves, whilst she rubbed herself against him. 'In the camp you'll be completely alone,' he said, and avoided the flames which were raging without warmth in the foliage around them. 'Not so long as you are my guardian,' she thought, and released her hold on the mind image, which remained visible for a few seconds with its bright green and reddish-gold colours before it disappeared. 'Strange things happen when my forest burns,' she said, half threatening, half triumphantly, before she let herself be led away by the red soldiers.

Translated by Janet Garton

HERBJØRG WASSMO

Dina's Book

Most men will proclaim every one his own goodness;
but a faithful man who can find?
The just man walketh in his integrity -
his children are blessed after him ...
Who can say, 'I have made my heart clean;
I am pure from my sin'?

— Proverbs 20:6-7, 9

*I am Dina who sees the sleigh with the person on it rush
headlong down the steep slope.*
At first I think I am the one lying there tied to the sleigh.
Because I feel pain more terrible than any I have ever known.
*Through crystal-clear reality, but beyond time and space, I am
in touch with the face on the sleigh. Moments later, the face
crashes against an ice-covered rock.*
The horse actually loosed the carriage shafts and escaped being

dragged down the slope! Amazing, how easily that happened!
It must be late in the autumn. Late for what?
I do not have a horse.

A woman found herself at the top of a cliff in cold morning light. The sun was not shining. Around her, the mountains rose dark and watchful. The cliff was so sheer that she could not see the landscape below.

Across the wide gorge, an even steeper range of mountains stood in silent witness.

She followed every movement of the sleigh. Until it finally came to a stop against the trunk of a large birch tree at the very edge of a precipice.

The sleigh teetered slightly toward the sheer drop. Beneath were steep bluffs. And, far below, thundering rapids.

The woman looked at the trail levelled by the sleigh as it plummeted down the slope. Pebbles, snow, clumps of heather, broken brushwood. As if a giant carpenter's plane had swept down, taking with it every protruding thing.

She was wearing leather trousers and a long, fitted jacket. Had it not been for her hair, one might have taken her for a man from a distance. She was very tall for a woman.

The right sleeve of her jacket hung in shreds. It had blood on it. From a wound.

Her left hand was still clenched tightly around a short-bladed knife, the type Lapp women wear in their belts.

The woman turned her face toward a sound. A horse's whinny. It seemed to awaken her. She hid the knife in a pocket of her jacket.

She hesitated a moment, then resolutely stepped over the stone wall at the side of the road. Toward the sleigh. It teetered less now. As if it had decided to save the person with the battered face.

She climbed down the slope quickly. In her haste she

dislodged loose stones. They formed a small avalanche, which rushed past the sleigh and over the edge of the precipice. She stared out into the unseen. As if she were in touch with the stones and followed them, even when she could no longer see them. As if she watched them until they reached a deep pool beneath the thundering rapids below.

She paused for a moment as new stones tumbled past the sleigh that bore the unmoving body. But only for a moment. Then she continued her descent until she could put her hand on the sheepskin covering the man and lift a corner of it.

Something that must once have been a handsome male face came into view. One eye was pushed in. Fresh blood flowed thick and evenly from many wounds on his head. During the few seconds she stood there, the man's head became completely red. The white sheepskin at his neck soaked up the blood.

She raised a long, narrow hand with well-formed pink nails. Lifted the man's eyelids. One after the other. Thrust her hand onto his chest. Was the man's heart still beating? Her fumbling hand could not tell.

The woman's face was a snow-covered world. Immobile. Except for the darting eyes under her half-lowered lids. Her hands became bloodstained, and she dried them on the man's chest. Then covered his face again with the corner of the sheepskin.

She crawled over the sleigh to the carriage-shaft fastenings. From each fastening she quickly pulled the remains of a piece of rope. She gathered them together carefully and put them into her jacket pocket along with the knife. Then she took out two frayed leather straps and coaxed them into the places where the ropes had been.

At one point she straightened up. Listened. The horse whinnied from the road. She hesitated, as if deciding whether her task was completed. Then she crawled back over the sleigh. The battered figure was still between her and the precipice.

The solid birch tree creaked from the cold and from the added weight of her body. She found a footing among the icy stones, then thrust her weight against the sleigh. Calculated the force needed, as if she had performed the same movement many times before.

As the sleigh left the ground, the sheepskin slid away from the man's face. He opened the eye that was not pushed in and looked straight at the woman. Speechless. A helpless, incredulous look.

It startled her. And an awkward tenderness flashed across her face.

Then everything became movement and air. It went quickly. The sounds echoed through the mountains long after everything was over.

The woman's face was blank. The landscape was itself again. Everything was fine.

I am Dina who feels the downward pull when the man on the sleigh reaches the deep, foaming pool. Then he crosses the vital boundary. I do not catch the final instant, which could have given me a glimpse of what everyone fears. The moment when time does not exist.

Who am I? Where are space and place and time? Am I doomed to this forever?

She drew erect and began resolutely to climb back up the slope. It was harder going up than down. Two hundred yards of icy terrain.

At the point where she could see the torrential autumn river, she turned and stared. The river curved before thundering out of view. Foaming masses of water. Nothing else.

She continued climbing. Rapidly. Gasping for breath. Her injured arm was giving her pain. Several times she nearly lost her balance and fell as the sleigh had.

Her hands grasped for heather, branches, stones. She made sure she always had a firm grip with one hand before moving the other upward. Strong, swift movements.

As she took hold of the stone wall by the roadside, she looked up. Met the large, shining eyes of the horse. It was no longer whinnying. Just stood there looking at her.

They faced each other, resting a little. Suddenly the horse bared its teeth and, angrily, bit into some tufts of grass at the side of the road. She had to use both arms to pull herself up onto the road, grimacing in pain as she did so.

The animal bowed its large head over her. The carriage shafts splayed at its sides. An empty decoration.

Finally, she reached for the horse's mane. Firmly, almost brutally, she pulled herself up to the resisting horse's head.

This woman was eighteen years old. With eyes as old as stones.

The shafts scraping against the ground were sounds outside the picture.

The horse stamped frozen blades of grass into the ground again.

She took off her jacket and rolled up the sleeves of her sweater and blouse. The injury appeared to be a knife wound. Perhaps she had been injured in a fight with the man on the sleigh?

She bent down quickly and dug into the frozen gravel road with her bare hands. Picked up sand and ice, grasses and debris. Rubbed them energetically into the knife wound. A look of intense pain crossed her face. Her mouth opened and let out dark, guttural sounds.

She repeated the movements. Repeated the sounds at regular intervals. Like a ritual. Her hand dug. Found gravel and sand.

Picked them up. Rubbed them into the wound. Time after time. Then she tore off her heavy sweater and her blouse and rubbed them on the road. Ripped and tore the sleeves. Rubbed and rubbed.

Her hands became covered with blood. She did not wipe them clean. Stood there outlined against the autumn sky in a thin lace bodice. But she did not appear to feel the cold. Calmly, she put on her clothes again. Examined her injury through the holes in her clothing. Smoothed her tattered sleeve. Grimaced with pain as she straightened her arm and tested if she could use it.

Her hat lay at the side of the road. Brown, narrow-brimmed, trimmed with green feathers. She gave it a quick glance before beginning to walk north along the rough sleigh road. In dim, silvery light.

The horse trudged after her, dragging the shafts. Soon caught up with her. Put its muzzle over her shoulder and nibbled at her hair.

She stopped walking and moved close to the animal. With a tug of her hand, she forced the horse down on its two front legs as if it were a camel. And seated herself astride the broad, black back.

The sound of horse's hooves. The shafts weeping against the gravel. The horse's easy breathing. The wind. Which did not know. Did not see.

It was the middle of the day. The horse and the woman had taken the steep road down the mountain and had come to a large estate. Tall, swaying rowan trees lined a broad lane, which stretched from the white main house down to the two red warehouses that faced each other near the stone pier.

The trees were already bare, with crimson berries. The fields yellow, sprinkled with patches of ice and snow. There were frequent breaks in the clouds. But still no sunshine.

As the horse and the woman entered the courtyard, the young man named Tomas came from the stable. Stood like a post in the ground when he saw the empty shafts and the woman's dishevelled hair and bloodstained clothing.

She slid off the horse slowly, without looking at him. Then she staggered step by step up the wide stairs to the main house. Opened one of the double doors. Stood motionless with her back to him while the light enveloped her. Then suddenly she turned around. As if she had become afraid of her own shadow.

Tomas ran after her. She stood in light from the house, warm and golden. From outside, cold, with bluish shadows from the mountains.

She no longer had any face.

There was great excitement. Women and men came running. Servants.

Mother Karen hobbled with a cane from one of the parlours. Her monocle dangled from an embroidered ribbon around her neck. A gleaming lens that tried in vain to make things cheerful.

The old woman creaked laboriously through the elegant hallway. With a gentle, omniscient look. Did she know anything?

Everyone flocked around the woman at the front door. A servant girl touched the woman's injured arm and offered to help remove the torn jacket. But she was brushed aside.

Then the clamour broke loose. Everyone talked at once. Questions poured over the woman without a face.

But she did not answer. Saw nothing. Had no eyes. Simply took hold of Tomas's arm so tightly that he moaned. Then she stumbled over to the man named Anders. A blond fellow with a strong chin. One of the foster sons on the estate. She took his arm, too, and made both men accompany her. Without saying a word.

Two horses from the stable were saddled. The third horse had no saddle. Was tired and sweaty after the ride down the mountain. The animal was unhitched from the shafts, wiped down, and watered.

The horse's large head lingered in the water bucket. People had to wait. It drank in well-deserved slurps. From time to time, it tossed its mane in the air and let its eyes glide from face to face.

The woman refused to change clothes or to have her wound bandaged. Just swung herself onto the horse. Tomas offered her a homespun coat, and she put it on. She still had not said a word.

She led them to the spot where the sleigh had skidded over the cliff. There was no mistaking the tracks. The ravaged slope, the flattened small birches, the uprooted heather. They all knew what was below. The sheer rock. The rapids. The gorge. The deep pool. The sleigh.

They summoned more people and searched in the foaming water. But found only the remnants of a crushed sleigh with frayed straps in the carriage-shaft fastenings.

The woman was mute.

The eyes of the Lord preserve knowledge,
and he overthroweth the words of the transgressor.
— Proverbs 22:12

Dina had to take her husband, Jacob, who had gangrene in one foot, to the doctor on the other side of the mountain. November. She was the only one who could handle the wild yearling, which was the fastest horse. And they needed to drive fast. On a rough, icy road.

Jacob's foot already stank. The smell had filled the house for a long time. The cook smelled it even in the pantry. An uneasy atmosphere pervaded every room. A feeling of anxiety.

No one at Reinsnes said anything about the smell of Jacob's foot before he left. Nor did they mention it after Blackie returned to the estate with empty shafts.

But aside from that, people talked. With disbelief and horror. On the neighbouring farms. In the parlours at Strandsted and along the sound. At the pastor's home. Quietly and confidentially.

About Dina, the young wife at Reinsnes, the only daughter of Sheriff Holm. She was like a horse-crazy boy. Even after she got married. Now she had suffered such a sad fate.

They told the story again and again. She had driven so fast that the snow crackled and spurted under the runners. Like a witch. Nevertheless, Jacob Grønelv did not get to the doctor's. Now he no longer existed. Friendly, generous Jacob, who never refused a request for help. Mother Karen's son, who came to Reinsnes when he was quite young.

Dead! No one could understand how such a terrible thing could have happened. That boats capsized, or people disappeared at sea, had to be accepted. But this was the devil's work. First getting gangrene in a fractured leg. Then dying on a sleigh that plunged into the rapids!

Dina had lost the power of speech, and old Mother Karen wept. Jacob's son from his first marriage wandered, fatherless, around Copenhagen, and Blackie could not stand the sight of sleighs.

The authorities came to the estate to conduct an inquiry into the events that had occurred up to the moment of death. Everything must be stated specifically and nothing hidden, they said.

Dina's father, the sheriff, brought two witnesses and a book for recording the proceedings. He said emphatically that he was there as one of the authorities, not as a father.

Mother Karen found it difficult to see a difference. But she did not say so.

No one brought Dina down from the second floor. Since she was so big and strong, they took no chance that she might resist and make a painful scene. They did not try to force her to come downstairs. Instead it was decided the authorities would go up to her large bedroom.

Extra chairs had been placed in the room. And the curtains on the canopy bed were thoroughly dusted. Heavy gold fabric patterned with rows of rich red flowers. Bought in Hamburg. Sewn for Dina and Jacob's wedding.

Oline and Mother Karen had tried to take the young wife in hand so she would not look completely unpresentable. Oline gave her herb tea with thick cream and plenty of sugar. It was her cure for all ills, from the scurvy to childlessness. Mother Karen assisted with praise, hair brushing, and cautious concern.

The servant girls did as they were told, while looking around with frightened glances.

The words stuck. Dina opened her mouth and formed them. But their sound was in another world. The authorities tried many different approaches.

The sheriff tried using a deep, dispassionate voice, peering into Dina's light-grey eyes. He could just as well have looked through a glass of water.

The witnesses also tried. Seated and standing. With both compassionate and commanding voices.

Finally, Dina laid her head of black, unruly hair on her arms. And she let out sounds that could have come from a half-strangled dog.

Feeling ashamed, the authorities withdrew to the downstairs rooms. In order to reach agreement about what had happened. How things had looked at the place in question. How the young woman had acted.

They decided that the whole matter was a tragedy for the community and the entire district. That Dina Grønelv was beside herself with grief. That she was not culpable and had lost her speech from the shock.

They decided that she had been racing to take her husband to the doctor. That she had taken the curve near the bridge too fast, or that the wild horse had bolted at the edge of the cliff and the shaft fastenings had pulled loose. Both of them.

This was neatly recorded in the official documents.

They did not find the body, at first. People said it had washed out to sea. But did not understand how. For the sea was nearly seven miles away through a rough, shallow riverbed. The rocks there would stop a dead body, which could do nothing itself to reach the sea.

To Mother Karen's despair, they gradually gave up the search.

A month later, an old pauper came to the estate and insisted that the body lay in Veslekulpen, a small backwater some distance below the rapids. Jacob lay crooked around a rock. Stiff as a rod. Battered and bloated, the old fellow said.

He proved to be right.

The water level had evidently subsided when the autumn rains ended. And one clear day in early December, the unfortunate body of Jacob Grønelv appeared. Right before the eyes of the old pauper, who was on his way across the mountain.

Afterward, people said the pauper was clairvoyant. And, in fact, always had been. This is why he had a quiet old age. Nobody wanted to quarrel with a clairvoyant. Even if he was a pauper.

Dina sat in her bedroom, the largest room on the second floor. With the curtains drawn. At first she did not even go to the stable to see her horse.

They left her in peace.

Mother Karen stopped crying, simply because she no longer had time for that. She had assumed the duties that the master and his wife had neglected. Both were dead, each in his or her own way.

Dina sat at the walnut table, staring. No one knew what else she did. Because she confided in no one. The sheets of music that had been piled around the bed were now stuffed away in the clothes closet. Her long dresses swept over them in the draught when she opened the door.

The shadows were deep in the bedroom. A cello stood in one corner, gathering dust. It had remained untouched since the day Jacob was carried from the house and laid on the sleigh.

The solid canopy bed with sumptuous bed curtains occupied much of the room. It was so high that one could lie on the pillows and look out through the windows at the sound. Or one could look at oneself in the large mirror with a black lacquered frame that could be tilted to different angles.

The big round stove roared all day. Behind a triple-panelled folding screen with an embroidered motif of beautiful Leda and the swan in an erotic embrace. Wings and arms. And Leda's long, blond hair spread virtuously over her lap.

A servant girl, Thea, brought wood four times a day. Even so, the supply barely lasted through the night.

No one knew when Dina slept, or if she slept. She paced back and forth in heavy shoes with metal-tipped heels, day and night. From wall to wall. Keeping the whole house awake.

Thea could report that the large family Bible, which Dina had inherited from her mother, always lay open.

Now and then the young wife laughed softly. It was an unpleasant sound. Thea did not know whether her mistress was laughing about the holy text or if she was thinking about something else.

Sometimes she angrily slammed together the thin-as-silk pages and threw the book away like the entrails from a dead fish.

Jacob was not buried until seven days after he was found. In the middle of December. There were so many arrangements to be made. So many people had to be notified. Relatives, friends, and prominent people had to be invited to the funeral. The weather stayed cold, so the battered and swollen corpse could easily remain in the barn during that time. Digging the grave, however, required the use of sledge-hammers and pickaxes.

The moon peered through the barn's tiny windows and observed Jacob's fate with its golden eye. Made no distinction between living and dead. Decorated the barn floor in silver and white. And nearby lay the hay, offering warmth and nourishment, smelling fragrantly of summer and splendour.

One morning before dawn, they dressed for the funeral. The boats were ready. Silence lay over the house like a strange piety. The moon was shining. No one waited for daylight at that time of year.

Dina leaned against the windowsill, as if steeling herself, when they entered her room to help her dress in the black clothes that had been sewn for the funeral. She had refused to try them on.

She seemed to be standing there sensing each muscle and each thought. The sombre, teary-eyed women did not see a single movement in her body.

Still, they did not give up at once. She had to change her clothes. She had to be part of the funeral procession. Anything else was unthinkable. But finally, they did think that thought. For with her guttural, animal-like sounds, she convinced everyone that she was not ready to be the widow at a funeral. At least not this particular day.

Terrified, the women fled the room. One after another. Mother Karen was the last to leave. She gave excuses and soothing explanations. To the aunts, the wives, the other women, and, not least of all, to Dina's father, the sheriff.

He was the hardest to convince. Bellowing loudly, he burst into Dina's room without knocking. Shook her and commanded her, slapped her cheeks with fatherly firmness while his words swarmed around her like angry bees.

Mother Karen had to intervene. The few who stood by kept their eyes lowered.

Then Dina let out the bestial sounds again. While she flailed her arms and tore her hair. The room was charged with something they did not understand. There was an aura of madness and power surrounding the young, half-dressed woman with dishevelled hair and crazed eyes.

Her screams reminded the sheriff of an event he carried with him always. Day and night. In his dreams and in his daily tasks. An event that still, after thirteen years, could make him wander restlessly around the estate. Looking for someone, or something, that could unburden him of his thoughts and feelings.

The people in the room thought Dina Grønelv had a harsh father. But on the other hand, it was not right that such a young woman refused to do what was expected of her.

She tired them out. People decided she was too sick to attend her husband's funeral. Mother Karen explained, loudly and clearly, to everyone she met:

'Dina is so distraught and ill she can't stand on her feet. She does nothing but weep. And the terrible thing is, she's not able to speak.'

First came the muffled shouts from the people who were going in the boats. Then came the scraping of wood against iron as the coffin was loaded onto the longboat with its juniper decorations and its weeping, black-clad women. Then the sounds and voices stiffened over the water like a thin crusting of beach ice. And disappeared between the sea and the mountains. Afterward, silence settled over the estate as though this were the true funeral procession. The house held its breath. Merely let out a small sigh among the rafters now and then. A sad, pitiful final honour to Jacob.

The pink waxed-paper carnations fluttered amid the pine and juniper boughs across the sound in a light breeze. There was no point in travelling quickly with such a burden. Death and its detached supporting cast took their time. It was not Blackie who pulled them. And it was not Dina who set the pace. The coffin was heavy. Those who bore it felt the weight. This was the only way to the church with such a burden.

Now five pairs of oars creaked in the oarlocks. The sail

flapped idly against the mast, refusing to unfurl. There was no sun. Grey clouds drifted across the sky. The raw air gradually became still.

The boats followed one another. A triumphal procession for Jacob Grønelv. Masts and oars pointed toward ocean and heaven. The ribbons on the wreaths fluttered restlessly. They had only a short time to be seen.

Mother Karen was a yellowed rag. Edged with lace, it is true.

The servant girls were wet balls of wool in the wind.

The men rowed, sweating behind their beards and moustaches. Rowing in rhythm.

At Reinsnes everything was prepared. The sandwiches were arranged on large platters. On the cellar floor and on shelves in the large entry were pewter plates filled with cakes and covered by cloths.

Under Oline's exacting supervision, the glasses had been rubbed to a glistening shine. Now the cups and glasses were arranged neatly in rows on the tables and in the pantry, protected by white linen towels bearing the monograms of Ingeborg Grønelv and Dina Grønelv. They had to use the linen belonging to both of Jacob's wives today.

Many guests were expected after the burial.

Dina stoked the fire like a madwoman, although there was not even frost on the windows. Her face, which had been grey that morning, began slowly to regain its colour.

She paced restlessly back and forth across the floor with a little smile on her lips. When the clock struck, she raised her head like an animal listening for enemies.

Tomas let the armload of wood drop into the wrought-iron basket with as little sound as possible. Then he took off his cap and clenched it between his strong hands. Embarrassed beyond all belief, because he was in the master bedroom, the room with the canopy bed and the cello, where Dina slept.

'Mother Karen sent me because I'm to stay at Reinsnes when the servants and everybody take Jacob to the churchyard,' he managed to stammer.

'I'm to give Dina a hand. If she needs it,' he added.

Tomas did not tell her, if he knew, that the sheriff and Mother Karen had agreed it was best to have a strong fellow there who could prevent Dina from harming herself while everyone was away.

She stood by the window with her back to him and did not even turn around.

The moon was a small pale ghost. A deformed foetus of a day tried in vain to break out to the north and west. But the windows' surfaces remained dark.

The boy took his cap and left. Realized he was not wanted.

However, when the funeral procession was far out on the sound, Tomas came to the room again. With a pitcher of fresh water. Would she like some? When she did not say thank you or give any indication that she saw him, he set the pitcher on the table by the door and turned toward her.

'You don't want help from me on the day of the funeral?' he asked in a low voice.

At that, she seemed to awaken. She went toward him quickly. Stood close to him. Half a head taller.

Then she lifted her hand and let her long fingers glide over his face. Like a blind person trying to see with her fingertips.

He felt as if he were being strangled. Because he forgot to breathe. So close! At first he did not understand what she wanted. Standing beside him exuding her fragrance. Tracing the lines in his face with her forefinger.

He slowly turned crimson. And found it impossible to look at her. He knew her eyes were waiting. Suddenly he took courage and looked straight at her.

She nodded and looked at him questioningly.

He nodded in return. Simply to have nodded. He wanted to leave.

Then she smiled and came even closer. Used the index and third fingers of her left hand to open his worn waistcoat.

He retreated two steps toward the stove. And did not know how he would escape before he got strangled or burned, or disappeared from the face of the earth.

She stood for a moment, sniffing his stable odour. Her nostrils were everywhere. They vibrated!

Then he nodded again. In utter confusion.

It was unbearable. Time stood still. He leaned over abruptly, opened the door of the stove, and threw a chunk of wood into the flames. Then he added three damp, sputtering birch logs. To stand up and meet her gaze again was a test of manhood.

All at once her mouth was on his. Her arms were stubborn willow branches filled with spring sap. Her aroma was so powerful that he had to close his eyes.

He could never have imagined it. Not in his wildest fantasies under his worn wool blanket in the servants' quarters. So he stood there, and all he could do was let it happen!

The colours of the embroidery on her dressing gown, the yellow walls with a vinelike design, the beamed ceiling, the deep-red drapes — they all fluttered into each other. Material merged with material. Limbs with limbs. Movements, furniture, air, skin.

He stood outside himself. And yet was inside. The smell and sound of bodies moving heavily. And deep, two-part breathing.

She put her hands on his chest and undid his buttons. Then she drew off his clothing. One piece after another. As if she had done it a thousand times.

He stood hunched forward, his arms hanging uselessly at his sides. As if ashamed that his underclothes were not completely clean and his shirt was missing three buttons. Actually, he did not know where he was, where he was standing, or how he was behaving.

She kissed the naked boy, opened her dressing gown, and let him in to her large, firm body.

It made him warm and brave. He felt the sparks from her skin as a physical pain. His skin tingled against hers, created a picture of her. He stood with closed eyes and saw each curve, each pore on her white body, until he went out of his mind completely.

When they were both naked, sitting on the sheepskin in front of the round black stove, he thought she would begin to speak. He was dizzy with embarrassment and desire. The seven lighted candles in the candelabra on the dressing table troubled him like a warning of hell. Their flickering light on the mirror's surface revealed everything.

She began to explore his body. Quite gently at first. Then wilder and wilder. As if driven by a great hunger.

At first he was simply frightened. He had never seen such intense craving. Finally, he gasped and rolled over on to the sheepskin. Let her pour oil on a fire greater than anything he had ever imagined.

In quick flashes he came to his senses again and to his horror felt himself pull her close and do things no one had taught him.

The air was dense with a woman's body.

His terror was vast as an ocean. But his desire, enormous as the heavens.

At the churchyard, the coffin decorated with wax flowers was lowered into the grave. Containing the earthly remains of innkeeper and cargoboat owner Jacob Grønelv.

The pastor tried to speak words that would allow the deceased to slip easily into paradise and not end up in hell's fire and brimstone. Yet the pastor knew that even though Jacob had been a good man, he certainly had not lived like a wax flower. No matter how sad an end he had met.

Some of the funeral guests stood with their grey jowls drooping in genuine sorrow. Others wondered what kind of weather they would have on the trip home. Still others just stood there. Took in everything halfheartedly. Most of them felt bitterly cold.

The pastor pronounced his ritual words and tossed his paltry spadefuls of earth in God's name. Then it was over.

Behind furrowed, serious faces, the men looked forward to the liqueur. The women, with tear-filled eyes, thought about the sandwiches. The servant girls wept openly. For the man in the coffin had been a loving master to them all.

Mother Karen was even more pale and transparent than in the boat. The eyes behind her black fringed shawl were dry as she stood supported by Anders and the sheriff. Each with his hat under his arm.

The hymn had an endless string of verses and was far from beautiful. In fact, it was barely endurable, until the deacon joined in with his untrained bass voice. He had a need to save every situation, the deacon.

In the large bedroom, behind drawn curtains, Tomas, the cotter's son, burned and blazed. In seventh heaven. Yet totally alive.

Moisture from human bodies collected on the windows and mirror. A faint odour clung to the sheepskin on the floor, the seats of the chairs, and the curtains.

The room welcomed Tomas the stableboy. Just as it once had welcomed Jacob Grønelv, when he was hospitably received for the first time by the widow of Reinsnes.

The widow was named Ingeborg. And she died one day when she leaned over to pet her cat. Now she had company where she was.

The bedroom was filled with heavy breathing, skin, and heat. Blood thundered through veins. Pounded against temples. Bodies were horses on broad plains. They galloped and galloped. The woman was already a practised rider. But he rode to exhaustion after her. The floorboards sang, the beams wept.

The family portraits and drawings swayed slightly in their black oval frames. The linen sheets in the bed felt abandoned and dry as dust. The stove stopped roaring. Just stood in its corner and listened openly, without embarrassment.

Downstairs, sandwiches and glasses stood waiting. For what? For Dina, the mistress of Reinsnes, to come sliding down the banister? Naked, her black hair like a half-opened umbrella above her large fragrant body? Yes!

And following her — half terrified, half in a dream — a powerful young boy clad in a sheet edged with French lace? Yes!

Tomas ran down the stairs on bare, hairy legs and sturdy toes with very dirty nails. He reeked so powerfully of ploughed fields that the demure inside air drew back.

They fetched sandwiches and wine. A large glass and a large carafe. A sandwich stolen here and there from the platters so it would not be noticed. They pretended they did not have permission to eat.

After they helped themselves from the platters, Dina gently rearranged the empty spaces. With long, quick fingers that smelled of salty earth and newly cleaned fish. Then she covered the plates again with the monogrammed cloths.

They stole up to the bedroom again like thieves. Sat down on the sheepskin in front of the stove. Tomas left the stove's double doors ajar.

Leda and the swan on the folding screen were a weak reflection of these two. The wine sparkled.

Greedily, Dina ate smoked salmon and salted meat. Bread crumbled across her firm breasts and down onto her round stomach.

Tomas realized he was in his mistress's room. He ate his food politely. But drank in Dina's body through his eyes, with watering mouth and many sighs.

Their eyes glistened over the same glass. It had a long green stem and had been a wedding present to Ingeborg and her first husband. The glass was not of the highest quality and had many bubbles in it. Bought before wealth entered the house through large cargo boats, dry fish, and powerful connections in Trondheim and Bergen.

Well before the funeral guests were expected to return the glass and the remaining wine were hidden away, far back in the clothes closet.

Two children, one worried and one wild, had fooled the grown-ups. Jacob's Chinese dice game was replaced in its silk-lined box. All traces were obliterated.

At the end, Tomas stood at the door completely clothed, with his hat in his hand. She scribbled some words on the black slate that she always kept close by, let him read them, then carefully erased them with a firm hand.

He nodded, looking nervously at the window. Listening for the sound of oars. Thinking he heard them. Suddenly he understood what he had done. Took all the guilt upon himself. Already felt the Lord's scourge upon his shoulders. Many deep lashes. Tomas's mouth trembled. But he could not feel regret.

Standing in the dark hallway, he knew he was no longer under anyone's protection. Like a gladiator who had fought joyfully against great odds. For one single experience!

Important beyond words.

He was doomed to lie on his straw mattress each night for months, feeling a woman's breath on his face. To lie with open eyes, reliving. The room. The smells.

And the thin blanket would rise in youthful, dreamlike ardour.

He was doomed also to the image of Jacob's coffin. That had to sway right along with them. And the great wave within him would combine all the impressions and send him straight to the northern lights. The wave would empty into his wretched bed, and he would not be able to prevent it.

Dina was calm and powdered pale when the boats glided in to the rocky beach. She lay in bed, thereby avoiding any fuss about putting in an appearance with the funeral guests downstairs.

Mother Karen came down from the bedroom and gave everyone complete details about Dina's condition. Her voice was honey on the sheriff's disposition. It blended lightly and sweetly with the liqueur.

Now that Jacob had been properly laid to rest, the sombre, sorrowful atmosphere lightened and improved. As the evening wore on, a sense of calm descended, and thoughts of temporal things and the hard day tomorrow crept into the quiet conversations.

Everyone went to bed early, as was fitting on such a day. Dina got up and played patience on the walnut table. After the third try, it came out. Then she sighed and yawned.

Translated by Nadia Christensen

CECILIE LØVEID

Double Delight

Dramatis personae:

SIRI, a medieval archeologist, 30
GUY, her husband, an archeologist, 40
KATARINA, called CAT, 16
TUTTI and FRUTTI, unemployed dancers, now field
    assistants at the dig
Three joggers
A SINGING PIG

*Siri's costume changes gradually during the course of the play
from modern dress until by the end she is wearing the costume
of a medieval queen.*

ACT I

The ruins of the Katarina convent, an archeological dig on the West coast of Norway. Earth, mud, everything is wet after rain. In the foreground soapstone graves, tarpaulins for covering the site.

A board game, still buried.

A washing area: a green hosepipe and a bucket.

The chapel lies below ground level with a wall round it, completely covered by tarpaulin. Underneath is hidden a large swan's wing.

A boat with the inside excavated, filled with water. Over it a tent of tarpaulin.

SIRI's hair is covered in a net of gold threads.

Blue spring night. Two figures move slowly towards each other: GUY and KATARINA (CAT). Move slowly away again.

Three voices over the loudspeakers: SIRI, TUTTI, FRUTTI. They mix with each other and with other sound effects: sea, birds, humming town noises.

SIRI

Sitting in bed waiting until morning. That is proof that he is glorious and loved. And who comes? Moonlight comes. White, mocking, merciless moon shining down to my bed.

TUTTI

If I'm sitting waiting until broad daylight, then that is proof that he is glorious and loved. If I'm sitting waiting until broad daylight.

FRUTTI

If I'm sitting waiting until broad daylight. Then that is proof that he is glorious, loved. Outside it's already beginning to grow light.

(*A baby whimpers, cries.*)

1

SIRI lying by the three graves in the foreground with the swaddled baby on her stomach. TUTTI and FRUTTI beside her.

A SINGING PIG comes dancing in from the background, playing a lute. Dawn.

SINGING PIG
    When temperate spring returns
    the trees grow green again, and birds
    join each after his fashion
    in the strains of the new song.
    Then it is best to turn your thoughts towards
    that which you most desire.

(*Exit.*)

SIRI (*SIRI's music.*)

A hundred boys I know who wanted me
A hundred boys wanted to go to the pictures
on the back row we would sit close up
petting

A hundred boys to go home too late with
A hundred boys who wanted to kiss kisses
and leave marks which wouldn't disappear
for weeks

I had to sit here with you, Cat,
I had to sit here with you

Whilst a hundred boys would rather go to the pictures
And I would rather go to the pictures
with a hundred boys
I couldn't
sit there with you

TUTTI
Isn't he coming?

FRUTTI
It'll soon be day.

TUTTI
Isn't he coming?

FRUTTI
They were going to have visitors, weren't they?

TUTTI
Who's that?

FRUTTI
Her sister.

TUTTI
Her sister? Then he'll not come.

FRUTTI
Cat.

TUTTI
Cat?

FRUTTI
She's called Cat.

TUTTI (*like the cat aria*)
Miaaaaow!

FRUTTI
Miaowmiaowmiaow!

(*They sing a duet.*)

TUTTI
She's afraid we'll look at him too long. Melt him.

FRUTTI
She has reason to be afraid of that!

(*They laugh.*)

TUTTI
Just because we didn't go along to the kitchen
to bake an apple pie. The apples are so sour,
she said, and looked at me as if I was Eve or
Lilith.

FRUTTI
Which of us is Eve and which is Lilith

only the birds know, but this place could
turn out to be Paradise? If we manage to dig
deep enough?

TUTTI
If we found the Sacred Snake, Saint Apple,
or perhaps the Sacred Rib!

FRUTTI
Or the Sacred Artichoke.

TUTTI
What artichoke?

FRUTTI
Just a joke, as I ever spoke!

TUTTI
I go soft between the legs when I think of him.

FRUTTI
Oh, how excessively shameful!

TUTTI
I go soft like two pillows of silk, I won't
say which. I shall take his head into me, I
can do no other when he wants to get in where he came
from, wet and red. When he shines and glistens
I can't resist, it must be the way I'm
made, the way Eve and Lilith were made, incapable
of saying no any of us...

FRUTTI
No, *we* never say no.

TUTTI
We always start with a YES!

FRUTTI
Well, what else can we say?

TUTTI
We dance, we sing, we slide up and down
over him, juggle with him, we stand up
and take in the earth, take in the spring, the whole earth!

FRUTTI
Deepgreen seas, yellow continents, pink cloud formations,
birds on the way down and fish on the way up.

TUTTI
This song we sing until our voices
reach the high attractive soprano...

FRUTTI
Become globe and continent ourselves,

TUTTI
Travel onwards,

FRUTTI
Sleeping, happy,

TUTTI
Innocently pure.

FRUTTI
Travel on to new meetings and a new YES.

TUTTI
But we haven't got time for this.

FRUTTI
No, we definitely haven't got time for this.
Miaaaow!
We who have to dig out a whole ship!

TUTTI
You know, if that voice belonged to a
pig it would be a sensation!

(*They laugh.*)
(*They get up and walk to the back of the stage, change into working clothes.*)
(*A jogger runs across the site.*)
(*Siri's music.*)

2

(*SIRI sits up and begins to scrape away a layer of earth. A board game emerges. GUY enters. Sits down by her.*)

SIRI
Give me a cigarette, Guy. Look, this must be a board game. Where were you last night? Is it chess?

GUY
You don't normally smoke out here. (*Gives her a cigarette, lights it.*) My sweet.

SIRI

I must have a smoke. I think it's a hnefatafl board.
What a name...
Where were you last night, my sweet?

GUY

You never know what you'll find. An elegant bear,
a piece made of iron with eight horns... Yes, the forms
vary.

SIRI

A person, a boat. With runes carved on it: 'Here sails the bold
seafarer.'

GUY

Some dice to cast.
Some nights you just can't sleep.

SIRI

But here, just here, there was water.

GUY

The sea came up to here. Boats from the whole world came
here.
('Roma caput mundi.' Rome the capital of the world.)

SIRI

Water, sea, salt, endless. Stretches right to
the edge of the earth, and then they sailed off!

GUY

Perhaps we'll find a boat.

SIRI

A boat in the ground. A boat mirrored in dancing waves,
sailing to the edge of the earth.
Where were you last night? You mustn't ...you mustn't be
too open with her. She must never know ... You've
sworn never to tell who her big sister
really is.

GUY

No, you can rely on that. But...
You can't decide what you're going to find.

SIRI

But you can decide where you're going to dig.

GUY

If you're digging, you're asking. She won't ask,
she suspects nothing. No-one here knows.

SIRI

Only you. Only you know what I did. Here. It was
the right thing?
We found a quayside with mooring ropes well preserved,
so we must be able to find a boat too.

GUY

Why precisely a boat? A boat precisely?
Why not a pair of wings from an angel?
They existed then?

SIRI

Oh, she should never have come. Sat and banged her head
against the bars of the cot. I had to take her
home to mummy. I had to become a sister.

GUY

Perhaps we'll find some playing pieces? That Kitty can
play with. (*He walks towards the field assistants.*) A bear
and some cattle! A fox and some hens!

SIRI

A flower grows inside me. A flower that wants to blossom
me out. A flower in a body is too much. That's why
a boat must come.
(*She crumbles earth between her fingers.*)
I must make ready for a journey across the sea.
'Here sails the bold seafarer.'
All my life I've tried to travel away from. But she follows
me like a little elf. A little laughing elf.
A little elf in my luggage. Go to your dancers.

(*GUY goes.*)

3

The SINGING PIG enters dancing.

SINGING PIG

    Neither letter nor message reaches me
    from the place where I found my joy.
    So my heart can neither rest nor laugh
    neither do I dare proceed
    before I know whether the outcome
    will be as I desire.

Exit.

(SIRI breastfeeding the baby KITTY. CAT enters. Stops by GUY and the assistants. He kisses her forehead. She is wearing a garland of flowers around her head.)

GUY
Over there is the Katarina hospital, over there, we think, lies the Katarina chapel, with the fresco of 'The Singing Pig' and here is where we think the well is. There are footprints here already before we put our feet down. Smelt together past and present, until it's gone, dizzily disappeared. We protect everything with tarpaulin.

CAT
How can you know that it is Saint Katarina's convent? Which Katarina? The southern one, the northern one?

GUY
You ask Cat, as if you're asking how we know what the stars are called! We get it from the archives of the North German seaports, quite simply. What do you think of my hair? Isn't it ... true, Cat, true I have raven-black hair?

CAT
Well, I think I would say ... more ... pepper and salt... What do you think of mine?

GUY
Children and brides let their hair flow free...
Have you met the assistants? This is Tutti, this is
Cat, Siri's sister. Little sister.

TUTTI
Hello pussycat!
Where were you last night?

GUY
And this is Frutti. They're unemployed dancers.
Wings and body are stiffened with lots of piano wire.

FRUTTI
Hi Cat!

CAT
Many times I dare more because I don't realise how difficult it
is.

FRUTTI
I dance in shoes when all the others dance barefoot.

CAT
Oh?

FRUTTI
Yes, you have to hop and hope that you're a Cat!

CAT
My mother wanted me to dance.
Why don't you use bigger spades?

TUTTI
I suppose you'd like us to use sandblasters too?

FRUTTI
We use quite different methods.

TUTTI
Index finger.

FRUTTI
Tongue tip.

TUTTI
Big toe.

FRUTTI
In this lovely spring which turns your thoughts towards what you most desire.

(*GUY makes notes in a notebook.*)

CAT
What are you writing?

TUTTI
He's noting something about the white spaces on the medieval map.

FRUTTI
Women are demons, he's writing.

CAT
What are you writing?

GUY
'Kiss me, my love.'

CAT
A speech from a bad film.

GUY
It's written on this runestick!
What do you want me to do, fool you or feel you?

CAT
To be a manly fool or a feeling man?

GUY
Exactly.

CAT
Both. My sorcerer.

(*GUY walks round with CAT, showing her the excavations.*)

TUTTI
She sleeps all day. Moons around and sleeps. Digs a bit here, fiddles a bit there. Sews herself strange headgear from medieval pictures. Swaddles the child in long bands. Strange.

FRUTTI
And when it's getting near dinner, she perks up and makes complicated dishes, lays the table beautifully, puts out candelabra, puts on a record with lute music or nuns singing, chatters away to him. Swaddles the child in long bands. Then she falls asleep again.

TUTTI
He is her high point.

FRUTTI
She must be sick.

4

(SIRI has finished feeding the baby. Crumbles earth between her fingers. CAT to SIRI, leaning over KITTY.)

CAT
Good morning! Hi!
(Leans eagerly over KITTY.)
Cwied and cwied last night I did, didn't get my milk I didn't, cwied and cwied, mummy.
Good morning, good night ... MARE!

SIRI
Mare? Good morning, Cat, you slept a long time, didn't you, it's late ... Who's brought you flowers? A suitor already?

CAT
Isn't it much more motherly to be a mother in French? Ma mare! I couldn't sleep last night. My first night on the run. Guy brought me flowers. It's not a deadly sin for a young virgin to like a loyal knight. I think. Isn't it lovely to have a baby? How did you manage it?

SIRI
I don't know. Couldn't you sleep? No, there's a lot going on in our house. That knight doesn't usually bring me flowers in the early morning.

CAT
Is Kitty like that every night?

SIRI
No. She's very sensitive to change.
New voices, faces. But in the short periods I get to
sleep, she gives me dreams.

CAT
Who is that?
(*Looks down into soapstone grave.*)

SIRI
A man. Almost 1000 years old.

CAT
That's a bit too old for me.

SIRI
Yes, marry him and you'll stay a virgin.
Dressed for a journey to the land of the dead.

(*Voices whisper, sing, voices from the past.*)

CAT
I caught him.

SIRI
Guy?

CAT
I am a cat after all. I think he was a little taken with me, yes.

SIRI
What are you saying? I can't hear, there are so many
voices here.

CAT
Many voices?
What do the voices tell you?

SIRI
They don't tell anything.

CAT
What do they say?

SIRI
Nothing to me.

CAT
But you're the only one who hears them. I can't hear a peep.

SIRI
I suppose they have their theatre.

CAT
Theatre?

SIRI
They're hospitable. They're entertaining me.

CAT
Would you like to be with them instead of us?

SIRI
I often hear voices out here. It's not so strange. They are here,
after all.

CAT
I caught him. I was the juggler who dropped an artichoke
in his lap.

SIRI
The Sacred Artichoke.
But it was him that walked through the room.

CAT
Of course. He was naked.

SIRI
Naked?

CAT
He was naked. It was almost morning. Violet.
It's all beginning again for me now. It's all beginning now.
My life. This morning. This lovely spring morning.
I got flowers from a man for the first time.
But he's a bit old, not exactly a thousand,
but ... it's just like in a film!

SIRI
You're sixteen, Cat, aren't you?

CAT
Nearly seventeen.
He didn't know I'd come. He didn't know
I was your sister. I was lying on the sofa in the lounge. He
walked past.

SIRI
You know it was me that changed your nappies when you were
little. It was me that started calling you Cat. Mother was

always at the theatre in the evenings. I was your little mother,
Cat. Don't forget that.

CAT
So that was why you didn't want children, because I was such
a nuisance to you?

SIRI
There's no need to be quite so frank. You're only a child.

CAT
To be with others at that time of night. Without sleep.
To be on the run. Be Puss-in-boots. The first night
on my great voyage out into the world.

SIRI
Can't you see that this is upsetting me?

CAT
You've borrowed so many men, you have, Siri, I know that.
Say that I'm going to Hollywood.

SIRI
It doesn't mean that my own is on loan.

CAT
I wouldn't do anything wrong. I don't, do I? In that way,
but not in *that* way. I just happened to be there. And he liked
me so much.

SIRI
Anyone would think it was you that was newborn.

CAT

But that's how I feel too! There's a strange scent in the house.
It makes something stir ...

SIRI

He was naked when he walked through the room.

CAT

He was naked when he made the world's best coffee! I said
nothing. I sat there and looked at him. I even believe I was
invisible.

SIRI

Pooh!
One night he came home with blood down his trousers.

CAT

Do you want more information? You have such cold hands,
Siri. Cold hands!
Not a lot of motherly warmth there, is there?

SIRI

Motherly warmth?
Naked. Were you also naked perhaps, in all innocence?
Was it only the spirit that mattered?
You'll soon be just as theatrical as mummy. Great primadonna
in a little theatre. Have you got a cigarette?

CAT

Yes I have, but I don't know if I'll give you one. You're
breast-feeding. No I haven't. (*Pause.*) Was that what you
thought?
That I was naked? He gave me coffee. Morning coffee after a
sleepless night in a silken shift in a medieval spring, he said...

I didn't forget you for a moment. We just wanted you to be left to sleep. To dream.

Afterwards I went out to the dig. I've been here once before, I thought. Many hundreds of years ago.

Then I went home to lie down again. And then ... the flowers were lying there.

SIRI
I don't know ... I must go ... I have to record something we found this morning ... fetch paper ...

CAT
Always go. Always go when there's a risk of something affecting you, getting close to you. I suppose you're going to dance. Alone in a room.

SIRI
My room is not alone.

CAT
Mine is...

(*SIRI takes KITTY and goes. CAT runs after them and lays the garland of flowers on the baby.*)

(*Two joggers run across the site.*)

Translated by Janet Garton

Bibliography

GERD BRANTENBERG

Opp alle jordens homofile (What Comes Naturally). Novel. Aschehoug, Oslo 1973.

Egalias døtre (The Daughters of Egalia). Novel. Aschehoug, Oslo
1977.

Ja, vi slutter (Yes, let's stop). Novel. Aschehoug, Oslo 1978.

Sangen om St. Croix (The Song of St. Croix). Novel. Aschehoug, Oslo
1979.

Favntak (Embrace). Novel. Aschehoug, Oslo 1983.

Ved fergestedet (At the Ferry Crossing). Novel. Aschehoug, Oslo
1985.

På sporet av den tapte lyst (On the Track of Lost Desire). Literary
criticism. Aschehoug, Oslo 1986.

For alle vinder (The Four Winds). Novel. Aschehoug, Oslo 1989.

Eremitt og entertainer (Hermit and Entertainer). Essays. Aschehoug,
Oslo 1991.

Published in English:

What Comes Naturally, trans. Gerd Brantenberg. The Women's
Press, London 1986.

The Daughters of Egalia, trans. Louis Mackay and Gerd
Brantenberg. Journeyman Press, London 1985/The Seal Press,
Seattle 1985.

The Four Winds, trans. Margaret Hayford O'Leary. Women in
Translation, USA 1995.

BERGLJOT HOBÆK HAFF
Raset (The Avalanche). Novel. Gyldendal, Oslo 1956.
Liv. Novel. Gyldendal, Oslo 1958.
Du finner ham aldri (You'll Never Find Him). Novel. Gyldendal, Oslo 1960.
Bålet (The Fire). Novel. Gyldendal, Oslo 1962.
Skjøgens bok (The Prostitute's Book). Novel. Gyldendal, Oslo 1965.
Den sorte kappe (The Black Cloak). Novel. Gyldendal, Oslo 1969.
Sønnen (The Son). Novel. Gyldendal, Oslo 1971.
Heksen (The Witch). Novel. Gyldendal, Oslo 1974.
Gudsmoren (The Mother of God). Gyldendal, Oslo 1977.
Jeg, Bakunin (I, Bakunin). Novel. Gyldendal, Oslo 1983.
Den guddommelige tragedie (The Divine Tragedy). Novel. Gyldendal, Oslo 1989.
Renhetens pris (The Price of Purity). Novel. Gyldendal, Oslo 1992.

LISBET HIIDE
Alices særegne opplevelse av natt (Alice's Peculiar Experience of Night). Short stories. Gyldendal, Oslo 1985.
Dame med nebb (Lady with Beak). Short stories. Gyldendal, Oslo 1988.

LIV KØLTZOW
Øyet i treet (The Eye in the Tree). Short stories. Aschehoug, Oslo 1970.
Hvem bestemmer over Bjørg og Unni? (Who Decides About Bjørg and Unni?) Novel. Aschehoug, Oslo 1972.
Historien om Eli (The Story of Eli). Novel. Aschehoug, Oslo 1975.
Løp, mann (Run, man). Novel. Aschehoug, Oslo 1980.
April/November. Two stories. Aschehoug, Oslo 1983.
Hvem har ditt ansikt? (Who Has Your Face?) Novel. Aschehoug, Oslo 1988.
Den unge Amalie Skram (The Young Amalie Skram). Biography. Gyldendal, Oslo 1992.

SISSEL LIE

Tigersmil (Tiger Smile). Short stories. Gyldendal, Oslo 1986.
Løvens hjerte (Lion's Heart). Novel. Gyldendal, Oslo 1988.
Sjelen har intet kjønn (The Soul Has No Gender). Aschehoug, Oslo 1988.
Granateple (Pomegranate). Novel. Gyldendal, Oslo 1990.
Reise gjennom brent sukker (Journey Through Burnt Sugar). Novel. Gyldendal, Oslo 1992.
Rød svane (Red Swan). Novel. Gyldendal, Oslo 1994.

Published in English:
Lion's Heart, trans. Anne Born. Orkney Press, Kirkwall 1990.

CECILIE LØVEID

Most. Novel. Gyldendal, Oslo 1972.
Tenk om isen skulle komme (What if the Ice Should Come). Novel. Gyldendal, Oslo 1974.
Alltid skyer over Askøy (Always Clouds over Askøy). Novel. Gyldendal, Oslo 1976.
Mørkets muligheter (The Possibilities of Darkness). Novel. Gyldendal, Oslo 1976.
Fanget villrose (Captured Wildrose). Poems/texts. Gyldendal, Oslo 1977.
Sug (Sea Swell). Novel/poem. Gyldendal, Oslo 1979.
Måkespisere (Seagull Eaters). Radio plays. Gyldendal, Oslo 1983.
Vift (Puff). Radio play. Solum, Oslo 1985.
Balansedame (Tightrope Lady). Play. Gyldendal, Oslo 1985.
Fornuftige dyr (Rational Animals). Play. Gyldendal, Oslo 1986.
Dobbel nytelse (Double Delight). Play. Gyldendal, Oslo 1988.
Badehuset (The Baths). Play. Gyldendal, Oslo 1990.
Lille Pille og Lille Fille i Den dype skogs teater (Little Pille and Little Fille in the Deep Wood's Theatre). Children's story. Gyldendal, Oslo 1990.
Tiden mellom tidene (Time inbetween Times). Play. Gyldendal, Oslo 1991.
Barock Friise (Baroque Frieze). Play. Gyldendal, Oslo 1993.

Maria Q. Play. Gyldendal, Oslo 1994.

Published in English:
'Captured Wildrose' (excerpt from *Fanget villrose*), trans. Nadia Christensen. In Katherine Hanson (ed.): *An Everyday Story.* The Seal Press, Seattle 1984.
Sea Swell, trans. Nadia Christensen. Fjord Press, London and New York 1986.
'Seagull Eaters', trans. Henning Sehmsdorf. In Janet Garton and Henning Sehmsdorf (eds.): *New Norwegian Plays.* Norvik Press, Norwich 1989.
Selected poems. In T.Johanssen (ed.): *20 Contemporary Norwegian Poets.* Universitetsforlaget, Oslo 1984.

ELDRID LUNDEN
f.eks. juli (e.g. July). Poems. Det norske samlaget, Oslo 1968.
Inneringa (Encircled). Poems. Det norske samlaget, Oslo 1975.
hard, mjuk (hard, soft). Poems. Det norske samlaget, Oslo 1976.
Mammy, blue. Poems. Det norske samlaget, Oslo 1977.
Essays. Det norske samlaget, Oslo 1982.
Gjenkjennelsen (Recognition). Poems. Det norske samlaget, Oslo 1982.
Det omvendt avhengige (Inverse dependency). Poems. Det norske samlaget, Oslo 1989.
Noen må ha vøre her før (Someone must have been here before). Poems. Det norske samlaget, Oslo 1990.

Published in English:
Selected poems. In T.Johanssen (ed.): *20 Contemporary Norwegian Poets.* Universitetsforlaget, Oslo 1984.

KARIN MOE
Kjønnskrift (Sextext). Poems/prose. Aschehoug, Oslo 1980.
39 FYK. Novel. Aschehoug, Oslo 1983.
Kyka/1984. Novel. Aschehoug, Oslo 1984.

Mordatter (Mother/daughter). Poems. Aschehoug, Oslo 1985.
Sjanger (Genre). Essays. Aschehoug, Oslo 1986.
BLOVE 1.bok. Novel. Aschehoug, Oslo 1990.
BLOVE 2.bok. Novel. Aschehoug, Oslo 1993.

Published in English:
'The Lady in the Coat' (from *Kjønnskrift*) and 'Eagle Wings' (from *39 FYK*), trans. Janet Rasmussen. In Katherine Hanson (ed.): *An Everyday Story*. The Seal Press, Seattle 1984.

MARI OSMUNDSEN
Vi klarer det! (We'll Make It!). Novel. Per Sivle forlag, Oslo 1978.
På vei mot himmelen (On the Way to Heaven). Novel. Oktober, Oslo 1979.
Wow. Short stories. Oktober, Oslo 1982.
Den grønne damen (The Green Lady). Children's book. Oktober, Oslo 1982.
Gode gjerninger (Good deeds). Novel. Oktober, Oslo 1984.
Familien (The Family). Novel. Oktober, Oslo 1985.
Den minste reven (The Smallest Fox). Oktober, Oslo 1986.
Drageegget (The Dragon's Egg). Short stories. Oktober, Oslo 1986.
Arv (Inheritance). Novel. Cappelen, Oslo 1988.
Gutten som slo tida ihjel (The Boy Who Killed Time). Novel. Oktober, Oslo 1990.
Absolvo te. Novel. Oktober, Oslo 1992.

MARIE TAKVAM
Dåp under sju stjerner (Christening under seven stars). Poems. Gyldendal, Oslo 1952.
Syngjande kjelder (Singing springs). Poems. Gyldendal, Oslo 1954.
Signal (Signal). Poems. Gyldendal, Oslo 1959.
Maria og katten i Venezia (Maria and the cat in Venice). Children's book. Gyldendal, Oslo 1960.
Merke etter liv (Marked by life). Poems. Gyldendal, Oslo 1962.
Mosaikk i lys (Mosaic in light). Poems. Gyldendal, Oslo 1965.

Idun. Play. Gyldendal, Oslo 1966.

Brød og tran (Bread and cod-liver oil). Poems. Gyldendal, Oslo 1969.

Dansaren (The Dancer). Novel. Gyldendal, Oslo 1975.

Auger, hender (Eyes, hands). Poems. Gyldendal, Oslo 1975.

Barn er så små (Children are so small). Anthology. Gyldendal, Stabekk 1979.

Falle og reise seg att (Fall and rise again). Poems. Gyldendal, Oslo 1980.

Brevet frå Alexandra (The Letter from Alexandra). Novel. Gyldendal, Oslo 1981.

Eg har røter i jord (I have roots in the earth). Poems. Gyldendal, Stabekk, 1981.

Aldrande drabantby (Elderly suburbia). Poems. Gyldendal, Oslo 1987.

Rognebær (Rowanberries). Poems. Gyldendal, Oslo 1990.

Published in English:

Selected poems. In T.Johanssen (ed.): *20 Contemporary Norwegian Poets.* Universitetsforlaget, Oslo 1984.

BJØRG VIK

Søndag ettermiddag (Sunday Afternoon). Short stories. Cappelen, Oslo 1963.

Nødrop fra en myk sofa (Cries For Help From a Soft Sofa). Short stories. Cappelen, Oslo 1966.

Det grådige hjerte (The Greedy Heart). Short stories. Cappelen, Oslo 1968.

Gråt, elskede mann (Cry, Beloved man). Novel. Cappelen, Oslo 1970.

Kvinneakvariet (An Aquarium of Women). Short stories. Cappelen, Oslo 1972.

Hurra, det ble en pike (Hurrah, it's a girl). Children's play. Cappelen, Oslo 1974.

To akter for fem kvinner (Two Acts for Five Women). Play. Cappelen, Oslo 1974.

En håndfull lengsel (Out of Season). Short stories. Cappelen, Oslo 1979.

Det trassige håp (Defiant Hope). Five radio plays. Cappelen, Oslo 1981.

Snart er det høst (Soon It Will Be Autumn). Short stories. Cappelen, Oslo 1982.

Fribillett til Soria Moria (Free Ticket to Soria Moria). Play. Cappelen, Oslo 1984.

En gjenglemt petunia (A Forgotten Petunia). Short stories. Cappelen, Oslo 1985.

Jørgen Bombasta. Children's book. Cappelen, Oslo 1987.

Små nøkler, store rom (Small keys, large room). Novel. Cappelen, Oslo 1988.

Vinterhagen (Winter Garden). Play. Cappelen, Oslo 1990.

Poplene på St.Hanshaugen (The Poplars on St. Hanshaugen). Novel. Cappelen, Oslo 1991.

Reisen til Venezia (The Trip to Venice). Play. Cappelen, Oslo 1992.

Elsi Lund. Novel. Cappelen, Oslo 1994.

Published in English:

An Aquarium of Women, trans. Janet Garton. Norvik Press, Norwich 1972.

'Tone - 16', trans. Ingrid Weatherhead. In Elizabeth Rokkan and Ingrid Weatherhead (eds.): *View from the Window*. Universitetsforlaget, Bergen, 1986.

Out of Season and other stories, trans. David McDuff and Patrick Browne. Sinclair Browne, London 1983.

'Daughters', trans. Janet Garton. In Janet Garton and Henning Sehmsdorf (eds.): *New Norwegian Plays*. Norvik Press, Norwich 1989.

HERBJØRG WASSMO

Vingeslag (Wingbeats). Poems. Gyldendal, Oslo 1976.

Flotid (Rising Tide). Poems. Gyldendal, Oslo 1977.

Huset med den blinde glassveranda (The House With the Blind Glass Windows). Novel. Gyldendal, Oslo 1981.

Det stumme rommet (The Silent Room). Novel. Gyldendal, Oslo 1983.

Veien å gå (The Way To Go). Documentary. Gyldendal, Oslo 1984.

Mellomlanding (Stop-over). Play. Gyldendal, Oslo 1985.

Hudløs himmel (Flayed Heavens). Novel. Gyldendal, Oslo 1986.

Dinas bok (Dina's Book). Novel. Gyldendal, Oslo 1989.

Lykkens sønn (The Son of Fortune). Novel. Gyldendal, Oslo 1992.

Published in English:

The House with the Blind Glass Windows, trans. Roseann Lloyd and Allen Simpson. The Seal Press, Seattle 1987.

Dina's Book, trans. Nadia Christensen. Arcade Publishing, New York 1994.